Love's
Surprise

Karen Ball

Love's Surprise

HENDRICKSON
PUBLISHERS

Love's Surprise

Hendrickson Publishers Marketing, LLC
P. O. Box 3473
Peabody, Massachusetts 01961-3473

ISBN 978-1-59856-691-8

First Hendrickson Edition Printing — November 2011

A NOTE TO READERS FROM

Karen Ball

MY MOTHER was the queen of celebrations and filled every holiday with fun and laughter. Valentine's Day meant the house was decorated top to bottom, and dinner was entirely red. Red food, red drink, red desserts. And there was always a little something special for each of us—my two brothers and Dad—at our plates. St. Pat's brought green and more green. April Fool's was a day to see who could play the most outrageous prank. I still have some of Mom's decorations, and they're almost as old as I am. I still remember putting them up with her, talking and sharing memories as we did so.

It's no wonder I love holidays as much as I do. And no wonder I was delighted to write novellas celebrating three of my favorite holidays: April Fool's Day, Christmas, and Valentine's Day! I wrote these short stories back in the late '90s. In fact, they were some of my first published works. So you can imagine my delight when Hendrickson Publishers asked if they could release them again in a new collection! I was even more delighted when they allowed me to update them. In fact, they let me completely rework all three stories, connecting them with a new thread. Mission: LOVE!

It's been great fun to revisit these stories and characters, and even more rewarding to bring new focus and refinement to them.

So what awaits you here are three new stories based on those original novellas and threaded together with common and sometimes wacky characters! Stories that celebrate holidays and family . . . and the wonder of *love's surprises.*

I hope you enjoy them!

Karen Ball

P.S. I always love hearing from readers, so please feel free to shoot me an email at kb4Him@gmail.com.

Jericho's Walls

1

An Unlikely Angel

95

Valentine Surprise

221

Jericho's Walls

MISSION CONTROL

"Mr. Hawk, you have a special delivery. A rather odd letter. I know I usually open the mail for you, but this is marked personal. And, well . . . I'm not sure what to do with it."

Brendan Hawk looked up from his drawing table and considered his secretary's hesitant words. "What kind of letter?"

She held it out to him, and he couldn't help a grin. The envelope was made of old newspapers, and his name and address were written, in permanent marker, across the front.

Gramps. It had to be. The man recycled everything.

He held out his hand. "I'll take it, Lisa."

His secretary eyed the letter as though it were some desiccated rodent, then handed it over. She left the office, and Brendan settled back in his chair and reached for a letter opener. For just a second he let his gaze rest on the logo across the handle of the stylish, acrylic letter opener: "Hawk's Eye Fine Art." Another smile. That promotional had worked like a charm. He'd had a host of inquiries from galleries after he'd sent them out with his press kits.

Slitting the top of the letter, he pulled the note free and opened it. A short bark of laughter. The message was pure Gramps. Short, concise, and definite.

Very definite.

"Come see me. Now."

He reached forward to press the intercom button.

"Yes, sir?" Lisa's response was as quick as usual.

"Lisa, cancel my appointments for today." Another smile crept across his lips. "It appears I have another one I've got to take."

"Um . . . Dr. Kylie, a . . . well, I guess it's a note just came for you."

Kylie Hawk looked up from the Siberian husky whose teeth she was inspecting. The dog's owner had the three-year-old ball of energy in a vise grip, doing his best to hold the dog still. "Shelley, I'm a bit busy here. Can it wait?"

The receptionist shrugged. "I suppose, but it came by special delivery, so I thought it might be important."

Kylie sighed and looked over the Sibe's head to the owner.

He gave her a sheepish grin. "I could take a break if you could."

She patted the dog's head, then she and the owner let loose the hound—who promptly jumped from the table, tail wagging. Kylie followed Shelley out to the empty reception area, then held out her hand. "Let's take a look at it."

"What's in it?"

Kylie turned to find Alan, one of her partner vets, peering over her shoulder at the envelope she now held. "I'll let you know in a sec." She turned the so-called envelope over in her hand, then grinned. A taped-up newspaper envelope? Her name and address in crayon?

"Gramps."

"He's in the envelope?"

She elbowed Alan, and he backed away, feigning injury. "No, but he sent it. I'm sure he did. It's just the kind of thing he'd do."

Alan took the handmade envelope and arched his brows. "What, is he senile?"

Kylie laughed out loud at that. "Not at all. He's just"—her lips twitched—"well, eccentric."

"That's a nice way of saying crazy. It happens when people age sometimes."

"Yeah, well, Gramps was born that way. He's amazing. My mom tells stories about when she was a kid. She thought everyone's parents were like hers."

"Come on, they couldn't have been that unique."

"Oh, yes, they can. It wasn't until Mom was in grade school that she realized it wasn't exactly the norm to have your father rise before the sun every day, brew a strong pot of coffee, and then go climb a ladder to the roof. There he'd sit, drinking the coffee from a thermos and reading the early-morning edition of the paper."

Alan's expression was priceless. "You're kidding me."

She nodded. "Nope. He sat up there every day. According to Mom, he said it was the best place in town to watch the day come to life."

"And your grandmother put up with it?"

"Not only that, she'd toss the paper up to him. And she has her own distinctions. She's always worn these beautiful, bright straw hats and colorful, gauzy dresses that swoosh when she floats by. Oh, yes, and she quotes Shakespeare or Longfellow or Hawthorne or a dozen other classical writers at the slightest provocation." Kylie wiggled her brows. "Sometimes, backward." She shook her head. "It's just Grams's way of carrying on a conversation."

Alan laughed. "OK, you win. They sound like a hoot."

"They are that." Kylie pulled the note from the envelope and four words jumped out at her: *Come see me. Now.* "Hey, Alan, do me a favor?"

"Anytime."

"Finish checking the Siberian's teeth for me, will you?"

His eyes widened. "You're handing off a Siberian? The 'most perfect breed in existence'?"

She batted at him with the note. Leave it to Alan to use her love for Siberians against her.

"Must be something really important. I thought you were here 'til six."

"I thought I was, too. Fortunately, Dasha was my last scheduled appointment today. So if you'll be an angel and finish her up, I can check this"—she waved the note in front of his face—"out."

"You're lucky to have me, you know that?"

She slipped her white lab coat off, hung it in the closet, and grabbed her jacket and purse. "So you keep telling me. Every day. Several times a day—"

"Sorry, no time to chat." Alan headed to the exam room. "Dedicated vet on his way to better a dog's life."

"You're my hero."

"And don't you forget it."

She tossed him a cheeky grin. "Ha! Like you'd ever let that happen." She grabbed her purse, pulled open the outside door, and trotted to her car. She had no idea what this note was about, but had a feeling Gramps's explanation would be one for the books.

She could hardly wait to hear it.

Brendan pulled into the driveway of his grandparents' house just in time to see his sister, Kylie, slide out of her car.

He pushed open his car door and stepped out. "Yo, sister mine. I take it you got a letter, too?"

She hurried over to give him a hug. "Newspaper. With crayon."

"Ditto. But with marker, not crayon."

"You've always been more sophisticated than I."

They walked up the cobblestone path to the front door.

"Any idea what's up?"

He glanced at his sister. He'd been pondering that very question during the crazy drive here. "I can only think of one thing."

She sighed. "Mom?"

"Mom."

Kylie pressed the doorbell, then grinned. "OK, what's the tune this time?"

He pressed the doorbell, listened, then nodded. "It's one of those golden oldies. . . . Oh yeah!" He swept Kylie into his arms for an impromptu dance, and sang out, "'Let me call you *Sweet*heart—'"

"I forgot your *naaaaame,*" she chimed in.

"That's not how the song goes, young lady, and you know it."

The siblings stopped their whirling and turned to grin at their grandfather standing in the now-open doorway.

"Come on in, you two." He stepped aside and swept his arm inward. "Grandmother put milk and cookies on the table for us before she went shopping."

"Fresh cookies?" Brendan let go of his sister so fast she almost fell over.

"Hey!"

He ignored Kylie's indignation and headed for the kitchen.

In short order, the three were situated around the kitchen table.

"So, Gramps—" Brendan spoke around a mouthful of still-warm-from-the-oven, melt-in-your-mouth grandma cookies. "What's so important you paid for two special deliveries to get us here?"

All humor left his grandfather's features. His whole body seemed to sag.

Brendan sat forward. "It's Mom, isn't it?"

Gramps's somber gaze said it all.

Kylie released a heavy sigh. "So it's time?"

Gramps inclined his head. "I'm afraid so. We just don't seem to have any other choice." He pulled several folded sheets of paper from his pocket and smoothed them out on the table. "These are your assignments." He handed a sheet of paper to each of them.

Brendan studied his paper, and couldn't restrain the slow grin easing across his mouth. "Brilliant. Devious, but brilliant."

Kylie looked up from hers and regarded her grandfather, new respect showing in her expression. "If I doubted it before, I won't do so again." She laid a hand on their grandfather's arm. "You are a genius."

"So—" Gramps reached out to cover Brendan's and Kylie's hands with his own. "It's unanimous. Operation Save Your Mom has officially begun."

The Mom Assignment

CHAPTER

One

*Kitty's eyes cracked, opened. She groaned. Ac-*knowledging the new morning was the last thing she wanted to do.

She had dreaded this particular day for weeks. Wished she could just sleep through it. Forget it existed.

But that wasn't possible.

Not with her devoted offspring, Kylie and Brendan, along with her parents, "watching over" her. They were all so determined to help her, to cheer her up.

It made her want to scream.

"Hope you're getting ready, Mom," her son, Brendan, had said a few days ago, that forced smile on his handsome face. "One more month until we *march* into April."

Of course he'd been trying to tug her out of the doldrums, trying to encourage her into their family tradition of making April Fool's a day of fun and celebration and laughter. Ever since the children were small, March 1 had been, for their family, the starting date for "marching" forward—and planning the biggest and best April Fool's caper of all.

How could she tell Brendan it was that very fact that triggered her depression? Yes, the other holidays since Dan's death had been difficult, but with her family's love and support, she'd managed to endure them. Rather admirably, she thought.

They'd even tried to make a go of it last April Fool's Day. They'd all said the right things and done the right things. And they'd all been loath to admit it was a colossal failure. Everything they attempted only seemed to bring Dan's absence back into stark focus.

She should have known it would be a waste of time to even try. April Fool's was *their* holiday. A tradition she and Dan started when they were dating. And one they'd continued—and worked hard to perfect—every year since. So when Kitty glanced at the calendar last week and realized it was only ten days to March . . . then thought about how April was on it's way . . . how this would be the third April Fool's Day without her husband . . . well, a bone-deep weariness had settled over her. All she felt was a bleak awareness of how horribly different that once-special day would be from now on.

Of course, it only made matters worse that April 1 also had been Dan's birthday.

And the day they got married.

It was so fitting. Dan was a man who knew how to live with enthusiasm and joy. Indeed, most days their household was steeped in "buffoonery and tomfoolery," as Dan loved to call it. It was a well-documented fact: Let a practical joke take place in the Hawk household, and Kitty could be sure that the instigator was as often her husband as it was their children. Kitty didn't mind. She enjoyed a good prank, though she usually played the role of spectator. Or victim.

A memory shoved its way into her mind, an image so clear and distinct she felt she could almost reach out and touch it. . . .

She had come up from the basement and found herself in the middle of a fierce water fight.

Inside the house.

In the living room.

Water dripped from the curtains and dribbled down the TV screen. A small pool was forming on the floor, held in check only by the cotton rug in front of the now-soggy couch. Her six-foot-three, forty-year-old husband was crouched behind the couch, full Super Soaker in hand.

"Daniel Willia—!" But her near-scream was cut short when what had to be an entire glass of water hit her full in the face.

Horrified silence filled the room for an instant. Then, "Way to go, genius sister. You just creamed Mom."

"Me? I didn't cream her! That was you!"

"Not a chance. Your signature idiocy at work, runt."

She turned to glare at her eldest child, her only son, Brendan, her firstborn, the one who was her constant ally in the onslaught of life—and could not believe the cheeky grin on his face.

"Yo, Mom, gotta learn to duck." He held out a handful of already damp paper towels.

"No, I need to *be* a duck." She snatched the proffered towels and tried to stem the stream of water dripping from her hair and off the tip of her nose.

An arm slid around her shoulders, and she glanced up at Dan's face, which bore his most winning smile. He didn't have a drop of water on him.

She narrowed her gaze. "Don't. Even. Try."

"I think you'll find this works better." He held a dry towel out to her.

She stared at it, not moving. Another drip off her elbow.

"You'll feel better if you dry off."

She hated it when he did that, talked to her in that low, sweet tone when she wanted to be outraged. He *knew* laughter—his or hers—was one of her greatest weaknesses.

Kitty looked away. "Forget it, Dan Juan. You aren't getting off so easily." She spread her hands toward the room. "What do you think this is? The lost city of Atlantis?"

He looked properly chastised—or he tried, anyway, but the twinkle in his hazel eyes belied his penitent demeanor. A rebellious swath of thick, honey-brown hair fell down on his forehead, and she fought the urge to reach out and brush it back.

"How did you stay so dry?"

"I learned to duck."

"Told you so, Mom," Brendan crowed.

She shook her head. "This room *will* be cleaned up."

"Yes, dear."

"And it will not be used for water fights in the future."

"Yes, Mom," her three troublemakers replied in chorus.

She took the towel from Dan, dried her face with it, then whipped it into a rope and snapped him with it. He jumped back, hands up. She met his laughing gaze. "And you will take me out to the restaurant of my choice to help me recover from the trauma I've suffered."

His slow smile warmed her from head to toe. "It would be my pleasure."

The sound of his voice, low and loving, echoed in her mind, as clear now as it ever had been. *No . . . no, the pleasure was all mine. And now it's gone.*

How exactly did one endure a birthday when the guest of honor was dead?

Fresh pain swept her and she rolled over, pulling the pillow over her head. "I can't do this anymore," she whispered to no one in particular. At least she told herself it was to no one. She absolutely, positively was *not* talking to God. Why bother? He clearly had stopped listening to her.

Otherwise, her husband would still be alive. Wouldn't he?

Despair slid into the bed beside her, covering as completely as the blanket she was clutching. She squeezed her eyes defiantly against the tears that pushed to escape.

She was tired of crying. She'd already cried a river. No, an ocean. No, *three* oceans. She gave a wobbly chuckle. How could one body hold so much water?

Get hold of yourself, Kitty! It's been two years. Twenty-four months. Seven hundred thirty days . . .

And every one of them a struggle. Oh, she got up each morning—well, most mornings anyway—and took up the business of living. But it wasn't the same. When Dan was alive, they'd relished their days together. They'd loved to go places. Whether on a trip, or just to the park or the library, they found things to do and enjoy. But without him . . .

Without Dan, Kitty was finding fewer and fewer reasons for going anywhere. It all just took so much effort. Or for getting up in the morning. Dan used to tease her about being such an early riser. Sleeping in meant not getting up until six a.m. Now she could hardly drag herself out of bed by ten. Or, on days like today, by noon.

Dan would be ashamed if he saw you like this! that same scolding voice nagged at her. *Get on with your life.*

Kitty clenched her fists. She wanted to hit something. So many well-meaning friends and family members had urged her to do that. Get on with her life. But no one could answer the question that continued to scream in her head: *What* life? What kind of life was left for her without the husband who had filled her days with love and laughter since she was eighteen. Nearly thirty years.

Twenty-eight, to be exact. We were married for twenty-eight years. And in all that time, he'd only made her cry twice: four years ago, when he told her he had cancer, then two years ago, when he died.

It had been, to Kitty's grief-dazed mind, the most unbeatable and horrible April Fool's joke of all.

The first April when Dan was gone, they'd all been so engulfed in grief none of them even noticed the date until the day was long past. Last year . . . well, that disaster was most likely at least a part of why it had hit her with such force this year.

Now all she wanted to do was hide.

If only she could be different. Follow Dan's lead. He'd believed so fully in the power of prayer and joy and laughter. "I know who's in control," he often said, even after his diagnosis, "so why should I get discouraged?"

True to his words, he hadn't allowed discouragement entrance into his heart or his home. Not once. Not in the midst of pain, not in the face of death. Amazingly, even as she was losing him, he'd filled Kitty's days with laughter, regaling her with tales of the nurses, the doctors, the other patients.

"There's so much joy all around us, Kitty." His once booming voice had grown weak and hoarse. "Don't ever forget that. Laughter is a gift from God, because he loves you so much. Don't let go of it, and don't let go of your dreams."

Laughter. Dreams. God. All a part of who Dan was. And all the things in life Kitty had lost.

I am with you.

The familiar words whispered through her mind, striking deep within her. She wanted to embrace them, to draw on them as a drowning man would draw on a tank of oxygen. But she couldn't. No, that wasn't true. She wouldn't.

I don't believe you. You aren't with me. You can't be. You let Dan die.

The creaking of the door alerted Kitty that she wasn't alone any longer.

"Mom?"

She didn't move or answer.

"Mom." The voice was closer now. Kylie. Sweet Kylie, the younger of their two children. Kitty had always shared a special connection with Kylie.

"She's your daughter, through and through," Dan often said. Kitty couldn't argue. For one thing, Kylie and Kitty both were dreamers. "Creative types," Brendan called them, usually with a self-effacing grin. After all, he was an artist himself. "Lots of imagination and no common sense." Some might be insulted at this, but Kitty didn't mind. As far as she was concerned, common sense was highly overrated.

Kylie also shared Kitty's deep love of animals. So much so that she'd studied veterinary medicine and was now one of the youngest—and most requested—vets at the local animal clinic. Kitty and Dan had been so proud of her.

As they'd been proud of their son. Brendan was a gifted artist. No matter the medium, he created such beauty with his hands. Galleries across the country showed his works. "The next Picasso," Dan would say with a grin. "Hurry up and make a million, Son, so your mother and I can retire!"

And yet, for all their professional successes, what pleased Dan most about their children was that they lived lives of faith. Kitty and Dan had raised them to do so, but in a world where so many voices clamor for a kid's attention, Dan had found it a special joy that his children stayed tuned to the voice of God.

"God's blessings to us have been abundant. And evident." It was Dan's favorite saying, especially when he was looking at or talking about their children.

"Mom?" Kylie's voice came again, a bit more insistent this time.

Go away. She didn't want to talk to anyone. *Go away, I'm asleep.* To prove it, she gave as realistic a snore as she could manage.

Her only reward was a snort of disbelief. "Nice try, Mom, but my room was next to Brendan's, remember? There's no way I'd buy that for a real snore. The walls aren't shaking." Her voice gentled. "Come on, Mom. I know you're awake, so you might as well sit up."

Kitty gritted her teeth and pushed the pillow away, peering at her daughter. "I thought I taught you children to be polite. Can't you see I'm . . . resting?"

Quick sorrow filled her daughter's eyes, and Kitty felt a stab of guilt. But she shoved it aside. Why should she feel guilty? Didn't she have the right to be left alone if she wished?

She started to say as much to Kylie when her daughter turned and walked toward the window, her steps determined. "Kylie." Kitty made the word forceful, hoping to stop her, but her daughter didn't pause.

"Looks like you forgot to open the curtains, Mom. You always told us you couldn't stand a room without sunshine." She took hold of the curtains and pulled them back, letting the light pour into the dark room.

"Don't!" But either her daughter had developed an acute case of deafness or she was ignoring Kitty. Kylie didn't even break her stride as she moved to the second window and set the daylight loose there as well.

Kitty pushed herself into a sitting position. "Kylie—"

"Wow, what a beautiful day. A good day for the park."

"*Kylie.*" Kitty let her tone grow ominous.

For all the good it did.

Kylie gave her a bright smile, pulled the curtains back on the last window, then moved to the doorway of the room.

"There you go, Mom."

Rotten child. She acted as though she'd just done Kitty some enormous favor. A quick, cutting retort jumped to her mind, but before she could voice it, Kylie lifted what looked like an animal carrier from the floor and plopped it on the bed.

"Anyway, I just stopped by to ask you a favor." Kylie opened the lid of the carrier.

"What—?" But whatever Kitty started to say stopped in her throat. Something small and furry darted out and dove under the covers.

"Awwwwk!" Kitty scrambled to get away from the creature, but it seemed to have decided it wanted to get to know her. Up close and personal. It crawled straight at her, and she pushed back until she slammed into the headboard. Folding her knees up against her chest, she looked around for a weapon.

Suddenly something clambered up her nightgown-covered legs. A yelp rose in her throat, but before she could scream the critter was there, perched on her knees, nose-to-nose with her. A pair of clever little eyes—small, black, and *beady*—scrutinized her with what appeared to be keen interest. A small pink nose twitched, whiskers all atremble.

Kitty stared in horrified silence for a second, then exploded from the bed with a screech. "A *rat*??! You put a *rat* in my bed??" She flattened against the wall. "Kylie Renae, have you gone stark-raving mad??"

"Mother!" Kylie frowned at her. "You frightened him!"

"I—!" Kitty stared at her daughter as though she'd turned purple. "*I* frightened *him*??"

Kylie didn't respond. She was busy looking under the covers, then under the pillows. Finally, she peered inside one of the pillows and a grin broke over her features. "There you are," she cooed, reaching down to scoop the animal up. She cradled the long, furry body against her, and gave Kitty a lopsided grin. "He's not a rat, Mom." She held the animal up for her perusal. "He's a ferret."

Kitty looked more closely, then arched a brow and pinned her daughter with a glare. "You'll have to forgive me, I left my field guide in my other nightgown."

Kylie chuckled. "You've seen ferrets before, Mother. We watched a special on the Discovery channel about them, remember?"

"I remember they're weasels." Kitty wasn't budging from the wall. The ferret hung from Kylie's hands, looking every inch a weasel. But, Kitty had to admit, a very cute, very patient weasel.

Its long, sleek body and bushy tail dangled loosely as it turned its head this way and that, taking in its surroundings. Its little paws were cupped over Kylie's fingers and folded over each other, almost as though the creature were praying. Its coloring actually was similar to a raccoon, with black and gray and white in the fur. It even had a black "bandit's mask" across its sharp, little eyes.

A disturbing realization hit Kitty. A few years ago Kylie had brought home a hedgehog. "They're all the rage for apartment pets," she'd claimed.

Kitty had been delighted and intrigued. In fact, she'd gone right over to pet the little animal, laughing at its antics. But now . . .

She closed her eyes. Now she just didn't have the energy. So she stood there, not moving, not speaking. Until her daughter's voice, so full of warmth and tenderness, whispered against her ear. "Go ahead and pet him, Mom. He's really soft."

Kitty opened her eyes. She wanted to refuse, to tell her daughter she saw right through her, that she was not going to get to her through this little bit of a fur ball—but she held her tongue, loath to wipe the hope from her daughter's face. With a sigh, she reached out a tentative hand.

The ferret watched her every move, sniffing at her finger as she touched its fur. Kylie was right, he was soft. Surprisingly so. She felt a smile tug at her lips as one little paw came to curl around her thumb, and a tiny, sandpaper tongue darted out to lick the tip of her finger.

Kitty met her daughter's laughing gaze. "OK, so he's not a rat."

"And?"

Why didn't she teach her daughter how to leave good enough alone? "Fine. And he's cute."

Kylie cradled the ferret in one arm and took hold of Kitty's nightgown sleeve with her free hand. "Come over here."

Kitty let her daughter tug her toward the chair near the window, then sat as directed.

"Here." Kylie handed her the ferret.

"Wait—"

Kylie didn't. She settled the small animal into Kitty's arms. She stiffened, waiting for it to bolt, but it just sniffed, then curled into a warm, furry ball, its tail draped over its pink nose, and gave a deep, contented sigh.

Kitty felt her heart melting. "So what's this favor you need to ask?" She reached out one finger to scratch the little head between the ears.

"He needs a home."

Kitty looked up ready to make a quick refusal, but Kylie held her hand up, forestalling the objection. "Not for good, Mom. Just . . . for a while. His name is Bosco. A family brought him in a couple of months ago because they couldn't keep him. I thought he'd find a home quickly, but he hasn't." Kylie looked down at the now sleeping ferret. "We've all had fun with him at the clinic, so he's gotten lots of handling, which is good. But Dr. Dupuis told us yesterday that we can't keep him any longer, that we needed to find a shelter for him."

"Why don't you keep him?"

Kylie shook her head. "One doesn't keep a ferret in the same home with Siberians. They'd think I'd brought home an hors d'oeuvre. I did check into ferret shelters or rescues in this area, but there don't seem to be any. I'd hate to see him destroyed. He's really a neat little guy."

Just then Bosco stretched, opened his mouth wide for a heartfelt yawn, then rolled onto his back, and snuggled into the protective circle of Kitty's arms. His front paws were folded together, as though in serene supplication.

Stop that! Stop being adorable. You are not going to make me like you.

"Please, Mom. You might even decide you enjoy him . . . or want to keep him." She gave Kitty the look. The one she'd perfected around age two, all puppy eyes and toddler entreaty.

It worked every time.

Kitty's mind screamed at her to push the sleeping bundle of fur back into her daughter's arms. Her heart cried out that it was too weary to care about anything. Determined, Kitty met her daughter's gaze and uttered her pronouncement. "For how long?"

The triumph lighting Kylie's face was the perfect foil for the disgusted defeat echoing in Kitty's head. *You're a cream puff. A waffle. Limp spaghetti has more of a backbone than you—*

"A few weeks. A month at the most."

"At the *most*," Kitty echoed firmly. "And just for the record, I won't want to keep him."

Her daughter leaned down to plant a kiss on her cheek. "Whatever you say, Mom." She sailed to the door. "And thanks. I'll go get his stuff from my car."

Kitty looked up. "Stuff? A ferret has stuff?"

"Oh, sure." Kylie waved a hand in the air. "A cage, his toys, litter box, his leash and halter—"

"Leash?" Kitty looked down at the animal. "For what?"

Kylie blinked. "Walks, of course. At least once a day." Her smile broadened. "Good thing the park is so close, huh?"

"Now, wait a minute! I never agreed to go to the park!"

But her daughter wasn't there to respond. She was bounding down the stairs, singing as she went, "Oh, what a *beyoo*-tiful moooorning! Oh, what a *beyoo*-tiful daaaaay! I've got a wonderful *feel*ing *ev*-'rything's go-ing my waaaaay."

Kitty settled back in the chair with a snort. "Little monster," she muttered, undecided whether she was referring to the ferret or her daughter.

CHAPTER
Two

It didn't take long for Kylie to coax Kitty to get dressed and come help her set up the cage in the living room. Together they got Bosco settled into his new home.

His temporary *home.* Kitty poked a finger into the cage to stroke the ferret's head. *He's not staying.*

"This is his food. These are his toys. He loves bananas as a treat, but don't give him too much." Kylie handed Kitty a book— *The Joy of Ferrets*—then made a beeline for the door. "And give me a call if you have any questions or problems. But I doubt you will. I think you two will get along like hot chocolate and marshmallows."

"Hmm." Kitty turned to look at Bosco, who was even now happily exploring his new digs. A new rush of panic hit her. Why had she let her daughter talk her into this?

"Kylie, wait! I don't think—"

But she was gone. The sound of her car starting up and driving away gave the ring of finality to the situation. No getting out of it now.

Kitty went to sit on the couch, watching Bosco as he pushed his way under the towel Kylie had put in the cage for him, then crawling up into the cloth hammock hanging from the top of the cage.

The animal had more sleeping arrangements than she did, for heaven's sake.

Kitty pulled her knees to her chest, encircling them with her arms. What was she thinking, letting Kylie leave the animal here? What if something happened? What if Kitty did something wrong and the animal got away? Or died? What if—?

Kitty . . . don't be afraid.

She caught her breath and closed her eyes against sudden tears. Just like that, she was thrown back to their last day. The day Dan left her for eternity. He'd taken her hand, brought it to his face. She had to lean close to hear his once-vibrant voice, now reduced to a whisper.

"Kitty, don't be afraid. You won't be alone. Not ever. There's so much love all around you." His eyes captured hers. "Hold onto wonder. Don't turn away, sweetheart. Let love find you. . . ."

Her heart breaking, she'd promised she would. Promised she'd go on, be open—

Enough. She stood, brushing away the tears along with the echoes, the memories that pierced her through, the knowledge that she'd broken each and every promise. . . .

She pushed it all away, forcing herself to focus on the here and now. On reality.

"So temporary roomies, huh?" She leaned forward and met Bosco's beady gaze. "Here's hoping we both survive it."

As Brendan sat waiting for a red light, his Bluetooth signaled a call. Before he could say anything, the caller spoke.

"Red Toad, this is Blue Dog. Phase One of the mission has been implemented. You're authorized to begin Phase Two."

He looked to the roof of his car. "And you're authorized to go to the nut house, sister dear."

Kylie laughed. "You just can't stand it that I'm more creative than you are. Wait'll you see what I did for Phase One."

She sounded so smug. Well, let her. She'd learn soon enough that his plans were beyond anything she could conceive. "I'm sure you think you've done something brilliant, but let's not forget who the true creative genius is here."

"Yeah, right!"

"Oh, trust me. Phase Two will rock your world."

"It's not *my* world that needs rocking."

Brendan started to chuckle. "It's taken care of, Sis. Phase Two is a guaranteed success."

Kitty leaned back against the cushions. She loved this couch. She and Dan had picked it out together. They'd hunted for weeks to find just the right one. When they discovered this couch at one of the finer furniture establishments in town, they made sure it was comfortable enough by lying down on it. In the showroom.

Of course, they'd taken their shoes off first. Didn't want to get it dirty.

Warmth filled her at the memory, followed by quick surprise. Such memories had brought a pang of pain and loss. This time, all she felt was gratitude for all she and Dan had shared.

A clattering drew her attention, and she glanced toward Bosco. Thank heaven! He was right where he should be, in his cage, playing with his water dish.

In the week since Kylie had deposited the animal into Kitty's life, he'd escaped his cage twice. How, Kitty had yet to fathom. She pinned him with a narrowed gaze. "I dare you to get out again." Not likely. She'd put extra fasteners on the door. That should keep him in place.

She hoped so, anyway. She'd learned the hard way that few things were as difficult to find as a gallivanting ferret. Amazing the places that animal could hide. His most recent trick? Chewing a hole through the fabric on the bottom of the sofa and crawling inside.

"He's a burrowing animal, Mom," Kylie explained when she came to extract him from the couch. "It's instinct."

"So is saving my sofa!"

At Kitty's retort, her daughter pursed her lips. "Mom, if he's too much trouble, I can find someone else to watch him."

"That won't be necessary." Kitty wasn't sure who was more surprised at her quick response, her daughter or herself. She scooped the squirming animal out of her daughter's hands and settled him back in his cage.

"So . . . starting to like the little guy, eh?"

She just might have admitted it was true if Kylie hadn't sounded so smug. "Don't be silly." She arranged Bosco's towel around him, then gave him a scritch behind the tiny ears before latching the cage door. "I promised my darling daughter I'd help her out, and that's what I'm going to do." She turned to meet her daughter's twinkling eyes. "No more, no less."

"Uh-huh."

That had been the extent of her daughter's response. Remarkable how so few words could speak volumes.

Kitty looked at Bosco. "Let her believe what she wants. You and I know the truth, and that's all that matters."

Bosco responded by coming to the side of the cage and going up on his hind legs, staring at her like an unjustly imprisoned captive pleading to be freed.

"Oh, no you don't, you rascal. You just stay where you are."

He continued to stare at her, those intent little eyes seemingly filled with entreaty.

"Oh . . ." Kitty sighed. He was just so darned cute! "Fine. You can go for a ride later."

She had to admire the little guy's tenacity. For all that he barely weighed three pounds, he didn't know the meaning of surrender. Or fear. He loved perching on Kitty's shoulder as she walked through the house. Generally, he was content to drape himself around her neck, like a living fur collar. But from time to time, he'd get overtaken with something her mother used to call "a wild hare," and make a kamikaze leap from her shoulder to whatever surface was handy.

The first time he did this he scared the wits out of Kitty. Fortunately, he landed on the couch, so no damage done. After that she started putting his harness and leash on him. Just for safety's sake, of course

He also loved to race around the house at top speed, slipping this way and that. He would run up to her, them back up, bobbing his head and making the most hilarious sounds.

She hadn't laughed in the last year as much as she'd done these last few days watching the little scamp's antics.

"But I'm not starting to like you, weasel. Not even a little."

Just then, the phone rang. It was Brendan. "Yo, mother mine. Just wanted to let you know I called the repairman."

Kitty frowned. "Repairman? For what?"

"For the various and sundry things you've been asking *me* to fix for months now. Like I have any idea what to do with a dripping faucet or a toilet that runs on and on and on. . . ."

"Not in a successful artist's pay grade, dear?"

"Definitely not."

"Is a repairman really necessary?" She cringed at the prospect of having someone she didn't know hanging around. Even if it *was* to fix her faucet. "I think I'm getting used to the drip. It's . . ." Oh dear. What would sound like a plausible reason for not fixing a dripping faucet? "Soothing." That was possible, wasn't it? Everyone said the sound of water was soothing. OK, not dripping, but still . . . "I kind of like listening to it at night."

"You're selling, Mom, but I'm not buying. 'Soothing'? Is this the same sound you told me was going to drive you up the wall?"

She had no answer for that.

"Don't worry. This guy is reasonably priced and highly dependable."

"*Now* who's selling something?"

Brendan ignored her. "He's a nice, old guy. His wife died some twenty years ago, Pastor David said. He joined the church six months ago or so. You'll like him, I'm sure."

First the ferret, now a repairman. How was it her children were so convinced they knew better than she what—and whom— she would like? Besides, she hadn't been to church in months. And she was supposed to let some little old man hang around, holding a mirror up for her to see how far she'd fallen from the days when Dan was alive? No, thank you. "Brendan, really—"

"Great! It's settled. He's coming this afternoon, so keep an eye out for him. His name is Kartz. Or Krantz. Or something like that."

"But I—"

"Okey dokey, Mom. Talk to you later. Love you!"

The dial tone sounded in Kitty's ear, and she held out the receiver, staring at it as though it had come to life.

A rattle of wire drew her attention back to Bosco, who was shoving his food dish around the cage with his nose.

"Well!" Kitty dropped the receiver in place. "How do you like that? It's my house and I'm being told who"—she glared at Bosco—"and *what* is coming over." She went to stand by the cage, her arms crossed. "Well, you and Mr. Kratz may get in the door, but neither of you is staying long."

She marched to the couch, flopped down on it, and opened the book on ferret care. "So don't bother getting too comfortable, my fine furry friend. This is a temporary arrangement. Just keep that in mind."

Bosco paused, looking at her as though considering her words, then suddenly exploded into action. He bounced forward, then bobbed back and forth, shaking his head from side to side and making the oddest noise.

Alarm swept her, and Kitty jumped up and rushed to the cage. "Are you OK?" *Please, please, don't let anything happen to him.*

The desperation of her inner plea startled her—and disturbed her. But a quick study told her the ferret wasn't in any pain or distress. In fact, he looked as though he were dancing.

Bosco chirped. No, it wasn't a chirp. It was more like a grunt. Like a little pig grunt . . . like a very happy little pig grunt.

Kitty narrowed her eyes. "What in the world are you doing?"

Bosco stopped his crazy dance, looked up at her, then came to the side of the cage and sniffed at her. His eyes were wide and curious, and he looked for all the world as though he were saying, "Hey there, don't worry, be happy!"

Kitty shook her head. "I never should have let Kylie talk me into this. I'm just not up to it!"

Bosco tipped his head, then ambled over to his hammock, sniffed it thoroughly, then climbed in and curled up with a deep sigh.

Kitty stood there, watching him, wishing she could be so content, so at peace. Suddenly, words drifted into her mind: *"I am with you."*

The words rolled over her, through her, deep within her. She tried to work up the anger, to fight against the reassurance as she'd done every time some passage from God's Word had come to her since Dan's death. But she couldn't. There was something stirring within her, something flaring into life as she watched Bosco's deep, even breathing and peaceful repose. He had no control over his life. He was at the mercy of those around him, those who decided if he lived or died . . . and yet he was at peace.

He's an animal! He hasn't got the brain power to be afraid! a mocking voice within her jeered.

True enough, but the ferret had something else working for him. Instinct. All animals could tell, instinctively, if they were in trouble or not. Bosco clearly sensed he was in caring hands.

So what? So an animal feels safe with you. What does that mean?

Kitty wasn't sure. Not exactly. But there was something rumbling around in her mind . . . something about trust, and faith, and knowing, instinctively, that she was safe in eternal, caring hands.

"Your unfailing love, O Lord, is as vast as the heavens." The psalm, long a favorite of hers, came to her like a tide, and she recited it in a whispered voice. "Your faithfulness reaches beyond the clouds, your righteousness is like the mighty mountains, your justice like the ocean depths." Tears slowly found their way down her cheeks. "You care for people and animals alike, O Lord. How precious is your unfailing love. All humanity finds shelter in the shadow of your wings . . . for you are the fountain of life, the light by which we see."

I am with you.

Raw emotion washed over her, crashing like a tidal wave on the rock that had been her heart, wearing it down until the sharp, jagged, angry edges finally, painfully, began to smooth.

"Oh, Jesus . . ." At the heart cry, light was set loose within her. It was as though—she let go a deep sigh—as though she was coming home.

Her gaze drifted back to Bosco, who was now fast asleep, lying on his back, his head dangling over the side of the hammock, the very tip of his pink tongue sticking out of his mouth. Kitty chuckled through her tears.

"I sure had you pegged wrong. Here I thought you were an intruding little weasel." She smiled. "Turns out you're an emissary from God." She expelled a soft breath. "Who knew?"

God did.

That nudged at her as she sat on the couch. God knew. He knew everything she struggled with. Every bit of loss and anger. Every bitterness and regret.

Kitty closed her eyes for a moment. It was all too much to think about. Too overwhelming. She needed . . . time. She opened her eyes and looked around for a distraction. There. The book on ferrets. She reached for it and opened the pages. "OK, let's get down to business."

It only took a moment of squinting at the page to realize she needed more light. She leaned over to turn on the lamp, but her hand paused in mid-reach. There, next to the lamp on the end table, was Dan's Bible. It had sat in that spot, untouched, since his death. Oh, she'd dusted it—she didn't want it to look unused—but that was all. She'd refused to open it. Or to open her own Bible, which was put away in a drawer upstairs.

I am with you.

Biting the side of her mouth, Kitty turned on the lamp. She wasn't ready—

I am with you.

She laid her hand on top of the Bible, fingering the worn, well-used leather cover. She could still see the way Dan's hands had held the Bible as he read it.

I am with you. . . . I will give you peace.

Kitty felt the prick of tears. Peace. How she longed for peace, for the sense of safety and shelter she'd known for so many years. How had she lost them?

The answer came to her, soft and gentle, yet filled with power. The power of truth.

Because they were based in Dan.

A small gasp escaped her. Everything within her wanted to deny it, but she couldn't. The more she let the thought penetrate, the more she knew it was so. Her security, her sense of being sheltered, even her faith had been based not on God, but on Dan.

The truth will set you free. . . .

How many times had she heard that in her life? Hundreds? More. And yet she'd never really understood. Not until this very moment. For as the truth filled her, something else happened—

The weight that had settled over her at Dan's deathbed, that had pressed on her heart and spirit every day since, began to lift. Kitty picked up Dan's Bible and held it against her chest. She let her eyes drift shut as she lifted her face to heaven. *Father, forgive me . . .*

And then—it was there. Peace. Engulfing her like a familiar, comforting quilt. She held Dan's Bible close a moment longer, then laid it in her lap, opened the cover, and fingered the thin pages.

"OK." She flipped the pages to Genesis. Chapter One. "Let's get down to business."

Three

Crash! Bang!

Kitty sat up with a jerk, sending the Bible flying to the floor. She blinked rapidly, trying to free her fogged mind. *Must have fallen asleep. . . .* She knelt to pick up the book. *None the worse for wear,* she decided.

Pushing herself upward, her hand touched the newspaper, spread across the floor. Kitty paused. She'd put the paper in a nice, neat pile next to the couch. How had it gotten spread out—?

Crash!

"What in the world . . . ?" She looked around. And then she saw it. Bosco's empty cage. Her mouth dropped open, and she stared at the open door of the ferret's cage.

"Oh, no! But how—?"

Bang!

She whirled and started for the sound, sudden awareness catching her attention. The living room looked like a tornado had hit it! The table lamp was knocked over and on the floor. That must have been what awakened her. But it wasn't the only evidence of the ferret's freedom. In addition to the paper and the lamp, couch pillows were scattered all about, as though someone had thrown them in the air in wild abandon.

Kitty clenched her teeth. "I hope you had fun, you little rat, because the party's over." She looked around, then frowned. "At least, it will be when I find you."

Crash!

Kitty spun in the direction of the noise. The kitchen. The little dickens was in the kitchen.

She rushed into the room, and the sight that met her there stopped her cold. Her containers of flour, sugar, and salt had been knocked over, and there was a blanket of the three substances covering the room. What wasn't blanketed had tiny, white ferret paw prints tracked across it. The dishes that had been stacked in the drainer to dry were scattered across the counter, and the window above the sink was now sporting a huge hole in the glass.

"Oh, *Bosco!*" She scanned the room. Speaking of the little devil, where *was* he?

A grunting sound drew her attention, and she turned and looked up. . . .

There, atop the refrigerator, whiskers and paws covered with flower, was Bosco. He bobbed his head, backing up and chattering gaily as though to say, "See, Mom? Look what I did for you!"

Kitty lunged, and the ferret squealed and scampered off the fridge and down onto the countertop.

"Bosco! *Come!*" Who was she kidding? Ferrets didn't come on command. Which Bosco set out to prove. He didn't even break stride as he scrambled across the kitchen counter. Kitty went after him, but the flour on the floor made it slick. Without warning, her feet suddenly shot out from under her, and she landed with a thump on her back.

Dazed from the fall, she stared up . . . and found a furry little face staring back at her. Bosco was balanced on the edge of the sink, peering at her, his nose whiskers twitching.

Ignoring twinges of pain, Kitty reached up slowly, slowly. . . .

Bosco sprang from the sink and landed right in the middle of Kitty's prone form. She yelped, then grabbed at him, but the ferret was already gone, scampering across the kitchen floor and out into the living room, chattering all the way.

Kitty scrambled up and went in hot pursuit. "Bosco, you little rat!"

That only seemed to spur the ferret into greater speed. He dashed around the room, leaving little white paw prints all over Kitty's blue carpeting. She followed his lead, over the fallen lamp, around the couch, through the potted floor plant, and then . . . he scooted under the couch.

"Oh, no!"

That couch weighed a ton! The last thing Kitty wanted to do was try to move it to grab her little escapee.

The doorbell rang.

"Brendan, where are you when I need your muscle?" Kitty wailed as she went to pull the door open.

"Mrs. Hawk?"

Kitty stared for a moment, then clapped her hands together. "Wonderful! A *man*! Just what I need." She reached out to grab the front of the man's jacket and pulled him inside.

"Excuse me?" He stared at her wide-eyed.

She tugged him toward the couch. "Hurry, over here."

"Whoa, lady, I'm just the repairman!"

She turned to regard him, and the shock on his face stopped her. She suddenly realized what she'd said and how it must have sounded to him. "Oh, my! No, no, no!" Heat flooded her cheeks. "When I said I needed a man I didn't mean—" Oh, good heavens. This was awful! "That is, I wasn't asking you—well, not exactly . . . what I mean is, well—"

"What"—he looked from her to the couch—"*did* you mean? Exactly?"

Her answer was cut off by a now-familiar baby pig grunt. Kitty spun to stare at Bosco, who had come out from under the couch and was standing there, watching them.

"Shhhh!!" Kitty planted her palm against the man's chest to ensure he didn't move. "Don't spook him!"

Too late.

At the sound of her voice, Bosco did his ferret fandango, then dashed back under the couch.

"Oh! Drat!" She looked at the repairman, then had to bite her lips to keep from laughing at the expression on his face.

His wide-eyed gaze was fixed on the spot where Bosco had been. "That was a weasel."

"Not quite. Bosco is a ferret."

The man turned to study her, and she was suddenly aware of very blue eyes, a thick mane of silvery hair, and a strong, square, clean-shaven jaw. He was tall and strongly built. Fiftyish, if she didn't miss her guess. But—

Where was the doddering old gentleman Brendan told her about? This man was . . . oh, my. He was not doddering.

Not one little bit.

"I take it your ferret doesn't belong under the couch?"

"My . . . what?" She blinked, still caught in her study of the man.

A faint glint of humor touched his eyes and he arched a brow.

"Oh!" She looked away. *Get a grip, Kitty.* "Of course, my ferret. Bosco." She shook her head. "No, he doesn't belong under the couch." She looked back at him, all business now. "That's where you come in."

He nodded. "You need me to lift the couch."

She smiled. "Bingo."

He inclined his head. "Well, then, let's see what we can do."

Jericho Katz walked toward the couch. What on earth had he gotten himself into? Kitty Hawk wasn't at all what he'd expected. For one thing, she was considerably younger than her son had led him to believe.

"My mother's a widow," Brendan Hawk had said over the phone, sounding all doting indulgence and concern. "She's recovering from my dad's death a few years ago and, well, she's grown rather frail. And a bit feeble at times. She really can't manage the house, but she can't bear to leave it—and the memories it still holds. I'm really very worried about her."

Jericho had leaned back in his chair with a sigh. He shouldn't take the job. His calendar was already full. But the image of a sweet, little white-haired elderly lady with a house full of repair needs and memories got to him.

Besides, he could still remember how hard it had been when his wife, Alice, died ten years ago. She'd been so young—only forty-five—and he'd been so lost. It took him a lot of years to feel as though he was on an even keel again.

He'd sighed. "OK, give me the address." It would be a pain to shuffle his jobs, but he'd managed.

Now, watching Kitty Hawk as she knelt in front of the couch and peered beneath it, he realized he'd been had. Oh, she was little enough. Petite, in fact. But elderly? Hardly. And feeble? Well, he could already see that particular word had nothing to do with this woman's physical state. As a matter of fact, since her son was in his thirties, that meant she was likely pretty close to Jericho's age—though she looked considerably younger.

Must be that wide-eyed expression of wonder on her face. His lips twitched. He hadn't had a woman look him over with such evident fascination in a long time. Not that there weren't women interested in him. He was considered quite a catch, actually. Or so he'd been told. But there had been something about her expression—about the way her lips parted and her cheeks tinged pink when she looked at him—that was as disconcerting as it was alluring.

He started. *Alluring?* "Whoa, buddy, get a grip!" he muttered, and she looked up at him.

"Excuse me?"

"I said, are you ready to get a grip on him?"

She nodded. "I think so."

Nice save, Katz, ol' boy. "OK, here we go."

He took a deep breath, bent at the knees, and hefted one end of the heavy couch. *Good thing I was here. She never would have—*

"Hey!" He shook his leg. Something was grasping the bottom of his pants. *"Hey!!"* he repeated on a roar as that something scampered up his leg, *inside* his pants.

"Look out!!" the so-called feeble widow yelped, jumping out of the way as he dropped the couch.

"Get this thing off me!" He grabbed for his belt buckle.

"Wait!"

"Wait?? Are you *nuts?* I've got a ferret in my pants!"

"You can't take your pants off here!"

"Lady," he said in as controlled a voice as he could. "I've got a *ferret* in my *pants!* One of us has to get out of them. Now!"

She jumped up, grabbed his arm, and dragged him across the living room, then shoved him into what looked like a guest bathroom near the front door.

He didn't even wait to see if she shut the door. He stripped his pants, dancing around as the small creature clawed at his leg.

Kitty Hawk's muffled voice came through the doorway. "Don't hurt him!"

"Don't—!" He clamped his lips shut. Unbelievable. Absolutely unbelievable.

He held his pants out in front of him, and there, clutching the material and swinging back and forth, was the infamous Bosco, tiny ears perked, whiskers twitching like mad, tail puffed out and looking like a bottle brush.

"Hello, weasel." He forced the greeting through gritted teeth.

"Don't frighten him!" came the woman's concerned voice again.

"Oh, heaven forbid." Would sarcasm get through the closed door? His movements slow and calculated, he reached for the long, dangling body—then let out a pent-up breath when his hand closed around the trembling animal. "I have no intention of frightening him," he called, then dropped his voice so only Bosco could hear him. "Fricasseeing, maybe. But certainly not frightening."

A quick inspection of his legs revealed some minor scratches, but nothing serious. He stepped toward the door, hid behind it, and pulled it open just enough to stick his hand—and the animal—out. "I believe this belongs to you."

"Oh, Bosco, you poor baby!" She snatched the ferret from his hand. "Did he hurt you?"

Jericho stood there, leaning his forehead against the door. *This is a test, Lord, right?* He shoved the door closed with a quick, frustrated motion, then turned to open the medicine cabinet. Fortunately, there was an antiseptic there, and he applied it liberally to his legs, grimacing as it stung.

"Serves me right for not listening to my common sense." He jerked his pants back on. "Next time, Katz, pay attention when you think you're too busy for something."

When he stepped out into the living room, Bosco was back in his cage, curled up in a small hammock, clearly exhausted from his ordeal.

"Are you all right?"

Jericho met the concerned gaze of the Widow Hawk and bit back any further sarcasm. "Fine." He was proud of the even tone of his voice. *Stick to the business at hand, Katz.* "A few scratches, but that's it."

She came forward to place a small hand on his arm. "I'm so sorry! I never dreamed he would . . . well . . ." She glanced back at the cage. "I'm watching him for my daughter. She's a vet. And he keeps escaping his cage."

He glanced down at her hand where it still rested on his arm, surprised at how much he liked the feel of it there.

So much for sticking to business.

She followed the direction of his gaze and jerked her hand away, stains of scarlet appearing on her cheeks as she stepped back.

Their gazes met, locked, and something stirred deep within him. He watched her face as emotions played across her pixie features. She had tiny wrinkles at the corners of her eyes, giving him the impression that she smiled often. Her face was framed by shoulder-length hair the color of aspen gold. There were streaks of white throughout, which only added a greater depth and beauty, far as he could tell.

No, Kitty Hawk was definitely not elderly.

But there was more to this woman than beauty. He saw that in her eyes. A shadow in those brown depths, a hint of some fathomless sorrow that wouldn't let her go.

Or that she wouldn't surrender.

She found her voice first. "I take it you're Mr. Kratz?"

He pulled his mind back to the reason he'd come there. What was wrong with him? In the space of fifteen minutes, this woman had jerked him into her house, subjected him to becoming a jungle gym for a weasel, and accused him of hurting the beast that had tried to turn his leg into shredded wheat.

And yet he stood there, looking at her like some love-struck kid, his brain turned to so much Malto Meal. This was not a good sign.

Katz, my man, if you have any common sense left at all, you'll turn around and run away from here as fast as your legs can carry you.

Kitty waited in silence for the man before her to respond. He had the oddest expression on his face. A kind of fascinated panic. It reminded her of a raccoon caught in the beam of a flashlight during a late-night raid on trash cans.

"Katz."

She angled a look at him. "Katz?"

He seemed to relax a bit, and extended his hand. "My name. It's Katz."

Though she'd never admit it, Kitty was acutely aware of the warmth and size of the man's hand as it engulfed hers.

"Jericho Katz."

Now there was a name you didn't hear every day. "Jericho?"

He held up his hands as though to stem any comments. "I know, I know, not your run-of-the-mill name. What can I say? My parents loved the Old Testament. My brother's name is Judah. My sister—"

"Let me guess. Jezebel?"

His deep chuckle surprised her. "Nice try, but no. Try Jochabed." He shook his head. "My parents loved being different."

"No more so than mine." She leaned against the back of the sofa. "My name is Kitty."

He thought for a moment, then nodded. "Kitty Hawk. I see what you mean."

"Hmm." She found herself smiling back at him. "My maiden name was worse."

"You're kidding."

She shook her head. "Kohrner." She gave it a moment to penetrate. "Kitty Kohrner. So believe me, I can relate."

"Kitty Kohrner," he echoed, saying the name slowly, as though relishing the sound of the name. "Even better."

They shared a smile, and a warm rush of pleasure filled her at the appreciative look in his eyes.

Stop it! She straightened. What was wrong with her?

Don't turn away.

The words stabbed through her, and she felt her heart constrict. No, oh no. She wasn't ready. She was not attracted to this man . . . not like that! Her reaction had to be something else. Maybe . . . of course. The simple fact that, unlike most people, he hadn't found her name completely bizarre.

She'd grown used to people reacting to her name with varying degrees of amusement or surprise. In fact, by the time she'd reached her teens, Kitty had been able to peg how people would react when they first heard her name. The most common responses were startled looks, amused grins, even double-takes.

From there it generally had gone one of several ways. The most common response was "Oh, my. How . . . interesting." And, once in a while, "Wow. So how long did it take you to forgive your parents?"

Kitty chuckled at the thought. Forgive her parents, indeed. Thank them was more like it.

Kitty's parents had been the anchor in her life, the two people she could always count on for love and support. They taught her how to stand on her own, how to walk forward with confidence and faith, how to take life by storm. They'd instilled in her the faith in God that had carried her through her most turbulent and painful times—

Like Dan's death?

A few hours ago, she hadn't been so sure. But now . . . Yes, faith would carry her. Even through this.

Jericho Katz's deep voice brought her out of her thoughts. "Let me guess. Your parents wanted to help you learn to laugh at yourself."

"Yes, as a matter of fact, they did." Hmm. The man had insight. "How did you know?"

He lifted his shoulders. "Mine, too." Wry amusement flickered in the eyes that met hers. "Are you sure we aren't long-lost brother and sister?"

A gamut of perplexing emotions ran through her, and she found it impossible not to return his disarming smile. "I sincerely doubt it." Why on earth was she so ridiculously happy about that?

Please, God. Please tell me I'm not becoming some desperate widow who's ready to waylay any man who comes her way.

"Well, it's refreshing all the same to meet someone else with a quirky name." Jericho glanced around the trashed room, then back at her. "Decorating courtesy of Bosco?"

She nodded. "Wait 'til you see the kitchen."

"Well, lead on, Mrs. Hawk. I'm all yours."

The casual comment—and the appealing image that sprang to life in her mind's eye—brought the warmth back into Kitty's cheeks. She pushed away from the couch. Jericho Katz was altogether too disturbing. If he was going to be around much—which was entirely likely, considering the number of things that needed to be done around here—she was just going to have to conquer her involuntary reactions to him.

No matter how hard that might be.

CHAPTER
Four

Kitty stood in the bathroom, staring at her reflection. "What's *wrong* with you?"

She set the brush down with a clatter and went to flop in the chair near the window. For the last week, since Kylie had brought Bosco into her life—and Brendan had brought Jericho Katz—she'd been fighting such . . . what was it? Restlessness? The sense that there was something unfinished. Something important she needed to do.

But what?

Lord, a bit of help here, please?

Her quick prayer brought a smile to her lips. She'd been doing that a lot since she started reading Dan's Bible. Praying. Talking to God. She'd done it often enough during her life, but this felt different. More . . . personal. As though she was talking to someone she knew rather than to someone Dan knew. She hadn't realized it until this last week, but she'd always had the feeling, deep inside, that God only listened to her because she was with Dan. Now . . .

Now she had the sense of being heard, and loved, just for herself.

It felt good.

So why am I so unsettled?

It was a good question, but one for which she had no answer. She glanced at Dan's Bible—which she was starting to think of as her Bible, now—where it lay on her nightstand. She went to pick it up and turn to the section of the book of John that she'd been reading early this morning.

"'Do you love me? . . . Then feed my lambs,'" she read out loud. The words seemed to resonate within, and she realized her heart was pounding. She trailed her finger down the page, then read again. "Do you love me? . . . Then take care of my sheep."

Yes.

The affirmation struck deep, stirring emotions she didn't fully understand. "What does it mean?"

Take care of my sheep.

She shook her head and set the Bible aside. A rattling sound came from downstairs, and she smiled. It was past time for Bosco's morning jaunt in the park. She stood and headed for the door.

Maybe some fresh air would help her clear her head. And her heart.

Kitty loved the park. During the last several months she'd almost forgotten how much.

But now that she was back, she found herself more aware than ever of the restorative effect it had on her. There was something fresh and alive and rejuvenating in this bit of country green in the middle of town.

Why had she stayed away so long?

Because you didn't want to go on to enjoy life, when Dan couldn't.

The truth hit her, and she stopped in her tracks. Bosco, however, kept going, until he hit the end of the leash and was jerked off his paws.

"Oh, I'm sorry, fella."

Bosco jumped up and faced her, then backed away in his little side-to-side jig, grunting. Clearly, he did not appreciate what had happened.

Smiling at the feisty little animal, Kitty started forward again, grateful that it was still early enough that there weren't a lot of people around. Over the last week she and Bosco had become park celebrities of sorts. There was something about walking a ferret on a leash that made people stop and stare. And talk.

The first time she came to the park, she'd come shortly after lunch, not realizing the stir her little companion would cause. She'd no sooner walked near the playground than a little boy stopped in mid-run and stood there staring with open-mouthed, wide-eyed amazement. He watched Bosco bouncing along in that loping way of his, then the boy spun around and raced to his mother. He tugged excitedly on her jeans until she looked down at him. "Mommy!" he exclaimed, half in horror, half in wonder. "What happened to that lady's *dog*?"

Within minutes Bosco was the main playground attraction. Children gathered around, hunching down to watch Bosco and giggle with delight at his undulating walk. At first Kitty had been mortified. Then a thought drifted into her mind, making her grin: Dan would have loved this! Suddenly she found herself laughing, talking with the children, and having a good time.

Now she looked forward to the morning walks she and Bosco shared as one of the highlights in her day. Today, though, with these troubling thoughts on her mind, Kitty hadn't paid attention to how far they had gone. Though several curious passers-by stopped them—one man practically fell off his bike when he saw Bosco, then did a U-turn and came to pet the happy ferret—Bosco had walked enough.

Kitty figured this out when the little fellow plopped down on the ground and refused to move. After a few tugs on the leash with no response, Kitty reached down to pick up the worn-out weasel.

"How about we take a rest, Bosco, my boy?" She glanced around, then headed for her favorite bench—the one facing the playground where children swarmed over the equipment. She sat down, Bosco cradled in her arms, and settled in with a sigh.

She'd really been hoping the morning outing would help her to see things more clearly. But she was no closer to understanding her inner struggle than she'd been before she left the house.

Take care of my lambs.

There it was again. *What does that mean, Father? I don't understand.*

"May I join you?"

Kitty turned to see a small, elderly woman standing there. From the mosaic of wrinkles on her face, Kitty guessed the woman was in her late seventies, early eighties. Her expression was warm and sweet, and intelligence and humor twinkled in those bright blue eyes.

The quintessential grandmother face.

Even the woman's garb reinforced the image of a sweet—albeit slightly eccentric—grandmother: a flowered blue dress topped with a pink sweater, elegant white gloves, and a broad-brimmed straw hat complete with a spray of silk lilies of the valley.

Hanging from the little woman's arm was one of the largest straw purses Kitty had ever seen, and it was bulging.

No . . . it was *moving.*

Kitty sat up straighter on the bench, and the woman glanced at her, then her face lit with a beautiful smile.

"Why, you have a ferret! How sweet."

Kitty smiled. Nice to find someone familiar with Bosco's sort. "Yes, he is sweet." The minute she said it, she realized she meant it. For all that he was a scamp, she enjoyed having the animal around. "His name is Bosco." She glanced down at the snoozing animal. "I'm afraid I wore him out this morning."

"Oh, my! Well, I know how the little tyke feels." The woman nodded toward the bench. "May I?"

"Oh! Of course." Kitty eyed the wriggling bag. "Please do."

The woman sat down with a sigh, and set the bag at her feet. She turned to Kitty and extended her hand. "May I introduce myself?" Kitty caught the hint of a southern accent. "I am Lily DuPont"—she pronounced the name *Dew*-pont—"of the Richmond DuPonts." Two dimples appeared in her furrowed cheeks. "But my friends just call me Miss Lily."

Balancing Bosco in one arm, Kitty took Miss Lily's hand, surprised by the strength of the small, gloved fingers. "Kitty. Kitty Hawk."

"Why, how utterly enchanting!" The twinkle in her clear eyes deepened. "How your parents must have loved you to gift you with such a delightful appellation."

"Yes, my parents loved me a great deal."

"If your tone of voice is any indication, I daresay you feel the same about them."

Kitty had the distinct impression her companion was pleased by this. She scratched Bosco behind the ears and settled back against the bench. "I do. My parents are wonderful."

"Well, if their choice of a name for you is any indication, I would guess they are people of great vision and purpose." Miss Lily's bubbly voice all but overflowed with approval.

"They are that."

"I would guess you are, as well, my dear."

Kitty smiled at the small woman. "I'd like to be. In fact, that's part of the reason I'm here today."

"Oh?"

Kitty opened her mouth, then hesitated. Was she really going to tell all this to a total stranger? "It sounds odd . . ."

"Not at all, dear. Go ahead."

"Well, I'm trying to decide what I want to be when I grow up." There. She'd said it. She waited for Miss Lily's arched brow, but instead the older woman nodded encouragement, so Kitty went on. "You see, my husband died a few years ago—"

"Oh, I'm so sorry."

"I am too. He was a wonderful man. He knew how to make a difference in people's lives. I thought I did, too, but I've recently realized I was just riding on his coattails, so to speak. Now I want to find what it is that *I'm* supposed to do. How I can make a difference in people's lives."

"A worthy quest, to say the least." The bag at Miss Lily's feet rustled again, and she looked down, her smile indulgent. She reached down into the bag and cooed, "There now, Sweetums, Mummy's right here."

Kitty's eyes widened. Good grief. Was the poor woman delusional? She looked around—maybe Miss Lily had an attendant nearby. When Miss Lily sat up straight again and turned those bright blue eyes on her, Kitty forced a smile to her lips, then felt her mouth drop open.

There, in the woman's hands, cradled close to her flowered bosom, was a small mass of fur and whiskers and pricked-up ears.

"Oh!" Kitty grinned. "A silky terrier! How adorable."

The woman smiled as though she were holding the greatest treasure in the world. "This is my Sweetums." Her fingers stroked the small creature's head, just behind its pointed ears. "He's a bit feisty, so you'll want to keep your little friend away from him, but he's a love all the same."

Kitty lifted her free hand toward the dog, then paused. The last thing she wanted was to suddenly find "Sweetums" attached to her hand or wrist. True, the dog was tiny—she couldn't weigh more than six or seven pounds—but Kitty knew terriers were notorious for being ready to take on any opponent, regardless of size.

Kylie had told her once about a client at the clinic whose Yorkshire terrier was constantly getting out of the house. The woman's greatest concern about that wasn't that the dog would get lost, but that it would end up facing down a car.

"I can see it now," Kylie had recounted with a laugh. "There would be Dusty, standing in the middle of the road, staring at the car and thinking, 'You're the biggest dog I've ever seen, but I think I can take you!'"

Kitty grinned at the memory, though it did make her cautious. "May I?" She nodded to the dog.

"Of course, my dear. Sweetums *loves* attention, don't you, little one?"

As Kitty stroked the silken fur, the tiny dog leaned into her hand, tipping her head so that Kitty's fingers hit just the right spot. She grinned at Miss Lily, who gave Kitty a wink.

"There, now, I knew you were trustworthy the moment I saw you. Sweetums has a highly refined sense of discernment." Kitty's grin widened at the definite note of pride in the woman's voice. "She can tell who is and isn't to be trusted." Miss Lily leaned down to press her cheek against the dog. "Can't you, darling?"

Being the center of so much attention was sending Sweetums into ecstatic wriggles, and his stub of a tail wagged so furiously that Kitty thought it might fall off.

"His discernment is further evident in the fact that he adores my children." Miss Lily's smile faded, like a cloud drifting by, blocking the sun. "If only my daughter weren't allergic to him." She sighed and looked at Kitty. "I rarely get to see my Eliza because of it. She lives too far away to come here often—her job simply doesn't allow for much time off. But I'm afraid I cannot bear the idea of leaving Sweetums in a kennel."

"Isn't there anyone who can watch him while you're gone?"

Miss Lily shook her head. "I'm afraid not. Many of my friends can't have animals where they live, or they have pets of their own and couldn't manage two." Her sigh echoed with sorrow. "I did call a few of those pet-sitting places, but all they do is come to your home to feed the animal and let it out twice a day. Why, Sweetums would be alone all day! That just wouldn't do."

Kitty straightened. Her senses sharpened, as though there were someone whispering in her ear and she couldn't quite catch

the words. She stared at the woman and her dog for a moment—
and understanding dawned.

Sweetums wasn't exactly a lamb, still . . . "What you need,"
Kitty eased each word out, "is someone who could take Sweetums
in. In a home setting, not a kennel."

Miss Lily's face lit up. "Oh, that would be lovely. But finding
someone like that, someone that I could trust with my Sweetums,
would be quite a task. Why, that person would have to be as honest as the day is long."

"She'd have to love animals," Kitty added.

"She?"

Kitty gave Miss Lily a wink. "Everyone knows women are the
nurturers."

The twinkle was back in Miss Lily's eyes. "Oh, of course. And
she'd have to have plenty of room, so the darling could run. A nice
big house with a nice big yard."

"She'd need access to a vet, just in case there were problems."
Kitty almost couldn't contain her excitement.

"Absolutely, and she would have to be willing to treat Sweetums as if he were her very own."

"And you would pay for this kind of service?"

Miss Lily looked at her, eyes wide. "For someone I could trust
to care for Sweetums while I'm gone? Absolutely. As a matter of
fact, I'm sure my friends with pets would feel the same. None of
them likes to leave their darlings at kennels."

Oh, Father, Kitty's heart sang out, *this is it! I can tell. I can feel
it's right.*

"Miss Lily, may I ask for your address and phone number?"

The woman regarded her for a moment, then nodded. "Of
course, my dear." She leaned over to rummage in her bag. "I believe I have a pencil and paper in here somewhere . . . ah. There
we go." She lifted the items, then handed them to Kitty and gave
her the information she'd requested.

Kitty folded the paper and slipped it into her pocket, then took Miss Lily's hand in hers. She wanted to lean over and give the woman a kiss, but thought better of getting Bosco that close to Sweetums. No point in testing fate!

"You've been an enormous help to me," she told the older woman. "In fact, I think God sent you here today. Thank you so much."

Miss Lily's eyes sparkled with sudden tears. "No, my dear, thank you. And please, let me know how things turn out."

Kitty grinned. "Miss Lily, you can count on it!"

Jericho stepped back to survey his work with a satisfied smile. There was something so gratifying in putting right things that had gone wrong.

In this particular case, he'd just finished replacing the window that Bosco had demolished during his mad bid for freedom last week. Jericho shook his head. He wasn't sure which one was crazier, Bosco or his keeper.

Jericho had been working at Kitty's house for nearly a week now. He'd no sooner check off an item on her son's list, than he—or Kitty herself—would add something else.

"You know, that garbage disposal hasn't been working quite right," Brendan had said when Jericho informed him he was almost finished.

That same day Kitty stopped him in the hallway. "Would you mind terribly repairing the handrail on the stairway?"

He shook his head. The only item left on the list now was the kitchen faucet, which shouldn't take any time at all. With any luck, this was his last day around Kitty Hawk.

You're a coward.

The accusation stung, but Jericho didn't deny it. "I don't need any complications in my life, OK?" he muttered, putting his tools away. "And if there's one thing this woman would be, it's a complication."

True, she was likable enough. Too likable, in fact. By far. All she had to do was come near him, and Jericho felt his heart rate pick up speed. The way she looked, the sound of her voice, even that faint scent of vanilla that seemed to follow her everywhere—she was getting to him.

So much so that every time she came around, he turned into a walking disaster. Yesterday she'd slipped up behind him and asked what he was doing just as he was swinging his hammer. Startled, he missed the nail entirely. His thumb, however, had been taught a severe lesson. As had the drywall the day she opened the front door as he was carrying a ladder through the room. He jumped back to avoid hitting her or the door. He'd succeeded, but the wall hadn't been so lucky. He'd rammed it with the bottom of the ladder, knocking a hole the size of a watermelon. Which of course had to be repaired.

Then there was the time early in the week when she asked him if he wanted coffee. He'd turned to answer her and knocked his wrench off the counter. Fortunately it hadn't damaged the floor tile. Unfortunately, that was because it landed on his foot.

If he were around her much longer, he'd end up on disability!

"Not only is she hazardous to my health, she'd drive me crazy," he told the pipes as he got ready to shut off the water. "She's about as organized as a teenager's bedroom. Her mind goes in forty different directions at once, and a single conversation can hit on a dozen different topics." He shook his head. "No, sir, that's one woman I can do without."

"Jericho?"

He jerked up, slamming his head on the pipes. He yelped, and she was suddenly there beside him.

"Are you OK?" Her tone was most solicitous.

He lay there, staring up at the offending pipes. "Oh, sure, I'm fine. No problem." His throbbing forehead disagreed, but he ignored it.

"Jericho, I was just wondering . . ."

He sighed heavily. She wasn't going to go away. "Hang on." As cautiously as possible, he slid out from under the sink, smiling when he completed the process without any further mishaps. He turned his head and found himself staring right into those warm brown eyes. She was kneeling beside him, so close he could feel her breath on his face.

He stared at her, suddenly struck dumb.

"Jericho?"

Who is Jericho?

She reached out to touch his hand. "Do—?"

The contact of her fingers against his hand shot through him like an electric shock. He jerked his hand away and scrambled to his feet. In the back of his mind was the image of that crazy robot on that old SciFi series, *Lost in Space*, waving its wobbly arms and intoning, "Danger, Will Robinson! Danger!"

Kitty stared at him as though he'd gone completely loony. Well, maybe he had. He shoved his hands into his pockets. "You were wondering?"

Her eyes lit up and she stood, clapping her hands together like a child at a birthday party. "Oh! Yes. I was wondering, do you do renovations?"

He narrowed his eyes. "Well, yes. Why?"

Her eager smile confirmed his fears. "I want to make some changes in my house."

"Changes?"

"I'm going to start my own business."

Her exuberance was contagious, and Jericho smiled in spite of himself. "Sounds pretty ambitious."

"Oh, it is. But it's not my ambition, it's God's."

He stared at her. "I beg your pardon."

She was so happy, she all but sang her explanation. "Isn't it great? It's all his doing. He told me to take care of his lambs, and that's exactly what I'm going to do." She fixed him with a look that warmed him all the way down to the soles of his boots. "And you're going to help me!"

He nodded, bemused. She was going to feed God's lambs, and he was going to—

Wait a minute!

"I'm what?" He scowled. "What do you mean I'm going to help you?"

"Of course." She took his arm and tugged him into the dining room where she had papers spread out all across the table. "God knew I'd need someone I can trust to do this, and that's why he brought you here. To help me."

Jericho shook his head. "Kitty, slow down. What on earth are you talking about?"

She laughed. "I'm sorry. I know I'm not making much sense." She took his arm again. "Come take a look at what I've drawn here."

The drawings were actually quite good. She'd sketched the floor plan of her home, showing both floors and the backyard. He leaned in closer, studying her notations, then turned to looked at her. Was this what he thought it was? "You're making your house into a kennel?"

"Only part of it. I'm putting a dog run in the backyard that will have both a free area and several separate cages." She pointed to the drawings. "I want you to change these downstairs rooms— the den and the two guest rooms. What I'd really like is to knock out the connecting walls—" She looked at him. "Is that possible?"

He gave a slow nod. "Sure, as long as it's not load bearing. But—"

"Good, then we can partition that area so that there are six or seven smaller enclosures, as well as a main area. That way I can use the enclosures for animals who need their own space, and the larger area for crates."

Jericho felt as though he'd been tossed into a Tilt-a-Whirl. "Kitty, hang on. These changes will take a lot of planning. And money."

"I know that. I can handle it. Dan left me—actually, I'm quite well off."

When did she become the bastion of confidences? "It's going to take a good deal of time, too. Between all these changes inside and out, it could take months to get it all done."

Her radiant grin was a thing of beauty. "Then we'd better get started, hadn't we? I'll need you to give me a list of supplies—"

"Whoa, slow down there!" Jericho straightened. "I've got other jobs lined up already, remember?" He'd made it very clear to her and her son that he couldn't do more work beyond this week.

Her velvety eyes came to rest on his face, a slight frown creasing her brow. He had to fight the urge to reach out and let his fingers caress it smooth again.

She tipped her head. "That could be a problem."

He gave a snort. "Yes, Kitty, it could." She looked up at him, disappointment starting to nudge the excitement from her face, and a twinge of guilt struck him.

He struck back. *This isn't my problem!*

His conscience wasn't buying it. *Right. That's why you feel so rotten? You know how much she's come to depend on you over the past few weeks. And you haven't done anything to stop it.*

True enough. He'd seen the change in Kitty, the way she'd light up when he got there in the mornings, the effort she put into having coffee waiting for him, fixed just the way he liked it. She'd even taken to making him his favorite sandwiches for lunch.

Pretty clear evidence that she was coming to look on him as a part of her family. He'd seen it and hadn't done a thing to dispel the image.

Because you liked it. You wanted it. For that matter, you nurtured it. Again, he knew it was the truth. Oh, sure, he'd done his best those first few days to get out of the house as quickly as he could. He'd been able to turn down her offers of a cup of coffee before he left without looking too cold. Or too panicked. Kitty was the loveliest woman he'd met in a very long time—inside and out, from what he could tell. But by the fifth or sixth refusal—he'd lost count in the whirlwind of her ideas—he somehow could not ignore her look of disappointment.

Finally, he couldn't take it any longer. She'd made hot cider, and the welcoming smell of cinnamon—and the warmth in her smile and in those tantalizing brown eyes—were more than he could refuse. "Just this once," he said, accepting the mug she offered him.

His inner voice had freaked. *Are you crazy?? Get out! Run!*

I've got a better idea, he responded, following Kitty to the living room. *Why don't you just sit down and shut up.*

And so it had begun. That was the first step in what became an established pattern of sitting and talking with her before he left each afternoon. He wasn't much of a talker, but that hadn't hindered them at all. She did most of the talking, almost as though she'd been cut off from people for months and was suddenly overflowing with the need to share. She told him about her childhood, her husband, and her kids. And as he listened, something awful happened.

He stared to care.

Stupid, stupid! He'd told himself that over and over. *Forget her. Get out, now!*

As much as he'd pretended otherwise, he knew leaving was the only thing he could do. It grew clearer every day: he and Kitty were as opposite as it got. He needed order, harmony, structure, routine, peace. And Kitty?

Kitty was chaos incarnate.

Wherever this dynamo went, pandemonium followed. Oh, sure, it was usually enjoyable, but it was pandemonium all the same. She didn't think or talk like he did—nothing about her made sense to his way of thinking.

But it wasn't thinking that got him into trouble. It was feeling. As far as his crazy heart was concerned, everything about this woman made perfect sense.

But nothing was going to happen. It couldn't. He just wasn't ready. Wasn't the right person for her. And through it all, he'd known this day would come, when he'd have to leave this woman who was starting to mean more to him than was good for either of them. The best thing he could do for her, and for himself, was to walk away and forget he'd ever known her.

All he had to do was figure out how.

"I know."

He turned startled eyes to her. "What?" Had she reached the point where she could read his thoughts?

"I know what we'll do." The shine was back in her eyes. She reached out to take his hand in hers. "We'll pray about it."

Exasperation slammed into him. "Come on, Kitty. Don't you think the God of the universe has more important things on his mind than my work schedule? Come into reality, woman. I can't—no, I *won't*—go crying to God to fix every little detail of my life. I don't work like that. *God* doesn't work like that."

He turned away from her, quick regret coming on the heels of his heated words. He didn't want to look at her, to see the hurt, the disappointment on her face.

"Jericho?"

He let his gaze meet hers—then stared. There wasn't even a hint of disappointment in her eyes. Quite the opposite. All he saw there was . . . what? Understanding? Compassion? Care? He wasn't sure.

A gentle smile eased over her features. "It's OK. I'll pray for both of us. I know God will have an answer."

Her faith was so sincere . . . so childlike. She was the oddest combination of maturity and innocence he'd ever encountered. He sighed. "OK, Kitty. You go ahead and pray. But don't blame me if you're disappointed."

She patted him on the arm. "Relax, Jericho. Everything will work out just fine."

Looking into those brown eyes, he could almost believe she was right.

That night, Kitty lay in bed, engrossed in her Bible reading. Suddenly she stopped, stared, and read the verse in front of her eyes again.

"Now the gates of Jericho were tightly shut because the people were afraid."

Pray for Jericho.

The urging was strong and undeniable.

Kitty slid from the bed and knelt beside it. God had brought down the walls of Jericho once before. Though this was a different Jericho, and the walls were a different sort, the problem seemed to be the same.

Fear. Her fear of letting go of the past. His fear of . . . well, she wasn't sure what he was afraid of. But she could tell he was afraid of something.

So she followed the leading of that still, small voice and brought the problem to the only place it could be solved: to her Father in heaven.

CHAPTER
Five

It was early morning a few days later when Kitty's phone rang.

She cast a glance at the clock, wondering who would be calling her so early. "Hello?"

"You win."

"Jericho?"

"Look, if you're going to gloat—"

"No, no. I wouldn't dream of it." She frowned. "But would you mind telling me what it is I'm not gloating over?"

Silence.

"Jericho?"

"I still don't think God is just sitting there, ready to jump in and take care of our every little problem. I just want that clear right up front, OK?"

Her heart started to beat faster. Was he saying what she thought he was saying? She forced her tone to remain even. "OK."

"All right. I got four calls yesterday. From clients."

"And?"

"And they want to postpone the work they contracted me to do for them."

"You're kidding!"

"I don't kid about my work, Kitty."

"Right." Good thing he wasn't there to see the grin spreading over her face. "That's true. Should have remembered that. So . . . ?"

"So I find myself with several months of open time and—"

"You'll do the work on my house!" She couldn't stop the glee that filled her words.

"You're gloating."

"I'm sorry. That wasn't gloating—it was happiness. But I'll behave." Though she blew that promise right out the window with the next breath. "Sooooo, kind of looks like God got involved after all, huh?"

"I'm hanging up now."

She laughed at the gloomy disgust in his tone. "OK, OK, I'll be good."

"That"—his tone grew even darker—"will be the day."

"Sourpuss."

"Pollyanna."

She laughed again. "See you in the morning?"

"Bright and early. You'd better have coffee."

"I always do. Tomorrow then." She knew she sounded revoltingly perky, but she didn't care. God was at work, and she was so excited she could hardly stand it.

CHAPTER

Six

"You want to do what?"

Jericho stared at Kitty. She couldn't be serious. *This is Kitty*, he reminded himself as he studied her face. *Of course she can.*

"I want to start bringing in clients."

"You mean animals."

"Right. That's what I said."

He looked away, the battle inside raging again. *She's crazy, Lord. I keep telling you that. Totally crazy.*

Lean not on your own understanding.

It's the understanding you gave me, Lord. And it's done just fine for fifty years. It's helped me build a successful business, supplied me with a good income and a nice home. Why change now?

The answer came from somewhere in the region of his heart: *It's not good for man to be alone.*

He closed his mind to the words and turned to give Kitty a stern look. "No way. The work's not done." His heart sank at the patient—and determined—glint in those chocolate eyes.

"Jericho, it's time."

"And you know this how, exactly?" But he knew what her answer would be. And sure enough—

"It's just a feeling."

Bingo.

"But it's a very clear feeling."

Oh, of course. That makes it so much better.

"God's ready for me to get started, Jericho. And I need to do so."

He wasn't going to win. Fine. He offered her a gloomy olive branch. "Just the upstairs. I'm nearly done up there. A few vent covers, some trim, a few touches of paint, and you're good to go."

The warmth of her smile was reflected in her voice. "Thank you."

"But you keep the critters quiet, under control, and out of my way, agreed?"

"Of course."

Gramps sat in his recliner and folded his hands in his lap. "OK, team, SitRep."

"SitRep?" Kylie folded her legs beneath her on the couch. "Gramps, this isn't a military mission!"

"I don't know." Brendan took another cookie from the plate on the coffee table in front of them. He could be a hundred years old and these would still be his favorite in the world. "I like the idea." He took a big bite, savoring the sweet treat. "Getting Mom back into life wasn't exactly a walk in the park."

His sister considered that, then nodded. "You're right. OK, a report on the situation it is."

"Glad we got that settled." Gramps leaned forward. "So? How's it going?"

Kylie offered a salute. "Everything's going according to plan, sir! It's been over six weeks since our plan was implemented, and Mom not only still has Bosco, but she told me yesterday she thinks she'll keep him."

"Brendan? How about your side of the plan?"

He allowed a smug smile. "An even bigger success than I'd hoped. Mom is moving forward with this new business plan of hers."

Gramps gave a slow nod. "I knew she had it in her. Has she started taking in any animals?"

Kylie looked positively gleeful. "The whole upstairs is full of them! As soon as people found out about her, she had more calls than she could handle. At last count, she had two kittens, a little dog, four ferrets—not counting Bosco—and the cat from hell."

Gramps started. "Excuse me?"

Brendan jumped in. "No kidding, sir. This cat is huge. He's got to weigh, what?"

"Thirty pounds, at least," Kylie supplied.

"Right. And every ounce is pure orneriness. Critter's name is Godfrey, but Jericho calls him Godzilla."

Gramps tented his fingers. "Speaking of Mr. Jericho . . . Brendan?"

He didn't even try to restrain his delight. "Let's just say I think Mom will be keeping more than just the ferret."

Gramps's eyes widened at that. "Your repairman?"

Brendan leaned back against the cushions. "No, at this point I'd say he's much more than Mom's repairman."

"Well done, kids." Warm approval sounded in Gramps's voice. "Well done, indeed."

"Outta my way!"

Kitty made a dive for the door. She slid through and slammed it shut behind her. The thud of something slamming into that door was followed by a sound that resembled a mix between a wailing banshee and a tortured set of bagpipes.

"I take it Godzilla didn't care for his din-din?"

She looked toward the stairs, where Jericho stood leaning against the wall.

"*Godfrey*"—she forced the name through gritted teeth—"won't care for din-din until it's me. Though he'd likely settle for just my head. On a platter."

She came to walk down the stairs with Jericho. She should have been tipped off that Godfrey wasn't an easy job when his owners called and begged her to watch the cat for them while they went on a week's vacation. She'd thought the desperation in their voices was because they couldn't find someone else.

Turns out they were just desperate to escape the beast themselves.

Thankfully, Godfrey wasn't her first client, or there may not have been a second. No, her first client was Sweetums, Miss Lily's terrier. Kitty had no sooner gotten the go-ahead from Jericho than she was on the phone.

"Miss Lily? How would you like to go visit your daughter?"

Sweetums was, even now, happily situated up in his room.

If only Godfrey were so easy to care for! His owners requested she pick the cat up at their apartment. Another clue she missed. They'd said the neighbor would let her in, and she'd find the cat's carrier on the kitchen counter. When Kitty arrived at the apartment, the neighbor did let her in—by throwing the door open and then running, muttering as he hurried off about crazy women who took their lives into their own hands.

Clue number three.

Still, it wasn't until Kitty went into the bedroom, where the owners told her she'd find their little cat, that she knew she was in trouble. The cat was ensconced under the bed, flanked on all sides by dust bunnies. He looked like he'd tried to burrow under them. When Kitty attempted the age-old, "Here, kitty, kitty, kitty," Godfrey's malevolent glare was topped only by the snarling hiss that emitted from deep in his throat.

She wondered if maybe she could get away with just taking the dust bunnies home.

After a half hour of ineffectual coaxing, she'd had it. "Look, cat"—she met him, glare for glare—"I'm bigger than you are, and smarter than you are. At least"—she swallowed at the evil glint in the cat's yellow eyes—"I hope so. So you might as well just give up now and come out."

No dice.

She found the cat's plastic food dish and filled it with food. That should help the cat warm up to her, right?

Yeah. Not so much.

As she slid the dish under the bed, Godfrey's hiss turned to a screech, and Kitty beat a hasty retreat. She came back twenty minutes later to find the shredded remains of the food dish. Of course, all the food was gone. Clearly, Godfrey didn't miss a meal if he could avoid it.

It took a call to Kylie for help, and a dose of sedative tucked into the cat's food (which Kitty placed in a new metal dish), to pry the beast from his sanctuary. Dragging the unconscious, over-sized feline out from under the bed was a task. As was getting him into his carrier. But Kitty managed, and finally, triumphant, got him to her house.

Fortunately, Jericho was there when she arrived, and he carried the massive cat up to his room. She got Godfrey settled in his sectioned-off sleeping area, and peace reigned again.

Until Godfrey awoke.

And went berserk.

The cat's bloodcurdling yowl and whirling-dervish reaction when she came in to feed it reminded Kitty of the Tasmanian devil on the Bugs Bunny cartoon. Maddened creature at her heels, Kitty scrambled up on top of a dresser, barely managing to evade the cat as he flew past her, claws flailing, out the door of the room.

Before she could react, Godfrey barreled into her bedroom and skidded under her bed. Kitty slammed the door shut behind the cat. Checking on Godfrey again could wait until the next morning. When Jericho arrived. She'd sleep elsewhere, thank you very much.

Together they'd opened the door, only to discover total mayhem. Her curtains were shredded, the lamp was on the floor, her books were scattered across the bed, and the pillows were decimated.

Bosco was an amateur compared to this fiend!

Jericho did his best to hold back his laughter, but he had little success. "You do realize you'll never get him out of there."

With a boldness born of utter desperation, she marched into the cat's territory, grabbed her Bible and a blanket, and stomped back out the door. "Not a problem." She hiked the blanket over her shoulder. "The couch is more comfortable than my bed anyway."

That was three days ago.

As she and Jericho reached the bottom of the stairs, he eyed the couch, where her blanket was neatly folded and new pillows were piled.

"Still sleeping down here, huh?"

She fixed him with a look, daring him to say more. He lifted his hands, signaling surrender, and she relented with a sigh.

"What can I say? I prefer remaining intact. Besides, he's the only problem child. The others aren't hard to care for at all."

Jericho met her gaze and grinned. "Give 'em time."

Later that day, Kitty went up to check on the ferrets in what was now the community room. She'd settled the four little imps into one of the "stalls," as Jericho called them.

She surveyed the room. Jericho had done a great job. He'd removed the connecting walls, then put in ten stalls with latching doors, one large open area for crates, and another large area for playtime.

At one end of the room, Sweetums was snoozing away. Two stalls down from her were Thelma and Louise, two cuddly little kittens. The ferrets were at the far end of the room.

After her escapades with Bosco, Kitty hadn't been sure how she'd do with four of the little mischief makers at once, but so far they'd been furry little angels—despite Jericho's dire warnings. He'd spent half an hour trying to talk Kitty into setting up a cage for the four.

"Their owner said he usually keeps them in a cage."

She'd crossed her arms over her chest. "Unless he's home. They'll be fine."

Jericho snorted. "Bosco wouldn't be fine."

"Bosco is an aberration of nature. I can't believe all ferrets are so predisposed to causing trouble."

She'd given them towels for curling in and an assortment of toys. The ferrets seemed thrilled with the set-up. They played together, wrestling and tussling until they tired themselves out. They were all trained to a little pan, so cleanup was minimal. All Kitty had to do was refill their water and food dishes and play with them a couple of times a day.

She'd come up with the great idea for a bed for them, too. A beanbag chair. "They'll love the thing," she'd told the still-doubting Jericho. And she was right. When they completely exhausted themselves playing, they'd curled up together in the middle of the bag and drifted off to peaceful slumber.

Ha! It felt good to be right for a change.

Still smiling, she opened the door to the ferrets' stall—and froze.

"Jericho!"

Her wail echoed off the walls, startling poor Sweetums awake and setting him to yapping. But she couldn't help it. What she found when she opened that door was . . .

Chaos.

The beanbag chair was nearly flat. It sported holes where the ferrets apparently had chewed through. The foam-bead filling was everywhere, covering the floor and adhering to the walls, thanks to static electricity.

Footsteps pounded up the stairs, and a wide-eyed Jericho bounded into the room. "What?"

She held out her hands. "Look."

He came to survey the damage. "The ferrets?"

She shrugged, scanning the mess for some sign of life, dread creeping into her heart. "They couldn't have gotten out . . . could they?"

He looked at her sideways. "They're ferrets."

The dread multiplied.

Suddenly a chorus of chirps and little grunts caught her ear, and Kitty looked to find two little foam-bead-covered ferret heads popping out of the deflated beanbag chair.

Even their twitching whiskers had beads on them!

But her dread shifted to relief when two more heads popped out. All four ferrets accounted for. They were safe, and that was what mattered.

Jericho shifted beside her. She held up a hand to forestall the impending "I told you so" that she knew she deserved but didn't want to hear. Even so . . . "You were right, Jericho. I'm sorry, I should have listened to you."

Their eyes met.

He considered her for a moment, then nodded and headed for the door. "You clean up the mess, and I'll be right back with a cage."

At least he had the grace to sound only a little smug.

Seven

What now? Jericho looked down from the top of the ladder when the doorbell pealed for the umpteenth time.

Kitty's voice drifted down from upstairs. "Can you get that? I'm giving Sweetums a bath."

"For the love of—" Jericho came down the ladder and headed for the door. "I'm a repairman"—he grabbed the door and jerked it open—"not a butler—"

The word froze on his lips. He stared, then went to the bottom of the stairs and called up. "Kitty, there's some clown at the door for you."

She appeared at the top, a soggy, suds-covered Sweetums cradled in her hands. "There's no need to be rude, Jericho."

"No, really," he said as she came down the stairs. "There's a clown there."

She jerked to a halt when she saw the man at her door. A fully decked-out circus clown—complete with red nose, big shoes, and a bouquet of balloons.

Jericho shrugged. Only at Kitty's house.

He walked back to the living room and the relative safety of his ladder when sudden chaos in the form of barking and growling and a frantic bellow spun him around.

The clown was now inside, waving his arms like a crazed conductor, which made the balloons attached to one wrist dance and bounce against the ceiling. He held one leg out and shook it.

At the end of that leg, attached to the clown's big, floppy shoe, was a snarling Sweetums. The usually docile animal was coming unglued.

The clown was *not* happy. "Get this oversized *rat* off my shoe!"

Jericho closed his eyes. Oh, boy. The guy insulted the dog. Not a good idea.

"*Rat?*" Kitty's outrage poured out of her. "Sweetums is nothing of the kind! I'll have you know she's from the purest line of—"

"Lady, do I look like I *care?*" The clown's eyes bulged and his face was turning redder by the minute.

Yeah. Welcome to my world, pal.

Jericho started toward the melee, but Kitty, who'd calmed down surprisingly fast, put up a hand to stop him.

"Get the stuffed sock."

He stared at her, as amazed at her calm as her request. "The what?"

"The stuffed sock. Sweetums's chew toy. On the couch."

Okaaay. He headed for the couch. Sure enough, a stuffed sock lay there. He scooped it up and felt something hard in the toe. A rubber ball, unless he missed his guess. He tossed the sock to Kitty.

She caught it, then turned to the clown. "Sir, stop trying to pull away."

"Are you nuts? He'll eat me alive! Lady, you're crazier than—"

Jericho had heard enough. He went to stand beside Kitty. "The lady asked you to stop." He straightened his shoulders, narrowed his eyes. "Now."

Sometimes it paid to be tall and broad shouldered. The clown took in Jericho's size, and stopped, his leg in the air, mid-shake.

Kitty nodded. "That's good, sir. Now please set your foot on the floor."

The clown obeyed. Jericho grinned. This was actually kind of fun.

As soon as the clown's foot hit the floor, Kitty waved the sock in front of the little dog's nose. "Hey, Sweetums! Get the sock!"

The dog launched at the toy, clamping onto it with the same ferocity it had chomped on the clown's shoe. Kitty lifted the sock, Sweetums and all, into her arms. The little dog chewed and shook the sock, seemingly content.

Jericho stared at Kitty, a new respect growing inside him. She'd handled that like a pro.

For her part, she was all smiles. "Jericho, why don't you see if our guest here was hurt while I put Sweetums in his room?"

She headed up the stairs. Jericho turned to the clown, who was standing there, a dazed look in his eyes.

"You hurt?"

The clown waggled his foot, then shook his head. "I guess not."

"So"—they both turned to find Kitty coming down the stairs—"everything all right?"

Jericho nodded. "I'm good." He turned to the clown. "You?"

The clown's head bobbed. "Yup. Good here."

"Well, then, Mr. Clown," from Kitty. "What may I do for you?"

The clown drew a deep breath, as though to compose himself, then said in a voice that would have done Sylvester the cat proud: *"Thay* there! Would you be the famouth Kitty Hawk?"

Jericho rolled his eyes.

Kitty just laughed as the clown danced around and honked his horn, singing off-key, "Let me call you *Thwee*heart, I've a gift for yooooouuu. . . ."

At the end of the song, he whipped out the balloons and handed them to her. "Happy April Fool's, one day early. From Brendan and Kylie."

"Um, thanks." Kitty's lips twitched. "You were . . . uh . . . great."

The clown didn't reply. But as he turned to leave, Jericho heard him mutter on the way to the door, "Be a clown, they said.

Make people laugh. You'll have fun." He snorted. "Who were they kidding?"

Jericho angled a look at Kitty. "Do you want to tell him, or shall I?"

She tipped her head. "What?"

He grinned. "You don't have to be a clown for fun and laughter. Just hang around with Kitty Hawk."

Her cheeks shifted into pink mode, but she pulled the balloons down to form a floating fan and batted her eyes at him. "Lan' sakes, Mistah Katz"—her Southern Belle was spot on—"you just gon' make my head spin with such fine praise."

She turned and sauntered, balloons in tow, toward the kitchen. Jericho stood there, watching her.

Frankly, my dear, I do give *a darn.* He shoved his hands in his pockets. *Far more than I should.*

"Thanks for the balloons, kids. They were great."

Kitty reached for her offsprings' hands around the table. They were out at one of their favorite restaurants together. The first time in a long time.

"Glad you liked them, Mom." Kylie squeezed her hand. "They reminded us of you."

"And of Dad."

Her son's quiet words made her throat catch, but only for a moment. She could think about Dan now without so much pain. "Me, too."

"So, Mom."

Uh-oh. She could tell from Brendan's tone that he was up to something.

"How's old Mr. Katz?"

She leaned back in her chair. "Not so old, but I think you know that. And he's fine."

"Just . . . fine?"

Kitty eyed her son, but he wasn't going to give up. He leaned his elbows on the table.

"Really, Mom. I want to know how you two are getting along."

Kylie jabbed him at that, but Kitty just laughed. She couldn't help it. She felt so . . . good. "We're getting along pretty well. In fact"—she watched her children's faces for any sign of dismay—"I'd say we're getting along very well."

There was no denying Kylie's delight, nor the pleasure on Brendan's features. Kitty released the breath she hadn't realized she was holding. "So, you don't mind? That I like this man?"

"Mind?" Brendan took a drink of his coffee. "Why do you think I chose him?"

Kitty arched her brows at that. "Oh, really?"

Her daughter's hand came to settle over hers. "Mom, we're glad. Really. We miss Daddy, but we all know he wouldn't have wanted you to be alone. And we want you . . ."

Kitty entwined her fingers with her daughter's. "What?"

"We wanted you to be happy again."

Kylie nodded her agreement to her brother's words, and Kitty knew she was the most blessed of mothers with these two.

"Although . . ."

Kitty looked at her son. "What? Is something wrong?" *No, Lord. Don't let him tell me something awful about Jericho. Please—*

"No, Mom." Brendan rested his elbows on the table, cupping his coffee mug. "But there is something you need to keep in mind."

"Oh? And what would that be?"

"Well, if you two end up being serious about each other . . ."

Kylie started to giggle. "Oh, that's perfect."

Kitty regarded them both. "What are you two talking about?"

Kylie leaned forward. "Mom, his name."

"Jericho?"

Kylie's brows lifted. "Jericho . . . ?"

"Katz." The moment she said Jericho's last name, she knew.

"That's right, Mom." Brendan was laughing now. "You need to be sure you love the guy enough to not mind going from Kitty Hawk—"

"—to Kitty Katz!" Kylie's peal of laughter had other diners looking their way. "Oh, Mom. What more proof could you want? This is a match made in heaven!"

Is it, Lord? Is this a match? Kitty knew her feelings for Jericho grew and deepened every day, but how did he feel about it? About her? There were times when she thought he cared too, but other times . . .

She just wasn't sure. He was so well protected. So encamped behind protective barriers.

"Mom, what is it?"

She met Kylie's worried eyes. "Nothing. Just . . . a few walls that need to come down."

Brendan set his cup down. "I thought all the walls were down."

"Not all." Kitty pulled herself from her thoughts and smiled at her children. "But there's no need to worry. God and I are working on it."

"Well, then, you're set." Brendan gave a solid nod. "Because if you've put your mind to something, it will happen."

She smiled at him over her coffee cup. *From your mouth to God's ear, Son.*

Jericho dropped his bag of groceries on the table in his kitchen and flipped on the light.

He stood still for a moment, savoring the silence. No animals grunting or barking or meowing. No phones ringing off the hook. No people coming to pick up their furry or feathered babies. No Kitty hollering for him when the next disaster strikes.

No Kitty . . .

Before the melancholy of that thought settled in, he started unloading groceries.

That's right. No Kitty. Just peace and quiet. Pure heaven. Just the way he liked it. Quiet. Silent. Really. Really.

Quiet.

He glanced around.

Too quiet.

Why hadn't he ever noticed before? This place was quiet as a tomb. Where was the life? The laughter? It was positively depressing here!

"Yeah, well"—he tossed his gloomy thoughts into the silence—"you'd better get used to it, bud. You don't want to get attached, so no complaining now that it's over."

And over it was. He had one more day of work left at Kitty's house. That was it.

He plopped in a chair and stared at the calendar on the wall.

Good grief. How fitting. Tomorrow, his last day with Kitty . . .

It was April Fool's Day.

CHAPTER
Eight

"Rowf! Rrrrrowf! Yap! Yap!"

"Kitty!"

"Bark! Bark-bark-bark! Yap!"

Jericho slammed down his hammer and stalked to the bottom of the stairs. The day had been frustrating enough without having to listen to that dustball of a dog yap.

He'd tried a dozen times to tell Kitty today that he was done. Leaving. Outta here. But every time he tried, the words stuck. And for some crazy reason, he'd had the same phrase repeating over and over in his head.

Tend my lamb.

Lamb? What, was the woman going to take in sheep now?

He'd done everything he could think of to make the words stop, to no avail. So, OK, he might not be able to shut that inner voice up, but he could sure do something about that darned dog. "Kitty!"

"I'm right here. You don't have to yell."

He spun around. She was right behind him. Close behind. Too close.

Her warm breath fanned his face. "Did you want to say something?"

Her sudden proximity made his head swim. He stepped back, forgetting about the stairs. The back of his boot hit the lowest step, and the next thing he knew he was going down.

"Look out!"

Kitty grabbed at him, but she only succeeded in being thrown off balance herself by his momentum. They landed with a thud, Jericho on the stairs, Kitty on his chest.

He lay there, groaning, uncertain what hurt more: his back—upon which, from top to bottom, the stairs were now imprinted—or his heart, where in some inexorable, impossible way, this woman was now imprinted

A feather-soft touch on his face. "Are you OK?"

He closed his eyes, savoring her nearness. The warmth of her fingers. The fragrance that was all her.

Get up, idiot. Get up and get your bearings back.

He should. But he couldn't. Not when all he wanted to do was—

"Bark! Yap-yap-yap! Rrrrrowf!"

His eyes flew open, and he shifted to a sitting position, then boosted Kitty to her feet. "*What* is *wrong* with that *dog?*"

Kitty patted him on the arm. "He must be missing Miss Lily. I'll see if I can find his sock."

"When you do," Jericho grumbled as she went up the stairs, "try stuffing it in his mouth."

Kitty entered the animal room and grimaced. Sweetums's sharp bark was enough to make your ears bleed.

Looking around, she spotted the terrier standing near the heating vent, barking furiously. "What is it, boy?"

The dog didn't even look at her. Drawing closer, Kitty saw that the vent cover was missing. She moved to pick Sweetums up, but the dog bolted away, then returned to the vent, barking with renewed fervor.

"Sweetums, enough already!"

Kitty glanced around for the dog's toy. Miss Lily was very clear. Sweetums *loved* that sock. He carried it everywhere, slept

with it, took it outside when he did his "business." If anything
could mollify the little dog it was that sock.

So where was it?

"Kitty, for cryin' out loud!" Jericho came into the room. "Shut
that walking dustmop up!"

"I would if I could." She tugged at his sleeve. "Help me find
his sock."

"Oh, for the love of— Fine. Whatever it takes."

They tore the room apart. No sock. Kitty pressed her hands to
her face. "It can't be just gone like that. What would have happe—"

Jericho's hand on her arm stopped the question cold. She
looked at him, then followed his gaze.

To the vent.

Kitty's eyes went wide. "Oh, you don't think . . . ?"

Jericho nodded. "The sock's in the vent. It's the only thing
that makes sense." He headed for the door, muttering all the way.
"I don't believe this. I just don't believe it."

Kitty scooped the dog up, grabbed his leash, and caught up
with Jericho. "Will it be hard to find?"

He fixed her with a glare.

"OK, OK. We'll go for a walk. Will half an hour do?"

No response.

"Right." She clipped the leash on Sweetums's collar. "An
hour it is."

"Lord"—was it prayer when it came through clenched teeth?—
"this woman is a disaster."

Jericho stomped out of the house, eyes scanning for access to
the crawl space. "Nothing goes right around her. She's crazy. But
I've told you that before."

There. The access door, held in place by four screws. He knelt
in front of it and pulled the screwdriver from his tool belt. With
each loosened screw, he continued down the list.

"Unorganized."

One.

"Flighty."

Two.

"Bounces from one crazy thing to another, like she's a—a *ping-pong ball* in a tornado."

Three.

"She drives me nuts, Lord, and I can't—I can't—"

The flow of frustrated words halted. Everything around him stilled. Jericho leaned his forehead against his arm and closed his eyes.

What was going on? What was this empty feeling in his gut?

"Lord, I can't."

He removed the final screw and jerked the door open, dropped to his belly, and crawled under the house, through the dirt and grime and spider webs. When he spotted the ductwork, he rolled over and stared at it, and as though it were a movie screen, images drifted through his mind.

Kitty the way he'd first seen her, covered with little white flour pawprints where Bosco had run across her as he raced for freedom . . .

Kitty's wide eyes as she stared at him for the first time . . .

"God, I can't." He tried to shake the images from his mind, but they kept coming.

Kitty's face, flushed and rueful when she discovered the ferrets had destroyed the beanbag chair . . .

Kitty scolding him, laughing with him, asking him for help, promising to pray for him . . .

"I can't, Lord. I can't . . . live without her."

As soon as the words escaped him, he knew they weren't true. Not quite. He could live without her.

He just didn't want to.

He rolled onto his stomach, staring at nothing. He hadn't thought it possible. He'd been so sure when Alice died that she'd been it for him. No way he'd ever find someone like Alice again. And that was true. Kitty was nothing like Alice. And yet . . .

Kitty touched him. Deep inside. Her joy in everyday life, the myriad expressions that played across her features, her core of tough determination. He spent more time than he'd been willing to admit thinking about her, wondering what she thought, what she felt.

Her mere presence brought him joy. It was that simple.

Tell her.

He worked the ductwork free and set it aside. Tell her? He could do that. But what if she didn't feel the same? What if she wasn't ready?

He reached inside the duct, fingers feeling until—

"Ha! Gotcha!"

He pulled the dog toy free. Easy as that. Just reach out and it was there, right where it should be.

Right where it should be.

He put the ductwork back together, then crawled out from under the house. With the access door secured again, he straightened, trying to brush some of the dirt off his clothes.

Maybe he should go home, take a shower, and change.

Tell her. Now.

He drew a deep breath and nodded. "OK, Lord, you win. I'll tell her." He made his way to the front door. "Just do me a favor, would you? Help her see she needs me."

He opened the door. "Almost as much as I need her."

CHAPTER
Nine

Kitty leaned down to lift the still-frantic Sweetums into her arms. She hoped an hour had been long enough. The look on Jericho's face when she left hadn't been encouraging. But she couldn't wait any longer.

She opened the door and stepped inside, then cupped her hand around Sweetums's muzzle. "Now hush up, you. Jericho will have your furry little head if you don't hush."

"I may do that anyway."

At the low, mumbled words, Kitty started. She looked up, then frowned at the sight that greeted her. Jericho was covered in dirt and dust. "What happened to you?"

"I met you."

"Ha ha." She unclipped the leash from Sweetums's collar.

His brows lifted, taking with them a strand of clinging spider web. "You think I'm kidding?"

She reached out to pluck the spider web free. "Never mind. Did you find the sock?"

He held out the sock, which was dirty as could be but seemed none the worse for its journey down the vent. Sweetums uttered a delighted yap and jumped from Kitty's arms, then ran to jump up on Jericho's legs.

"Do you know the term 'drop kick,' doggie?"

Kitty plucked the dirty sock toy from his hand. "Don't be such a sourpuss." She dropped the sock down to Sweetums.

"No! Wait—!"

She jumped at Jericho's yell. What on earth?

Sweetums grabbed the sock toy and bounded up the stairs.

"Stop him!"

Kitty scrambled to obey the bellowed command, but the little dog had too much of a head start. He hit the top of the stairs and paused just long enough to look down at Kitty and Jericho as they bounded after him. But the moment they were within reach, the dog spun and darted to his room.

"Come back here, you little rat!"

What was *wrong* with the man?

They chased Sweetums to his room, entering just in time to see the terrier standing at the edge of the still uncovered floor vent.

Sudden understanding hit Kitty between the eyes. "Oh, no!"

Jericho looked at her. "Wanna bet?"

As though he understood their every word, Sweetums held the sock over the vent. And let go. Kitty and Jericho stood there, staring at the now joyfully yapping dog and listening to the toy bounce its way to the depths of the heating ductwork.

Kitty bit her lip, afraid to look at the man beside her.

It started low, and then grew. Deep, rich laughter, filling the room. Kitty turned and found Jericho leaning against the door-jamb, laughing so hard now that tears ran down his face, leaving little trails in the dust on his cheeks.

Then it hit her too. Laughter that rose from deep within, joining his to fill the room.

He held out a hand to her. She didn't hesitate to take it and let him draw her into the circle of his arms.

He cradled her against his chest, and when she met his eyes there was such tenderness there it took her breath away. His hands cupped her face and then, as though it was the most natural thing in the world, he leaned down and pressed a soft kiss to her lips. And just like that . . .

She was lost. And found.

Lost in the wonder of all Jericho was. Found with all he'd brought back into her life. Of renewed love and rediscovered joy.

When he drew away, her knees had gone so weak she had to grip his shirt to keep from falling. His deep chuckle warmed her, as did the hand that caressed her face.

"I love you."

His simple words were an explosion of joy inside her. She looked up at him, and said the first thing that came to her dazed mind. "Please tell me this isn't an April Fool's joke."

He laughed. "The only joke was in me thinking I could walk away from you. But you're stuck with me, woman. Like it or not."

"Oh"—she let her love shine in her gaze—"I like it. It's always nice when the man you love loves you back." She sighed and rested her cheek against his chest. "It finally happened, didn't it?"

"What's that?"

"The walls came crashing down."

He didn't even ask her what she meant. When she looked up at him, she could see in his eyes that he knew.

"I did everything I could to keep you out, Kitty. But there was no resisting you. And God. And all this crazy, wonderful chaos. I'm well and truly in love with you, Kitty Hawk. And I'm going to marry you. We belong together, now"—he caressed her face— "and for as many days as God gives us."

"Oh," she breathed the word out on a sigh, "that's what I want. And I don't even mind."

"Mind?"

"That you'll make my name more outrageous than it's even been."

She felt his chuckle, deep in his chest. "It's only fair, consider-ing what you're going to do to my nice, ordered life."

He kissed her again, and she knew. God had given her everything she'd been missing, restored everything she thought she'd lost.

Even April Fool's.

Ten

"Your mom is a lovely summer bride."

Kylie and Brendan glanced at the small, elderly woman in front of them. They both broke out in smiles when they saw the little dog she held cradled in one arm.

Kylie took the small, gloved hand the woman extended. "You must be Miss Lily."

"I am, indeed."

"I'm so happy you could make it. Mom said it wouldn't be the same without you. And Sweetums."

Brendan looked to where their mother stood with her new husband. "You're absolutely right, Miss Lily. Mom's beautiful."

"And so radiant." The woman's sparkling eyes moved from Brendan to Kylie. "It's just delightful that she chose to have her wedding in the park. Sweetums would have hated to miss this auspicious occasion." Miss Lily followed Brendan's gaze back to the wedding couple. "And I must say, her new beau looks so happy."

"They do, indeed."

Kylie nudged her brother at the smug tone in his voice.

"How good of God to bring them together." Miss Lily patted their hands, then moved away, holding a piece of wedding cake out for Sweetums to nibble on as she walked.

Kylie shot her brother a look. "Ha! Miss Lily got you good with that one."

He shook his head. "Put in my place by a little woman who talks to her dog."

Kylie laughed. "I only hope I'm half so elegant and sweet when I'm Miss Lily's age."

"Congratulations, team."

They turned at the hearty call and found Gramps coming up behind them. He held three plastic goblets of punch. They each took a goblet.

"A toast." Gramps lifted his goblet high.

"To us," Brendan said.

"To Mom and Jericho," Kylie added.

"To a mission well accomplished." Gramps's eyes were glowing.

They clinked their glasses together, then drained them.

Brendan looked around. "Pity there's no fireplace to cast them into."

"Not necessary." Gramps took their empty goblets from them. "I'll just put these away in case I need them again."

Kylie frowned. "For what?"

"Oh, you never can tell." Gramps patted the coat pocket where he'd put the goblets. "There may come another time when we need them to celebrate a successful mission."

"Gramps, Mom's doing great." Brendan loosened his tie. "She's not going to need us again."

"True."

Kylie wasn't sure she liked the serene smile on her grandfather's face. What was he up to?

"But there are others who may yet need help." He patted them each on the arm, then drifted away.

"Others?" Kylie called after him.

Gramps kept moving, but his words reached them all the same. "People who aren't settled yet, who are wrapped up in their careers, who need to find happiness as much as your mother did."

Brendan shook his head. "I pity the poor fools, whoever they are."

Kylie still watched her grandfather. "You know Gramps. He won't give up until they're 'settled.'"

A small frown creased her brother's forehead. "Who do we know that's wrapped up in their jobs?"

"No one." Kylie noted that Gramps was now deep in conversation with Mom and Jericho. All three glanced at her and Brendan. "But it's clear he's up to something."

"Maybe they're moving on to you," Brendan said with a laugh.

Kylie crossed her arms. "Not a chance. I'm too busy for relationships right now. I mean, it's fine for Mom. She needs a man around. But me?" She waved the thought away. "Last thing I need is a man underfoot, needing me, wanting to spend time with me, looking at me the way Jericho looks at Mom, like she's some kind of early Christmas present. Besides, I don't exactly have any prospects. And with all the hours I work you can bet I won't have any for a good long time. Which wouldn't be so bad if I wasn't standing here watching my mother get married before I do. My *mother*, for heaven's sake—"

She looked away, astonished to find herself blinking away tears. What was with her today? And what was with this ache inside? She cleared her throat and turned back to Brendan. "Anyway, you know what I mean."

The small crease tugging at her brother's brow said he wasn't so sure. "You OK, Sis?"

"Fine." Whoa! That came out way too forceful. She dropped her tone a notch. "Fine, really. Weddings always get to me."

"Are you sur—?"

"So, you ready for some cake? I sure am." She didn't wait for a reply. She spun on her heel and started for the cake table.

Brendan fell into step beside her. "Don't worry, Sis. I'm sure whoever Gramps is talking about doesn't concern us. We're good, right?"

"Right, of course." She linked her arm with her brother's. "We're adults. We'll know when it's time to take the step into a relationship."

"Exactly."

Kylie gave her brother a bright smile, and herself a quick kick in the mental pants. *Buck up, girl. Today isn't the day to feel sorry for yourself. Today is about Mom and Jericho. You'll have plenty of time later to get all morose. At home. By yourself.*

Like always.

"Kylie, Brendan!"

She started from her thoughts and looked around. Mom waved at them from where she stood, a growing crowd of women behind her. She was positively glowing.

"Come on, you two. It's time to throw the bouquet."

Brendan shot Kylie a look, but she straightened her shoulders and pasted a broad smile on her features.

"You don't have to—"

She brushed her brother's concern aside. "Don't be silly. I wouldn't miss it for the world."

No matter how much she might want to.

She made her way to the back of the crowd. She should be safe here.

"Everyone ready?"

The chorus of giggles was enough to drive anyone crazy—

"Here goes!"

A wave of movement surged through the women as they lifted their hands, fingers outstretched.

"I got it!" The woman beside Kylie pushed off of Kylie's shoulder as she jumped up. The unexpected impact sent Kylie flying backward, and she landed on her backside with a resounding "Oomph!"

She looked up to give the woman a piece of her mind—and just managed to avoid getting beaned with the bouquet, which landed square in her lap.

All the women screamed and gathered around Kylie, pulling her to her feet and hugging her. She clutched the bouquet, about to run screaming for cover, when a gentle hand touched her face.

Mom.

She enfolded Kylie in her arms, hugging her close. "Sweetie, are you all right?"

For a moment, Kylie stiffened, then she melted against her mother, letting the warmth and love overflow her. She buried her head in her mother's neck.

Mom led her away from the crowd, to two empty chairs. She took Kylie's hand in her own. They sat in silence, and Kylie felt peace flowing through her.

Mom must be praying for her.

She looked up and smiled at her mom. "You look so happy."

"I am."

"Jericho's a wonderful man. He's so perfect for you."

"Just as perfect as your man will be for you someday."

Her mother knew her so well. "I wish I were as sure as you, Mom."

"That he'll be perfect?"

"That he exists!"

Her mother's laughter danced around her, easing the tightness in her heart.

"Oh, Kylie. Of course he does. You know how I know?"

"How?"

Her mother stood, holding a hand out to her. Kylie took her hand and let herself be pulled to her feet. Together, they started walking back toward the reception crowd.

"I know, my darling girl, because I've prayed for that man since the day you were born."

Kylie stopped. "Really?"

Her mother's nod was firm. "Really. And God let me know, many years ago, that he was working on it. So I know, when the time is right"—she touched Kylie's cheek—"when it's God's perfect timing for you *and* for that very lucky man, it will happen."

Kylie forced words past the lump in her throat. "You promise?"

Her mom slipped her arm through Kylie's. "Absolutely."

That settled it. Because if there was one thing Kylie could count on, it was that her mother always kept her promises.

An Unlikely Angel

MISSION CONTROL

"Any idea what your dad is up to?"

Kitty turned to Jericho. "You're kidding, right?"

Those handsome lips twitched, and she felt his fingers tighten on hers for a moment. "You're right. I may have been a part of this family only for a few months now, but I should know better."

Kitty leaned her head back against the car seat. Yes, only a few months, and yet it felt as though she'd been with Jericho forever. Not that she'd ever forget Dan. But God had given her this second chance at love, and it still amazed her how quickly Jericho had become a part of the fabric of her life.

And her heart. She turned her head to look at him, remembering how well he'd fit into their family's Thanksgiving celebration the previous afternoon.

"Still, when your dad asked us after dinner yesterday if we could stop by today, he sounded pretty serious."

Kitty pursed her lips. "What he sounded like was he's up to some scheme or another. And that worries me."

Jericho's deep laughter filled the car, wrapping her in warmth. "Oh, I don't know." He tugged on her hand, drawing it to his mouth to place a kiss on her knuckles. "His last scheme turned out pretty great." He released her hand and turned the car into the driveway of her parents' home.

Hmmm . . . Brendan's car sat in the driveway. So this wasn't about him—

"Wow."

Kitty looked at her husband of three months. "Wow?"

He pushed open the car door and got out. Kitty did the same, then followed his gaze—and grinned. "Welcome to holidays at the Hawk household."

The house was decked, roof to foundation, with Christmas lights and decorations. As was the driveway. And the yard.

Kitty and Jericho walked hand in hand to the front door, but before Jericho could press the bell, the door flew open.

"Welcome!"

Kitty's son, Brendan, engulfed the two of them in bear hugs, then hustled them inside. "You're just in time. Grams just put a plate of crullers on the table, along with some of her homemade hot chocolate."

He didn't have to say that twice. Within minutes, Jericho and Kitty were settled in, still-warm crullers in hand, listening as Kitty's dad explained the reason they were there.

In a word, her daughter, Kylie.

"She's just not been quite right since your wedding, sweetie."

Kitty hesitated, cruller midway to her mouth. "But she seemed so happy I was marrying again."

"Oh, she is." Brendan reached for another crunchy treat. "Thrilled. Ecstatic." He licked the powdered sugar from the edges of the cruller. "That's the problem. She sees how happy you are. . . ."

Kitty set the cruller back on her plate. "And wonders when it will happen for her."

Jericho slid his arm around her shoulders. "It's been a tough few months for her, what with losing Sasha and all. She and that dog were so connected."

Kylie's Siberian had made it to the ripe old age of fourteen. But that hadn't made losing her any easier. "It helps that she's got Zsuzsi."

"I'll say." Brendan brushed powdered sugar from his fingers. "I've never seen a dog so tuned in to people before. I mean, the way Zsuzsi is with owners at Kylie's clinic when they've lost a pet . . ."

Kitty hadn't been surprised when Kylie got another dog within weeks of Sasha's death. But she *had* been surprised when her daughter brought home a komondor rather than another Siberian.

"God brought her to me," Kylie had said. "Besides, I think I needed a change."

But that change wasn't enough. As healing as it had been for Kylie to have Zsuzsi, it was clear she needed something more. Kitty straightened in her chair. "So, troops, what are we going to do?"

"Actually"—Brendan leaned forward—"I've got an idea."

As he unfolded his plan, the heaviness that had settled in Kitty's heart lifted. It was perfect. Better than perfect—

It was heaven-sent.

"So we're agreed?"

At Dad's question, they looked at each other, then all reached for the crullers.

"So be it—" Dad held his cruller high, and the others followed the motion. They tapped them together to a fall of more powdered sugar, then all took a bite in replication of a toast.

Dad smacked his lips, then grinned. "Operation Kylie is hereby activated."

PROJECT CHRISTMAS

CHAPTER
One

Snow fell outside, blanketing the night in sparkling white and giving the city a stunning, almost storybook appearance. Men and women stopped their holiday shopping and stared at the glittering window displays. Children squealed and lifted mittened hands to capture the large, fluffy flakes floating down on their upturned faces and waiting tongues.

It was enough to make a man gag.

Mackenzie St. Clair turned away from his high vantage point at the window, back to the partygoers milling around the spacious, elegantly decorated ballroom on the top floor of the Hirsch, Tesler & St. Clair building. He couldn't help his grin. It still got to him. Having his name on a building.

Let the everyday people below have their winter wonderland. It couldn't compete with the elegance and glamour of the annual employee Christmas party of Seattle's most prestigious efficiency consultant firm. Snowfalls were commonplace. This party? Hardly. Everyone knew that.

Or at least, almost everyone.

Mackenzie had noticed one young woman, dressed in a stunning sequined gown of electric blue showcasing her slim figure. It wasn't the dress or her shape that caught his attention, but the fact that she'd pressed her perfectly made-up nose against the glass of a tall, beveled window and stared at the sparkling display like a kid seeing Santa for the first time.

Another woman, this one dressed to the nines and a hard edge to her expression, came up beside the gawker. "Andrea, get a grip. It's just snow."

Mackenzie stepped back, a large decorative tree blocking him from the two women's view. He, on the other hand, could still see the two friends. At least he assumed there was a friendship. It was hard to tell with women. Sometimes they just hunted together.

At Miss Nines's tart reprimand, Blue Dress swiveled around. "But it's so beautiful! Even you have to admit that, Maris."

OK. Nines is Maris, Blue Dress is Andrea. And she talks in exclamation points.

"Actually"—Maris arched dark, perfect brows—"I don't. Nor do you, unless you want everyone at the party to know just how new you are to the city."

That hit home. Even from this distance Mackenzie caught the flush that crept into Andrea's cheeks, and she glanced around.

"Oh, don't worry." Maris brushed a crumb from her sleeve. "I was able to stop you before you made too much of a fool of yourself. But, really, Andrea you must learn to get some control. You're working at one of the largest, most successful firms in Seattle now. Don't you think it's time you started acting a bit more . . . well, professional?"

The woman's gaze swept the room, and Mackenzie inched back a step. He had no trouble recognizing that glint in her eyes. Pure calculation.

"Believe me, darling, men like these won't have the patience for sweet, naïve little girls. They'd chew you up in a second."

Sad, but true. The men in Mackenzie's employ knew it was a dog-eat-dog world. Especially in the current economy.

"I know." Andrea's sad, wistful sigh struck Mackenzie. Hard. She sounded just like—

He shook the thought away. He'd come to this party to forget the job he'd just finished, not be reminded of it. Time to find someone else to entertain him. He started to move, but caught the sparkle of Andrea's blue dress as she moved back to the window. She lifted a hand, pressed it to the glass.

Like a caged bird longing for freedom.

"But it's so beautiful—"

"For heaven's sake!" Maris took the younger woman's arm in a firm grip and propelled her toward the buffet table. Mackenzie waited a beat, then followed, picking up a plate and lingering just far enough away that they wouldn't know he was listening.

"Look around you!" Maris's cold, rational tone was even more familiar. Mackenzie used it all the time.

"This is your chance, Andrea," she went on. "These men are sophisticated, intelligent, and ridiculously well paid. Some are even single."

From the corner of his eye, Mackenzie saw Andrea glance around. "But does any of that really matter if he doesn't"—she shrugged—"you know, make your toes curl?"

Mackenzie fought a chuckle. This girl was so . . . innocent.

"Like him, for example."

Maris turned to inspect Andrea's supposed toe-curler, and Mackenzie realized with a jolt that they were looking at him.

She turned back to Andrea, then cast her gaze to the ceiling. "Oh, good grief. *Any*one but him."

Mackenzie frowned.

"Why? He's very clearly wealthy—"

Darn right.

"Yes, quite." Maris picked up a crystal punch glass. "That's Mackenzie St. Clair. As in Hirsh, Tesler, and . . ." She pursed a lip. "He's one of the partners."

Andrea's brows lifted. Well, at least she was impressed with that bit of news.

"Really?" She studied Mackenzie again. "*That's* Mackenzie St. Clair? I thought he was an old man."

Oh, give me a break!

"Only at heart, dear. Only at heart."

Andrea, seemingly his saving grace, tipped her head. "Not handsome, but good-looking—"

Hmm. Well, he could live with that.

"—tall, broad-shouldered, wealthy—"

He was really starting to like this woman.

"—single?"

Maris snorted. "Count on it."

That woman, he could do without.

"Well, then, what on earth is wrong with him?"

Yeah. Do tell.

"Oh, not much. Just that he's cold as ice, unfeeling, demanding. You know, basically inhuman."

Mackenzie's fingers tightened on the plate as he pretended to select another canapé.

"Come on! He can't be that bad."

"Probably worse." Maris sipped at her drink. "Look, Andrea, I've been with this company for almost five years, and if there's one thing I've learned, it's to stay as far away from that man as possible."

Now there was some good news.

"I thought he was supposed to be the best of the best."

"Oh, he is that. No better efficiency or management consultant in the field."

Finally, some recognition for what he'd accomplished.

"When a company calls him in, they know they'll get their money's worth, and then some. He knows exactly what to do to bring a company back to life and fiscal viability. And he doesn't let anything get in his way. Not compassion. Not consequences to others. Not anything."

Andrea visibly shuddered. "He sounds perfectly horrid."

He did, at that. Was that what people thought of him?

"Bingo." Maris ladled more punch from a crystal bowl into her glass, capturing one of the floating cherries as she did so. "I was assigned to work for him a few months last year, when his regular secretary was out on maternity leave."

Mackenzie took another sideways look at the one called Maris. She'd worked with him? Why didn't she look familiar? At least her name should ring a bell—

"It was an interesting job, but not one I'd care to take on for long."

"Too much work?"

"For one thing, the man never got my name right. Kept calling me Mary."

Of course. Mary. Now he remembered—

Maris grabbed a toothpick and speared an hors d'oeuvre. "How hard is it to remember someone's name, for heaven's sake? For another, too much hostility. I received dozens of calls from angry people. 'Idiots and malcontents,' St. Clair calls them." She pursed her lips again. "Among other things. But they all had one thing in common: they wanted to give the man a piece of their minds. Several left messages. I recall one in particular, from an older man who wanted to . . . let's see, what did he say? Oh, yes, 'rip the devil's heart out.'"

Andrea's eyes widened. "How did Mr. St. Clair react when you told him?"

"He didn't even blink. But I wasn't too surprised. I mean, it was hardly a believable threat."

"Why? Wasn't the caller serious?"

Maris brushed back a stray hair. "Oh, he sounded quite serious. But he made a tactical error."

"What was that?"

Maris angled a look across the room at her distinguished employer. "If there is one thing Mackenzie St. Clair does *not* have, it's a heart."

Mackenzie set his plate down on the buffet. Hard. Enough was—

"Heartless and hopeless, huh?" Andrea gave another sad sigh. "I pity the woman who falls for him one day."

Maris almost choked on her punch. "Trust me, dear, she'd have to be a total saint. Either that, or a total fool!"

Mackenzie pinned Maris with a narrow-eyed glare. Andrea noticed it first, and went still. Maris looked at her companion, then followed her wide-eyed gaze. When her eyes met Mackenzie's, she stiffened . . . then paled.

That's right, ladies. Heard every word.

He held her gaze captive for a heartbeat longer, then walked toward them, stopping when he was right next to them. Both women stood like gazelles frozen in fear, waiting for the death strike.

He smiled and leaned his head close to them. "Enjoy the party, ladies." With that, he straightened and moved on, leaving them staring after him. But he could tell it had worked.

That spark of fear in Maris's eyes asked if his intended message was, "It will be your last."

It was well past midnight when Mackenzie finally quit his company's Christmas party. His two partners pressed him every year with the fact that his presence at such events was important, a "morale builder."

Clearly, *some* of his employees disagreed. As much as he'd tried to brush aside Maris's comments on his humanity—or lack thereof—he was more than irritated.

Morale builder, my foot. Monumental waste of time is more like it. He stepped out of the elevator onto the marbled floor of the lobby, his mood growing darker by the minute. "Just like Christmas. And the whole month of December."

"You were saying, sir?" The doorman didn't wait for an answer. "A good evening to you, sir. Your car is waiting." The man knew him well enough not to offer the ubiquitous "Merry Christmas" as Mackenzie exited the building.

He handed the parking attendant a five-dollar bill, then slid onto the leather seat of his Infiniti, sinking into its familiar comfort. This was more like it. Quiet. Solitude. A totally controlled environment where he was alone, isolated, not expected to make inane conversation with people he didn't know—or care one whit to know. Especially perky ones in shiny blue dresses.

The half-hour drive to his house went by quickly. That was one benefit of driving at midnight: Seattle's normal gridlock was over and done with. Another benefit of the late hour was that, at least for tonight, he wouldn't have to watch people bustling about, caught in the frenetic shopping fever that this time of year seemed to spawn. It was barely the beginning of December, but Mackenzie had had his fill of watching adults and children alike staring at Christmas displays in storefront windows as though they'd never seen such a wondrous sight before.

"Same ridiculous displays every year." Shaking his head, he reminded himself he was free. For an entire month. Until three years ago, he'd hated the arrival of December. The moment that month dawned, his job became next to impossible. Something about the Christmas season made people in business lose their nerve.

Not Mackenzie. He thrived on bringing new life to a company on the edge of bankruptcy. Sure, he'd made enemies along the way. That even bothered him . . . at first. He'd agonized over cuts and layoffs, wondering how people would react, how they would survive.

Then he'd lost the client for the firm because, the man said, Mackenzie wouldn't make hard decisions.

"He's so worried about the employees that my business is going down the tubes!" the angry owner had fumed. Back then Mackenzie had only been with Hirsch and Tesler for a few years, so he figured a pink slip was coming. Instead, the two older men took him out to lunch. They said they'd been watching him, that he held great promise—but that he needed to toughen up.

"You're not a babysitter, Mackenzie." There'd been such confidence in Abe Tesler's quiet tone. "Corporations don't call you in to help them deal with their people. They want you to save their businesses. No matter what it takes."

Hard lesson, but he'd learned it. Within the next year he'd become the most-requested consultant at the firm. Three years later, he'd been offered partnership. And he'd never looked back.

Well, really? So why do you keep remembering scenes from the job you just finished?

Mackenzie's grip on the steering wheel tightened. OK, so he had to consider the emotional impact once in a while. It helped him with his strategy.

That's what you call it? Strategy?

Hey, sad but true. Sometimes people had to be sacrificed to keep a company afloat. Management understood and followed his recommendations to the letter. It was the others who got emotional—

Oh, you mean the people whose lives you've just ruined?

As though on cue, the images of the consultation he'd just completed flooded his mind. A smallish corporation with two hundred employees . . . when he first arrived, that was. By the time he left, they were pared down to half. Everything had been going according to plan until the last day. He'd been on his way to his car in the parking lot when an older man hailed him.

"Mr. St. Clair?"

Mackenzie had turned, and the man was there beside him. Though Mackenzie only dealt with executives at the corporation, he recognized this employee. Mr. Hendricks had been with the company for thirty years. He was in his late 60s, just shy of full retirement. Though he wasn't a tall man, his straight back and square shoulders bespoke confidence. And the man's face always seemed so . . . kind. *Probably why he'd never gotten higher than supervisor.*

Mackenzie had come across him several times in a hallway or office, always with someone who'd just found out he or she had gotten "the news." It appeared he was consoling those people. Mackenzie found that interesting, since this man had been one of the first to be let go. Early retirement, they called it. Because of this man's seniority, Mackenzie had made sure the man was as well taken care of as possible. Not full benefits, by any means. But he would be better off than most. He now probably wanted to thank Mackenzie.

Mackenzie faced the man. "Yes? It's Hendricks, isn't it?"

He nodded. "Sir, I understand you decided who kept their jobs and who didn't?"

Uh-oh. Mackenzie squared his shoulders. "No, not true. I made recommendations, that's all."

"Did they follow your recommendations?"

Of course they did. To the letter. But Mackenzie wasn't about to tell this man that.

Mr. Hendricks nodded again. "I can see from your expression they did."

Irritation singed Mackenzie's nerves. "Listen, I'm sorry you lost your job, but the company did take good care of you—"

"They did, and I'm grateful."

That stopped Mackenzie. That and the sincerity in the man's gaze. He really was grateful. So what was this about?

"I'm not worried myself, Son. I'm worried about you."

Son? Mackenzie frowned, irritated once more. "Me?"

"I've been watching you these last few days."

"Watching me?" He sounded like an idiot, echoing the man's words. But none of this was making sense. "Why?"

"What you do, it can't be easy. You impact lives, Mr. St. Clair. And I'm guessing that impact is almost always negative. As it was here."

Mackenzie crossed his arms over his chest, readying himself for an onslaught of condemnation. But this man's eyes held no anger. All Mackenzie saw was . . . what? Concern? "Please, Mr. Hendricks, what is it you want to say to me?"

"You didn't seem affected by what took place here. I looked for some glimmer of compassion, something to show you under-stood what people were going through, and it just wasn't there."

What did the man want? Mackenzie sobbing in a corner for doing his job? "I wasn't hired to feel anything."

"What happened to you, Son? What made you this way?"

Mackenzie couldn't have been more stunned than if the man had punched him in the gut. "What?"

"It's one thing to keep a professional demeanor, but that's not what you're doing. You simply . . . don't feel. And that's not good. Not for the people you impact. But more important, it's not good for you."

Mackenzie was feeling plenty. Mostly anger. "I'm sorry, Mr. Hendricks, but you don't know a thing about me."

The man smiled. Smiled! "No, I don't. But someone else does. Someone who has given me a glimpse into the emptiness inside you. Who prompted me to say something to you."

Oh, this was too much. "Are you saying God told you to talk to me?"

"I am."

Mackenzie shook his head. "Well, then, you've done your duty. And I have someplace to be, so if you'll forgive me, I'm leav-ing." He snatched the car door handle.

"I'll do more than forgive you, Son."

The quiet words stopped Mackenzie, and he glanced over at the man standing there.

"I'll pray for you."

I'll pray for you. The words had been so full of compassion and concern. *I'll pray for you.* How arrogant could a person be? Like that man had any idea what Mackenzie needed.

I'll pray for you. I'll pray for—

Stop! Mac beat a fist against the steering wheel. What was wrong with him? He didn't let things like this get to him. It had to be the time of year. The minute this month hit, even his normally attentive, acquiescent executives balked.

"I can't fire him, it's Christmas!"

"Let her go? How can I let her go now? It's Christmas!"

"What do you mean, 'downsize'? Don't you know this is Christmas? What will they do? What will they think of me?"

Mac rubbed his aching temples. What was this fascination people had with this time of the year? Yes, it was the celebration of Jesus' birth. That accounted for Christmas Day. Maybe even Christmas Eve. But why couldn't people keep things in perspective? He had faith, but it stayed where it belonged—in church on Sunday morning.

He saw the worst in humans every day. Let a company fall into serious financial trouble, and its executives scrambled, abandoning honor and integrity, in the name of the bottom line. Let a rumor of cutbacks float on the air, and employees began saying one thing to a person's face then cutting that person down to the quick when he left the room. Mac started out believing in the importance of treating others fairly and with honor, but those things couldn't endure when a company faced financial ruin. Far better to concentrate on the nitty-gritty. Logic was the name of the game, not compassion.

Do what had to be done, and let someone else worry about how those involved *felt* about it.

Which only made his inner wrestling match that much more infuriating. OK, it *had* to be December. This month-long indulgence in frivolity hidden under the guise of "holiday cheer" was enough to drive a man crazy. Particularly him. That's why, a few years back, he went to his partners with a proposal. Rather than beat his head against the Christmas spirit, Mac would take the month off. Use the time to review the past year, to evaluate the direction of his professional and personal life, and prepare for the coming year. The partners were all for it.

So far it had worked well. Every December he ended up with a list of goals that he tracked throughout the year. It made life much easier, more organized, more logical.

That's what he needed now. To immerse himself in analysis. Logic. Goals. Maybe that would shut the inner voice up.

You think it's that easy?

He'd *make* it so. He turned his car onto his street and snorted at the holiday frippery on the houses and lawns. At least a few of his neighbors showed some restraint, sticking to white lights on the trees and elegant wreaths on the doors. Others, however, had gone all out. Ornaments and lights dangled from the eaves of the houses, and Santa or crèche displays leaving scant inches of lawn without some kind of holiday raiment. All of which had the irksome effect of turning Mac's normally quiet, refined neighborhood into some kind of mutant carnival gone wild.

Couldn't these people find a better way to utilize their time than putting plastic reindeer on their lawns?

He pulled into his driveway, noting with a certain measure of satisfaction that his home alone retained its bare, unadorned sophistication.

If only the rest of the world would fall in line.

But as he eased out of his car, Mackenzie knew he was asking too much. The rest of the world would never see things his way—especially during the peace-on-earth, have-a-holly-jolly holidays. They were too busy sopping up good cheer to see straight.

Mackenzie cast one last glance at his neighbors' lawns as he drove into the garage.

"Thank heaven Christmas comes only once a year." The dark words matched his mood as he punched the button to close the garage door.

CHAPTER

Two

"*I wish Christmas would last forever!*" Kylie Hawk wrapped her arms around herself. "What do you say, Zsuzsi? Isn't this the greatest time of year? Don't you wish it would just go on and on?"

The large white dog sitting beside Kylie's rocking chair responded with a happy *Woof!* Kylie grinned at the komondor, then uttered a contented sigh as she rocked back and forth. She gazed out the bedroom window at the early morning, noting the cloud-covered sky. "Looks as though we're going to have snow again today, girl."

The dog tilted her head, as though considering her mistress's words. Kylie laughed, reaching out to rub the dog's long ears, loving the feel of her soft, corded coat.

She glanced down to the Bible in her lap. Several years ago she decided to read through Isaiah during the Christmas season. It had been so moving that she'd made it a tradition. Normally she settled for reading two or three chapters a day. But this morning she'd found herself paging through the book, as though looking for something. And so she had. Once again she read over the section in Isaiah 40 that had seemed to jump out to her when she'd turned to it:

A voice says, "Call out." Then he answered, "What shall I call out?" . . . Get yourself up on a high mountain, O Zion, bearer of good news, Lift up your voice mightily, O Jerusalem, bearer of good news; Lift it up, do not fear. Say to the cities of Judah, Here is your God!

A shiver passed over Kylie. She'd been reading the Bible for most of her life, but seldom had she felt such a strong impression— as though the Lord wanted her, Kylie Hawk, on this specific day in early December, to read these specific words. As though he had something special in store. "I'm listening, Father."

A strong, sweet awareness swept over her, and she closed her eyes, filled with wonder. God was there. She could feel him touching her heart and spirit, flowing over her with his presence. And a certain conviction settled in her heart that this Scripture was more than just a morning reading. It was a message she needed to share.

But with whom?

"Show me, Lord—"

Be-weep!

The sharp sound startled Kylie from her whispered prayer, and she glanced out the window. The neighbor was walking toward his sleek, expensive car. He must have just disabled the alarm. She watched as he opened the car door . . . and took in the man's tall frame, confident stance, and no-doubt tailor-made overcoat.

Mackenzie St. Clair, the quintessential "man who has everything." She started to turn back to her prayer, but something stopped her.

"Call out."

She frowned, watching the man as he retrieved a file folder, then pushed the door shut and reset the alarm.

"Call out . . . say to the cities of Judah, 'Here is your God.'"

Kylie's breath caught in her throat, and her eyes widened. "You've got to be kidding, Lord!"

"Call out."

She shook her head. "No way. Not this man." She lifted her gaze heavenward. "I've tried before, Father. You know I have."

She'd tried to be friendly after moving in next door. Every conversation she tried to start had been met with monosyllabic responses. The record to date was a three-minute conversation in which he'd stopped her while she was on a walk with Zsuzsi and asked her to please keep her sunflowers from leaning over the back fence into his yard.

"They drop seeds." The distaste in his expression was echoed in his tone. "And the birds are all over them."

"I know." Kylie offered her most winning smile. "Aren't the birds fun to watch?"

His eyebrows arched a fraction. "Fun? You like having birds spreading seeds all over your lawn?"

"Well, yes. That's the point."

His dark eyes when he turned back to her were pure bafflement. She wasn't sure if she wanted to laugh or cry. She tried to explain. "More flowers means more birds."

"And more mess."

She'd opened her mouth to debate but realized it was no use. He just didn't get it. And so she told him she'd do her best to keep the flowers on her side of the fence.

"I'd appreciate it."

Nearly every other encounter she'd had with him had ended in the same way: with him looking at her as though she were from Mars, and her sighing and shrugging her shoulders.

"He thinks I'm a nut, Lord!"

The room resonated with silence, and after a moment Kylie let out a slow, deep breath. "OK, if you say so." She let her fingers stroke Zsuzsi's broad head, finding comfort in the action. "But I sure hope you intend to send me some help with this. Because one thing's for sure, I'll never get through to Mackenzie St. Clair on my own!"

CHAPTER
Three

The next afternoon Mackenzie had just finished preparing his usual lunch of salmon salad when the doorbell rang. Frowning, he went to glance out the window. He wasn't expecting visitors. Certainly not during his month off.

A bright red Mustang sat in the driveway. Lindsay.

He opened the front door and found himself staring at a large, full, blue spruce.

"Merry Christmas, brother mine!" a sweet voice sang out from behind the branches. "I come bearing gifts."

"How nice"—he stepped aside as she staggered inside, tree in tow—"you brought me a bush."

"A *bush*? This, my poor, unenlightened brother, is a Christmas tree of the finest quality."

"Ah. Of course." He watched her deposit the tree in the middle of his Berber rug. "And what exactly am I supposed to do with it?"

She dimpled. "Decorate it, you goon. Now stop being obtuse and come give your sister a kiss."

Chuckling, he leaned down to give her a quick peck on her smooth cheek, and she threw her arms around him in an exuberant hug.

She was petite, but she was strong.

"Lindsay, give the ribs a break."

She giggled and stepped back. "If this beauty doesn't get you into the Christmas spirit, I'm inclined to think you're hopeless." The gaze she turned on the tree held an adoration that most women—at least, those he knew—generally reserved for precious gems.

"I keep telling you that's the case, Changeling. The sooner you realize it, the happier we both will be."

"Not so, Bear." She grinned at him, and he shook his head. He'd given up trying to quell the nickname years ago. An avid Winnie the Pooh fan, Lindsay had decided, at the ripe old age of five, that her big brother reminded her of Pooh. "You're cute and cuddly."

"And I have very little brain, that it?"

"Yes!"

He'd argued for a short time, but there was no putting a lid on Lindsay when she had her mind and heart set on something. She'd been adamant that he needed a nickname, something with "personality," she said. Fortunately, she'd been willing to compromise, so "Pooh" (a name that still made Mackenzie shudder) gave way to "Bear." Exactly why it was so vitally important, he'd never fully understood—but then, not understanding Lindsay was par for the course.

Ten years his junior, Lindsay was a lovable mystery. She lived life to the hilt, going from one adventure to the next, finding and producing delight everywhere she went. Mackenzie couldn't remember the last time he'd seen her without a smile on her face.

Hard to believe they were related.

She stood on tiptoe and tweaked his nose. "I know there's a heart in there somewhere, dear brother." She headed for the kitchen, and he followed, closing cupboard doors and drawers in her wake as she helped herself to sandwich fixings.

"Mmmmmmm." She applied another helping of Miracle Whip to her bread. "Peanut butter, Miracle Whip, and pickles. A lunch fit for a queen."

Mackenzie grimaced, but she ignored him. Sandwich in hand, she made a beeline for the breakfast nook, pulled out a chair, and plopped down. "So, what do you hear from the aunts lately?"

Ah, the aunts. The siblings had been raised by the three of them after their parents died in a car accident. Mackenzie had been fifteen, Lindsay, five. Celie was a physicist; Ophelia, a law researcher; and Amelia, a senior professor of mathematics and statistical methods at the university. All three were known as somber, cerebral, and introspective individuals.

"The usual. They're in high demand as speakers and as dinner guests." He moved over to the counter to start a pot of coffee. "They told you, didn't they, that they've been invited to a forum on modern philosophy?"

"Hmm," she said around a mouthful of her monstrous sandwich creation. "That's right. Paris, isn't it?" She paused a moment to swallow. "They'll be gone all month. Ah, yes, nothing so enjoyable as stimulating discourse with the intellectual elite, is there?"

Actually, Mackenzie thought said discourse sounded inviting. Like the aunts, his and Lindsay's parents were university professors. Their positions in the world of academia had been established long before either he or Lindsay had come on the scene. When Mackenzie was born, they simply brought him along. Quiet and undemanding even as an infant, he fit in perfectly. When most children his age were racing around playgrounds, he was content to sit and listen. By the time he was ten, he was even taking part in some of the discussions, demonstrating a remarkable grasp of logic and reasoning. A fact that delighted his parents to no end.

Then—Lindsay. A complete surprise from the get-go and as different in nature from the rest of them as humanly possible. Impulsive, dramatic, emotional, she took their family by storm. Neither Mackenzie nor his parents could begin to understand her. By the time she was a toddler, Mackenzie was convinced she was some sort of alien, planted in their family to keep things in an uproar. Hence her nickname: Changeling. She brought chaos—and in spite of themselves, uproarious laughter—into their home.

So it was that by the time Lindsay was four, Mackenzie and his parents shrugged their shoulders and accepted her as an enchanting anomaly. They couldn't explain or comprehend her, but they had no trouble at all adoring her.

An adoration that the aunts shared, thank goodness. They'd always doted on both him and Lindsay, so though they'd all been devastated by their parents' deaths, it hadn't taken too long to feel at home with the aunts. There'd been adjustments, especially for him. Going from having a dad to being the only male in a household of women had been a struggle. But the aunts were loving—in their own way—and patient, and he'd finally come to realize just how blessed he and Lindsay were.

Mackenzie pulled himself from his thoughts and joined his sister at the table as she polished off her sandwich. He took a few bites of his salmon salad, thinking his aunts weren't the only ones who adored Lindsay. He might be skeptical about a lot of things, but this he knew: he loved his sister, and she was going places. As an up-and-coming creative consultant, she'd been gaining steady recognition for the work she was doing around the Seattle area. Her design concepts were being touted as some of the most innovative and imaginative to hit the city in a long time. Considering how unique Lindsay was, that came as no surprise to Mackenzie.

"So I guess that leaves just you and me for Christmas, eh, Bear?"

He opened his mouth to reply when the air was split by loud, raucous barking. Mackenzie groaned, but Lindsay's face lit up. "Kylie's outside, huh?"

Mackenzie grimaced. "She must be. The creature only sounds that excited when they're outside together." Lindsay jumped up and went to peer out the window.

"You've got to stop spying on my neighbors, Lindsay." He followed her over to the window. When Kylie Hawk had moved to the house next door last spring, she'd piqued his sister's considerable curiosity. Before long the two were getting together on a fairly regular basis to share tea and conversation.

Apparently Lindsay had found a kindred soul.

"You've got to see this!"

He came up beside Lindsay and glanced out, his eyes growing wide as he took in the scene next door. "She's . . . building a snowman."

Lindsay laughed. "She is indeed."

"Where did she ever find that monstrosity?"

"What monstrosity? Her dog?"

"You call *that* a dog? Looks more like some kind of mutant dust mop!" The beast had to weigh a hundred pounds or more and was covered with a white, corded coat that danced and bounced it as it circled around her mistress and whatever it was she was constructing.

"For your information, I think Zsuzsi's cute."

"You think anything with four legs and fur is cute. I'm telling you, that animal is some kind of genetic experiment. A twisted mix between a lion and an unmade bed." He shook his head. "Not that the beast doesn't fit her well. Her hair is as out of control as her dog's!"

"Her hair is to die for!" Lindsay exclaimed, turning to stare at him like he was some kind of clueless alien. "It's like a hair care commercial. You know, 'Use our product and your hair will look like this, all curls and waves and sun-kissed golden highlights cascading down almost to your waist. . . .'" She angled a look at the neighbor, then back to her brother. "Face it, Bro. She's gorgeous. As is her hair."

"She's peculiar." He studied the petite, slender woman who was rolling what apparently would be the head toward her snow creation. "I realize she's a vet—"

"She started her own clinic." Lindsay's tone was one patient tolerance. "She owns it. She's very successful, though she doesn't flaunt it." She smiled, a tinge of admiration in her expression. "Kylie happens to be that rare combination of talent and humility."

"With more than a touch of oddity thrown in. I swear, she doesn't follow any kind of a work schedule. There's no telling when she'll be home and when she'll be at that clinic. And that rag mop dog of hers goes with her everywhere."

"Kylie Hawk is the perfect blend of professional and woman. She's doesn't give in to the tyranny of the deadline and is comfortable in her own skin. . . ." Lindsay fixed him with a wry gaze. "Which explains why you don't get it."

His eyebrows arched. "Oh, I *do* get it. Relaxed. At ease. Spontaneous." He looked upward. "All nice little metaphors for undisciplined and wanton."

"*Wanton?*" Lindsay hooted. "Did you just say *wanton*? Nobody uses that term anymore. Besides—" she struggled to contain her mirth—"if there's anyone who isn't wanton, it's Kylie."

"Ah, yes. The paragon of Christian virtue."

Lindsay nudged him with her elbow. "Be nice. She's the real thing."

"So you've told me."

Lindsay leaned back against the wall, crossing her arms and studying him. "She really gets to you, doesn't she?"

"Not at all. I just find her . . . peculiar. And the way she talks about God is—"

"Intimate?"

"Overly familiar."

"It's the way I often talk about him. And the way you used to—"

"That was a long time ago. I was much younger, more naïve then."

"Seems to me you could use a bit more naïveté in your life. You've grown . . . well, hard, Bear. Sometimes I'm not quite sure who you are anymore."

He turned away, not wanting to see the pained expression he knew would be in her eyes. They'd had this discussion several times over the last year. Actually, ever since Kylie arrived on the scene.

"You know how I feel about faith issues." He kept his tone light.

"It's how you feel about God that concerns me."

Et tu, Lindsay? "Come on, Linds. It's not bad enough I've got this voice in my head bugging me about things, now you have to join in?"

"Voice in your—"

Never should have said that. "Look, I believe in God and in Jesus. A man would have to be blind or a fool not to. I am neither. But I'm not as convinced as you are that God is so very interested or involved in our everyday lives. Too many people are doing too many rotten things to each other. If God's so involved, why is all that happening?" He met her troubled gaze. "I've talked with people who profess faith, who talk about prayer and God as though it's all a big part of their lives, and I've watched those same people act and speak in ways that make *me* blush!"

"Bear, you can't base your feelings about God on a bunch of desperate corporate managers and owners—"

"I know that." He stopped, drew a breath, and softened his tone. None of this was Lindsay's fault. "I'm not. It's across the board, management on down. My last job? There was an older gentleman at a small business who told me that he was praying for me, asking God to give me wisdom. But when he lost his job, he just gave me this look. Like . . ." Mackenzie turned away. He didn't want to talk about this. Think about it.

"Like?"

"I don't know, like he was disappointed. Not in losing his job, but in me." He turned back to her. "In me, Linds. When all I did was what I was hired to do."

Her small hand was warm on his arm. "There wasn't anything else you could do, Bear."

He saw the trust in her eyes, the belief that he'd done his best for everyone concerned.

Everyone who mattered to your firm, anyway.

Shut. Up. "That doesn't matter. Not to them. I had a guy last year who had a Bible at work and Scripture verses posted all over his cubicle, but when he was among the laid off, he called the office, ranting about me being the devil and needing to have my heart ripped out." He shook his head. "I've seen too many people who just toss their faith out the window if circumstances aren't to their liking."

"Kylie's not like that, Bear. And neither am I."

He looked at her. "I know that. About you, anyway. But it's all made me a whole lot less sure." He held up his hand to stop her flow of words. "Not of God, Linds. But of people. And I just don't believe in talking about the Almighty as though he's some . . . some pal you knew when you both were kids."

"But in many ways that's exactly what he is. You used to believe that. I remember it. I remember how open you used to be, how full of life and laughter . . ."

"Like the Bible says, 'When I was a child I thought like a child, I reasoned like a child.'"

"That's *not* what that verse means."

"'When I became a man, I put childish ways behind me.'" He returned to the coffee maker, grabbing a coffee mug off the counter. "Want some?" He waved the mug, hoping for a diversion.

She ignored it. "This life of yours . . . this unemotional, untouched world where everything is ordered and controlled, that's not you, Bear. I know it's not."

"Lindsay—"

"Think about it. You weren't like this until . . ."

He frowned at her hesitation. "Until what?"

She bit her lip. "Until Mom and Dad died. That's when you changed."

He'd had enough. He loved his sister, but this conversation was a waste of time. Hers and his. He was who he was. She was just going to have to accept that. "Face it, Linds. You see life different than I do. But you're . . . well, you're you."

At his sister's shaky laugh he turned to her, and a pang shot through him when he saw her eyes and the unshed tears. "That's what I like about you, brother mine. That keen sense of the obvious."

He tapped her nose with a finger. "You know what I mean. You have the heart of a child. And that's a good thing. My heart? Contrary to popular belief, it does exist. It's just not so inclined to buy into some things."

"Like God's love."

"Like his involvement." At the forlorn look on her face, he set down his coffee mug and pulled her into a comforting hug. "Don't look so worried. We'll be OK." He leaned away and smiled down at her. "Who knows? Maybe you and Miss Loves-Dogs-and-Children are right, and I'm all wet. If so, I'm sure God will let me know."

That brought her smile out again. "You can count on it. After all, Kylie and I pray for you often enough. God's bound to do something."

He clamped down on the groan. "You two *pray* for me?"

She leaned her cheek against his chest. "All the time. Does that bother you?"

"If it did, would you stop?"

Lindsay delivered a light punch to his rib cage. "Of course not, idiot. You'd need it more than ever."

"Well, then, you do what you think is best, and I'll just put up with it. After all, you're family. I love you no matter how emotional, excitable, and extreme you get. As for your ditsy friend out there, well, she's another matter entirely." He stepped away from her and carried his coffee back to the table, where salmon salad waited. "She's certifiable. You do realize that, don't you?"

"Bear—"

"Do you know what your pal did yesterday?"

"Something awful, I'm sure."

Fork again in hand, he fixed her with what he hoped was a somber stare. "She was out there, with that weirdo canine barking full volume and jumping around while she had a snowball fight with the neighbor kids. *All* of them." He shuddered. "She was waving to anyone she could see to join them. There were screaming, snowsuit-clad midgets everywhere." He fixed his now grinning sister with a glare and stuffed in a bite. "The woman clearly doesn't know the meaning of the word *restraint.*" He spoke around his food. "Or order. Not only that, she's so . . . so *happy* all the time. I've always assumed her eternal good mood stems from being more than a bit removed from reality."

Lindsay chuckled. "Removed from your reality, maybe. But she's quite in touch with her own. And quite content." She leaned against the counter. "All the more reason for you to ask the woman out."

He stared at her. There were no words.

"After all, it's the first time I've seen you take a real interest in the right kind of woman."

He shook his head. "An *interest* . . . in *what* woman? When?"

"Just now. In Kylie."

"I was not—"

"Argue all you want, Brother, but you stood there a good ten minutes watching her. Analyzing her dog. Her hair. Her behavior." She crossed her arms and gave him a sage nod. "That's interest."

"More like morbid fascination."

Lindsay was back at the window and waved him over. Almost in spite of himself, he walked back over to the snowman scene. The head was now in place, complete with eyes, a big stone smile, and an old hat. As for his neighbor, she was kneeling in the snow, hugging her ridiculous dog, face rosy from the cold and wind, a grin stretched from ear to ear.

The woman was a lunatic.

Mackenzie turned back to his sister. "Seriously, can you see me with a woman like that?"

"Only in my dreams."

He felt his jaw go slack. She couldn't be serious. Even his slightly nutty sister couldn't think such a match could work.

The gleam in her eyes told him otherwise. "If you ask me, that woman is exactly what the doctor ordered. Much more so than that human computer you've decided is the apple of your eye. No pun intended, of course."

He turned his back on the window and moved back to the table. "Amanda is not a human computer."

Lindsay followed him. "Of course she is. She's even more structured than you are, though I didn't think that was possible until I met her. Good grief, she thinks you're frivolous! I'll bet she hasn't got a spontaneous bone in that sleek, sophisticated body of hers."

Forget lunch. He was no longer hungry. He picked up the rest of the salad, wrapped the bowl with plastic wrap, and stuck it in the fridge. "Listen, Changeling, Amanda and I suit each other well. As for your animal doctor friend, we'd have nothing in common."

"At least you'd have fun."

He moved into the living room and sank down on the couch. "Fun isn't enough, Lindsay. Kylie is *always* smiling and laughing. Last summer, when my windows were open, I could her singing."

"Clear evidence she's a psycho."

"Lindsay, I watched that woman sitting in her backyard once, picking daisies and making them into some kind of necklace. From what you've said she must be making good money. Why on earth wouldn't she just buy jewelry? Why form it out of *weeds*? She probably got aphids."

"Better aphids than frostbite." At his dark look, she hung her head. "I'm sorry, Bear. Kylie's always telling me I need to control my tongue." She sighed. "It's just that Amanda is so . . . regulated." She shuddered. "I can't imagine her feeling passion, let alone expressing it."

"Amanda's passion is none of your concern." That came out more sharply than he'd intended.

"No, it isn't. But it should concern you. Do you really want to spend the rest of your life in this austere house living a ho-hum life with Ice Queen at your side? What kind of life would that be? I think God has better plans for you. At least, I'm pretty sure he does."

Caught off guard by her words, he leaned his head back and stared at the ceiling. So now he was heartless *and* ho-hum? It was a wonder anyone could stand him.

The memory of Kylie sitting in the grass floated through his mind—as it had many times since the day he'd seen her, surrounded by flowers, the picture of serene contentment, cheeks kissed with the sun, golden hair cascading down her shoulders.

The image filled him with an odd sense of restlessness. He pushed it away and regarded his sister. She was looking at a piece of paper with a slightly stunned expression on her face.

"Lindsay?"

Her gaze moved to meet his. She was clearly upset. "I don't believe you."

The hurt tone in her voice startled him, and he sat up quickly. She handed him the sheet. It was his to-do list for the next month. He frowned, his gaze returning to his sister's now-flushed face. "I'm sorry, I don't understand."

"That much is painfully evident."

At the hurt in those whispered words, he frowned. "Lindsay, please. What have I done that's so terrible?"

"Item number five." Her tone was flat.

He looked down. "'Propose to Amanda.' So you have a problem with that, as you've just told me?" When she didn't respond, he looked up to see her staring at him as though he were some stranger. "It's my life—"

"Bear—" she broke in, then sat back, her breath coming out in a frustrated hiss. "You've got to be kidding. I mean, it's one thing that you're thinking about marrying that woman. That alone would make me nervous. But you've *got the proposal on your to-do list!*"

"What's wrong with putting that on my list?"

"It's number *five*, Bear! One of the most important decisions of your life, and you've got it listed as number five! After—" she leaned forward and grabbed the list from his hands—"*after* grocery shopping and balancing your checkbook!" She threw the list at him and stood. "What ever happened to you, Mac?"

What happened to you, Son? What made you this way?

He clenched his teeth. "I grew up."

She strode to the door and pulled it open, then paused and looked back. Mackenzie was stunned to see tears—and disappointment—in her eyes. "I'm sorry." Her voice was husky. "It's your life. But if a man was going to propose to me, I'd sure want to be more important to him than grocery shopping."

Before he could formulate an appropriate response, she was gone.

CHAPTER

Four

Lindsay leaned against the side of her brother's house, tears running down her face.

Her brother was hopeless. It was time she admitted and accepted it.

"Hopeless," she whispered, unleashing another wave of tears.

"Nothing is hopeless, Lindsay."

She looked up to see Kylie watching her, compassion clear in her green eyes as she leaned on the white fence separating her yard from Mackenzie's. "Wanna talk?"

Lindsay took a deep breath and wiped the tears from her cheeks. She pushed away from the wall and shrugged, pulling her coat closer about her as she moved over to the fence. "He's so sure he's right."

"Your brother?"

"Who else? He's bound and determined to wreck his life, and he doesn't even see it."

"Wreck his life?"

Lindsay crossed her arms. "He's going to ask that woman to marry him." Her heart felt torn in two by anger and regret.

Kylie's eyes opened wide. "You mean Amanda Carr?"

Lindsay nodded. She met Kylie's concerned gaze. "He can't do it, Kylie! She's not the right woman for him. I just know she isn't. But he's so blind—he can't see how wrong it would be for him to do this."

Kylie reached out and took her hand in a warm grasp. "God sees, and he cares about your brother even more than you do." She tugged on Lindsay's hand. "Leave it to the Lord, Lindsay."

"I know I should." Tears misted her eyes again. "It's just that Mac's so wonderful, and I care so much, and I want everything to go right for him."

Kylie leaned on her arms along the top of the fence. "I'm sure they will. As much as you love your brother, it's only a fraction of the love of God for him. And he's at work on Mac's behalf." Her lips twitched. "In fact, from what I know about your brother, God's probably mobilized two or three brigades of angels already."

"Hey, Kylie! Are we gonna play hide 'n' seek or what?"

Kylie glanced behind her, then patted Lindsay's arm. "Sorry, friend. Got to go. The munchkins await."

Lindsay looked toward Kylie's backyard and saw a group of neighborhood kids. With a wave of her hand, Kylie went to join them in their game. Zsuzsi dashed and dodged playfully, tail wagging.

Lindsay smiled as she went to her car. The laughter from Kylie's backyard floated around her as she slid in and reached forward to put the key in the ignition, then let her hand fall into her lap. She closed her eyes.

"Lord, is she right? Have you set a brigade of angels on my brother?" She hoped so. Oh, how she hoped so.

Would even that be enough to get Mac to open his eyes?

The next morning, Mackenzie did the unthinkable. He ignored his five-thirty alarm. Instead of throwing back the covers and getting started with the day, he rolled over and stared at the ceiling.

He hadn't had a night this bad in years. His eyes felt like they were full of sand, his mouth, like he'd been sucking on sweat socks. He'd tossed and turned, exhausted and in need of sleep. But every time he closed his eyes, Lindsay's face, so full of disappointment, filled his mind.

He'd hurt her. If only he could understand why.

It's not that hard to understand, and you know it.

He pulled his pillow over his head. Not again. Not another day of hearing those heart whispers—

The sound of the doorbell brought him to his feet, and he jumped up, pulling on a shirt and jeans as he hurried to the door. It had to be Lindsay. She couldn't stand a fight between them any more than he could. He pulled the door open, then stood and stared.

"Merry Christmas!" It was Kylie, dog in tow. A brown suede crusher was pulled down over her unruly hair, but rebellious wisps snuck out to frame her face with a golden glow.

She grinned at him, holding out a plate wrapped with brightly colored cellophane and topped with a large Christmas bow. Mackenzie stared at her, then the plate, then back at her. The smile broadened. "May I come in?"

He stepped aside, but looked at the dog at her side.

"Don't worry, Zsuzsi will wait right her on the mat, won't you, sweetheart?" She rested her fingers on the dog's broad, furry head. "Stay, girl." With that, she sailed into the kitchen.

Mackenzie followed Kylie as she placed the cookies on the counter. He cast one glance back at the dog. It sat there, perfectly content, regarding him with the oddest expression. If he hadn't known better, he'd swear the beast was looking at him with a strange sort of pity in its dark eyes. He shook his head. This conflict with Lindsay—and a totally rotten night—was making him imagine things.

"Normally I'd never invade someone's home this early in the morning," Kylie was saying in that lilting voice of hers. "But Lindsay told me you get up at five-thirty most days—"

"Every day."

She eyed him at the correction. "Right. Every day. So I figured you wouldn't mind if we stopped by on the way to work."

"Not at all." A tantalizing fragrance tickled his nose. Was it whatever was on the plate? He lifted the cellophane and peered beneath it. "What are these?"

"Christmas cookies. It just isn't Christmas without them."

Sugar cookies, from the look of them, all decorated with frosting and sprinkles. He sniffed. Nope, they weren't the source of the scent.

Kylie leaned her elbows on the counter, cupping her chin in her hands. "To be perfectly honest, I didn't think you'd be all that thrilled to receive them, but God disagreed, so there you have it."

God disagreed . . . ?

She went on. "There are Santas, snowmen, stars, reindeer—" she indicated the cookie on top—"even a Rudolph complete with red candy nose. Brendan, my brother, always saved his Rudolph until last. But I couldn't. He was always the first to go. Rudolph, I mean, not my brother." She leaned toward Mackenzie. "There was something *so* satisfying in biting off his nose."

What kind of response could one make to that?

Fortunately, Kylie didn't seem to expect one. She straightened up and glanced around. "What a beautiful place you have here. A nice clean palette just ready to be brought to life." She angled a compassionate look his way. "I know you haven't been around much. You really do work too much, you know."

He opened his mouth to inform her it was NOYB how much he worked, but she sailed on.

"Maybe you can take a few days during the holiday to start fixing everything up."

Mackenzie frowned. "It's already fixed up."

Her surprised gaze roamed the spartan room, as though searching for something to confirm his words. He felt himself growing just a bit defensive. "This is how I like it."

She continued her careful study.

"It's simple," he insisted. "Well ordered."

Her brows drew together, and he had the oddest sense she was pained.

When her wide-eyed gaze came back to meet his, the slight disappointment he saw there took him aback—then annoyed him.

"It's certainly . . . clean."

Wow. Had to really dig for that, didn't you? "It's perfect for me." His words came out more forcefully than he'd intended.

She looked away, then her whole face lit up. "Oh! What a beautiful tree!"

Before Mackenzie could respond, she was in the living room and had buried her face in the needles. When she lifted her head and looked at him, her eyes glowed with a kind of relief. "You must have just brought it in. It still smells of the forest and the cold."

Could the woman be any more confusing? Why on earth should Kylie Hawk care what his home looked—or, for that matter, smelled—like? "I wasn't aware it smelled at all."

She stepped back, inspecting each branch, fingering the needles. "Yes, it's perfect. It quite suits you. Big. Bold. Full of strength and vitality."

Unexpected pleasure stirred at this assessment of his character.

"I can hardly wait to see it decorated!"

He cleared his throat. Decorated? He was expected to decorate it?

"Well, thanks so much for inviting me in."

Inviting her in? He didn't recall getting the chance.

She breezed past him, not seeming the least bit fazed by his pointed glance. "But Zsuzsi and I have to be going."

He followed her to the door, feeling a bit as though a small tornado had just swept through his house. There was that fragrance again. What *was* that? Vanilla?

And there was the dog, waiting just inside the door as ordered. Kylie glanced at him over her shoulder and apparently saw how he stared at the beast. "Pretty unique, isn't she?"

Unique was not the word he had in mind.

"She's a komondor, a Hungarian breed."

His brows arched at that. "You mean someone intentionally bred a dog to look like that?"

She laughed—a soft, silvery sound that drifted around him. "Actually, they've bred a lot of dogs to look this way. Komondors are growing more popular all the time." She scratched the animal's ears. "They're intelligent, loyal, and protective, which is pretty common for herding dogs, isn't it, sweetie?"

Zsuzsi gave a deep "Woof!" as though to agree with her mistress's assertion. Kylie laughed again.

"So the fur is supposed to look like that?" The question came out before he'd realized he was going to ask.

Kylie nodded. "It helps them blend in with the sheep. Can you imagine being a predator moving in on a seemingly defenseless herd of sheep when one of these beasties suddenly jumps up to take you on?" She sounded like a proud mama. "A hundred pounds of protective fury, that's what she would be. Well, see you later. Time to get to work."

He moved to hold the door for her, and as she stepped past him, he caught on. The fragrance. It was . . . her.

The realization left him staring after her as she led the happy dog to her car. He closed the door, then turned to study Lindsay's tree. He strolled toward it, leaned forward, and took a deep breath.

Son of a gun. It *did* smell like the forest and the cold.

He moved to pour himself a cup of coffee, then sat at his desk, flipped on his computer, and prepared to get to work. December wouldn't last forever, and he had a lot to accomplish. *His to-do list.* That shut everything down for a while.

Later he realized he was staring at the blank computer screen in a daze. He pushed to his feet. Why was it so difficult to concentrate? And why did the image of Kylie's face and the echo of her laughter keep nudging at him? And that fragrance . . .

He smelled it everywhere now.

He flopped down into a wide leather chair, staring into the dark fireplace. Pursing his lips, he went over her visit, recalling the way she talked about God, in those intimate tones, as though he was her close, lifelong friend.

Was that what made her seem so different? So ... alive?

The longer he pondered, the more he became aware of something nagging at him, deep inside. Some vague sense that he was ... missing out.

With a whoosh of air he catapulted himself out of the chair and strode to his computer. He knew he was punching the keys with more force than was necessary, but the action felt good.

Far better than sitting around and getting morose over some imaginary lack in my life. He set his shoulders, a decision made.

The next time Kylie Hawk appeared on his doorstep, he would courteously but firmly shut the door—on her *and* the doggone dog.

CHAPTER
Five

"What a day."

Kylie sank into a chair in the clinic lounge and propped her feet up on the coffee table. She closed her weary eyes, only to have them fly open again when the robust fragrance of coffee filled her senses.

A coffee cup, its steam wafting up into her face, was being held in front of her. She accepted it on a grateful sigh. "Alan, you're the best."

"Of course I am."

Her partner settled into the chair opposite her, propping his feet up on the table as well. "Whew! Appointments all day long, plus walk-ins, plus your emergency case. If we never have another day like this one, it'll be too soon."

She lifted her cup to him. "Amen, Brother."

He glanced at Zsuzsi lying on her cushion, snoring away. "Looks like your pal is equally pooped."

Kylie sipped the nicely strong brew. "She was great today. Especially with those two kids."

The hardest part about what she did was helping pet owners accept that their animal friends couldn't be healed, that it was time to let them go. Today had been especially tough. The emergency had been a family bringing in a terrier who had suddenly started vomiting blood. Kylie's fears were confirmed by the tests. Cancer. The family had to say good-bye to a terrier they'd had for sixteen years. As hard as it had been for the adults—and it had been hard—it was heartbreaking for the kids, a ten-year-old girl and her fourteen-year-old brother. When it was over, both children were in tears, even the boy.

That's where Zsuzsi came in.

Kylie had discovered the komondor's special skill shortly after finding her. Kylie discovered the dog, one hot summer afternoon, at a rest stop on Interstate 5. She'd just stepped from her car when she spotted the collarless animal walking toward her. It was evident from the dog's emaciated condition and the burrs in its fur that the komondor had been abandoned. Without even thinking, Kylie dropped to her knees, opened her arms, and called to the dog.

Zsuzsi didn't hesitate. She ran into Kylie's embrace.

A thorough search revealed no form of ID. Kylie took the dog to her clinic, cleaned her up, and cared for her. She put out notices, but when it became clear no one was going to claim the dog, Kylie brought Zsuzsi home.

Good thing, because in those few weeks at the clinic the two of them had adopted each other.

Maybe it was because Kylie still had been recovering from the loss just a month previous of her Siberian, Sasha. Or maybe it was one of those magical moments when two of God's creations were supposed to be together. Whatever the case, Kylie knew the moment she saw Zsuzsi that the komondor was her dog.

Over the following months, that feeling was confirmed over and over. But never so much as the day Zsuzsi came into an exam room just as Kylie helped an older, sobbing woman, whose cat had just died, to a chair. As though knowing exactly what the woman needed, Zsuzsi came to the woman, touching her trembling, veined hands with a cool nose. The woman started, and Kylie tensed, ready to hurry the komondor from the room. But then the woman threw her arms around the dog's neck, sobbing into the komondor's unusual soft and corded coat. Zsuzsi had leaned forward, resting her massive head against the woman, and sat there. Silent comfort for a grieving woman.

From that day, it was as though the dog knew when she was needed. No sooner would a pet breathe its last than Zsuzsi was there, beside the distraught owner, bringing much-needed comfort and, inexplicably enough, peace.

It was the peace those two kids needed today. Especially the teenager. He'd stood there, fists clenched, features frozen.

"It's what's best for Rufus, Jarod."

The boy didn't even look at his mother. "He could get better."

The mother cast a pleading glance at Kylie who repeated what she'd already told them, making it firm, but gentle. "I'm sorry, but he can't. His body is just worn out." She waited until the boy looked at her. "He's tired, Jarod. He fought the cancer a long time, but he doesn't have anything left."

He started to respond, but the door to the room opened—and Zsuzsi entered. She moved to stand between the two children, leaning a solid shoulder against Jarod's leg. Kylie watched him try to resist the dog's touch, then it was as though the tension in him just flowed out. He went down to his knees and threw his arms around the komondor's solid neck, burying his face in Zsuzsi's fur.

"OK."

That one muffled word spoke volumes. She heard it all, the boy's pain mixed with the desire to do what was right for his friend. Kylie nodded—and within seconds it was over.

She left Zsuzsi with the grieving family and stepped from the room. When they finally came out, Jarod's hand rested on Zsuzsi's broad head. He met Kylie's gaze.

"I'm sorry I got mad."

Kylie touched his arm. "It's OK. I understand."

With one last pat to Zsuzsi's head, the boy turned away. But as he started to follow his family out the door, he looked back. "Thank you." His words thickened. "For taking care of Rufus."

"You're welcome."

Yes, that was tough. But Zsuzsi made it easier. On all of them.

"So, you heading home soon?" Alan's query brought her back to the present.

Kylie took another sip of her coffee. "Absolutely. I think Zsuzsi and I are both ready for a night without drama or excitement."

Alan grinned. "Like that ever happens with you two."

She pushed to her feet. "Tonight it will." She straightened her shoulders. "I'm determined."

"Well, then, knowing you two"—Alan's laughing eyes peered at her over his coffee cup—"I guess it's settled."

Kylie made a face at her teasing friend. Let him laugh all he wanted. She meant what she said.

Tonight was going to be blissfully boring.

Mackenzie stepped back to admire his handiwork. His dining table had been transformed by a white linen tablecloth, elegant china plates and bowls flanked by filigreed silver utensils, and sparkling crystal glasses reflecting the glow of tall tapers in the middle of a fresh-flower centerpiece. Well, it was the florist who had done it up just right, but he'd put the order in and specified exactly what he wanted. Romantic music played in the background. A delicious meal waited to be served. One he'd mostly crafted himself.

"Ha. Let's see you call *this* ho-hum, Lindsay."

No denying it. Everything was perfect.

Tonight, he would cross item number five off his list. "So there you have it." At the sound of the doorbell he strolled over to pull the door open. "Good evening, Madame. Your dinner awaits." He added a sweeping bow in his best Cary Grant impression.

Amanda Carr stood on the threshold, the image of refined beauty. Her facial features were delicately carved, her mouth full, her bearing poised. Mackenzie first met her at an art gallery opening. They'd collided while studying a sculpture. Startled from his contemplation, he'd turned and found himself staring into a pair of beautiful, blue eyes. The rest of the woman was equally impressive—as was her intelligence, which he discovered while they shared their interpretations of what the sculpture was trying to express. Before he'd realized he was going to do so, Mackenzie asked Amanda out to dinner. Much to his surprise, she accepted.

As their relationship progressed it became clear that they were a good match. Capable, reasonable, well-read, intelligent, prone to logic over emotion . . . every facet seemed to mesh. As well as the fact she was the only daughter of business tycoon Alexander Carr. Amanda might be a bit more driven, a bit more determined than Mackenzie, but she had to be. After all, it wasn't easy to become a female CEO in a prestigious Seattle advertising firm. Those same beautiful blue eyes that had so captured his attention could turn positively glacial, which characteristic had helped her face down more than one stunned male in the board room. Amanda knew what she wanted and went after it with steely determination. She never allowed herself to be distracted by sentimentality or misplaced altruism.

As if we came from the same mold.

Oddly, he felt a slight uncertainty at that thought.

"Mackenzie, dear," she remarked now as she stepped inside and tilted her head back, inviting him to kiss one smooth cheek. He did as expected, noting the fragrance from an expensive perfume he had bought for her, then reached for her dripping raincoat and umbrella. In spite of the weather, not a strand of her silky black hair was out of place.

Quite a contrast to Kylie Hawk. She'd probably be dripping wet and loving every minute of it. The thought—and the sudden picture in his mind of his neighbor's golden, unruly hair—startled him.

Amanda caught sight of the carefully laid table, tipped her head to listen to the music, then turned to him. "Darling, really. Such extravagance."

The hint of censure in her voice made him frown.

"I'll bet she hasn't got a spontaneous bone in that sleek, sophisticated body of hers." He pushed Lindsay's words away as he pulled out Amanda's chair for her. "It's a special occasion."

"So you said when you invited me." She smoothed her pants, then laid a cloth napkin on her lap and smoothed that as well.

"I can't even imagine her feeling passion. . . ."

He shook his head to dislodge the unwelcome memory, with little effect. Drawing a steadying breath, he settled into his own chair.

Amanda's appraising gaze rested on him. "Really, dear, isn't it time you told me what's going on? You know how much I dislike being kept in the dark."

"Austere . . . ho-hum . . ."

"I . . . wanted to ask . . ." He tried to swallow, but his suddenly dry and constricted throat didn't want to cooperate.

"Yes?"

"Ice Queen . . . rest of your life . . . God has better plans. . . ."

"Shut up!"

Amanda stiffened. "I *beg* your pardon."

Oh, good grief. "No, I'm sorry, Amanda. . . ."

She sat there, features frozen, and he fought the urge to pound his forehead on the table. This wasn't going at all as he'd planned.

The doorbell sounded, and Mackenzie jumped to his feet. "Excuse me—back in a minute." He'd take any reprieve right now and be glad of it. He crossed the room and jerked the door open.

No one was there. Was this some kind of prank? He looked to the sides, then down—

What on earth?

There was a wolf on his stoop! A soggy, muddy, whining wolf.

Mackenzie stared at the beast. No, not a wolf. A dog. With heavy reddish-brown and white fur, large pointed ears atop a squarish head, and staring eyes—one brown, one ice-blue. *A dog with mismatched eyes? Some kind of mutant?*

Mackenzie inspected the animal. A sled dog, maybe? Mackenzie was far from an expert. He glanced around again. No one in sight. He stepped out to look farther down the street through the evening shadows. Nothing. He looked back at the dog, whose pathetic whines had lessened, but only a bit.

"Beat it. Go away. Lassie, go home." He pointed a finger as emphatic as his voice.

Those intense eyes fixed on him. Then, as though in supplication, the animal lifted one soggy paw and placed it on Mackenzie's leg.

He brushed the paw away and stepped back inside, shutting the door.

"Who was it, darling?" Amanda seemed to have gotten over his slip of the tongue

"No one." He sat down in his chair. "What do you say we eat before the food gets cold?" The smile he offered her felt pasted on. "Then we'll talk."

"If you say so."

Mackenzie nodded and picked up his fork. All he needed was some food in his system to clear out his fogged brain. And a little time to figure out exactly what he wanted to say.

Two bites later, a horrific and sorrowful sound reverberated through the house. The dog was howling. Right outside his front door.

"What in the world?" Amanda's delicate brows lifted. Mackenzie gritted his teeth and held up a hand.

"Just . . . a minute." He went to the door again, pulled it open, and stepped out, closing the door behind him.

"GO AWAY!"

That bellowed, he composed his features, turned, and opened the door—only to run right into Amanda.

She stepped around him and glanced outside. The dog was sitting there, a morose look on its furry face. "What on earth is *that?*"

"It's a dog."

She swiveled her gaze to him. "I can see it's a dog, Mackenzie. Whose is it?"

"Your guess is as good as mine."

She crossed her arms. "You don't need to get emotional about it."

"I am not getting emotional."

Clearly startled by his tone, Amanda stepped back.

He looked down, closing his eyes. "Amanda—"

"Perhaps you should call the police, Mackenzie. That seems the most logical solution."

She was right. He moved to the phone and returned a few moments later. "The police transferred my call to Animal Control."

"Good. When will they be here?"

Mackenzie shrugged. "They told me to watch the dog, and they'll get here as soon as they can."

"Well, if that's the best you can do . . ."

"It's the best they can do, Amanda."

She lifted a shoulder and brushed her hand over her hair. "Then shall we finish our dinner and have our little talk?"

Half an hour later, the dog was still howling, and Mackenzie was wishing Kylie was home. He'd figured she'd show up when the dog started its caterwauling and had fully intended to hand the creature over to her, but no luck. Why couldn't his neighbor be around when he actually wanted her to be?

"Mackenzie, isn't there something you can do?" Amanda lifted her fingers to probe her temples. "That creature's unholy racket has given me the most horrendous headache."

What, exactly, did she expect him to do? Tossing his napkin on the table, he went to the door again and jerked it open.

The dog had stopped howling and was now lying in the darkness, chin resting on his paws. His heavy fur looked soaking wet. He looked up at Mackenzie. At the woeful expression in the animal's eyes, something inside of Mackenzie gave.

No one should be treated like this. Not even a dog.

He knelt down and extended a hand. The dog lifted his head and licked Mackenzie's hand. Maybe in forgiveness?

An unfamiliar tightness formed in Mackenzie's chest, and he felt beneath the fur to the dog's neck. A collar? He examined it, but found no tags. Instead, what he discovered was a piece of clothesline tied from the collar to the railing of his porch. The dog was tied to the railing!

"Who did this to you, fella?" The dog stared at him in sorrowful silence. Making a sudden decision, Mackenzie untied the clothesline and stepped inside. The dog followed him without hesitation.

"Mackenzie! What in the world? You can't bring that awful creature in here!"

Now who was getting emotional? "He's wet, Amanda, and cold. I can at least get him dried off."

"With what? I hope you don't plan to use any good towels on that—that thing!"

He tied the clothesline to the door knob and the dog sat down on the rug. "I've got some old towels I use to wash the car." He went to the garage, grabbed them from a box, then returned. The dog was still sitting there, looking every inch the perfect gentleman. Mackenzie shook out the towels, directing a positive look at Amanda. "See? This won't be so bad." He stepped forward, the towel spread open—

The dog promptly stood and shook himself. Mud and water flew everywhere.

Mackenzie dove for the dog, trying to throw the towels over him and protect his mostly white furniture and walls. The dog scrambled back, tugging on the line with such force that it came untied. Realizing it was free, the animal tore away, his claws scrabbling over the polished wood floor.

"Come back here!"

Mackenzie's bellow only served to alarm the dog more. With a yelp, the beast vaulted the coffee table, his muddy paws touching down just long enough to smear everything in his path.

Thus began a wild chase.

Mackenzie followed the rampaging animal as it jumped the couch, scrambled across the tiled kitchen floor, circled and knocked down a screeching Amanda, raced down the hallway, and leaped into the middle of Mackenzie's king-sized waterbed.

Momentarily startled by the uncertain footing, the dog paused, which gave Mackenzie the opening he'd been watching for. Quickly he grasped the edges of the silk comforter and lifted, enveloping the dog as neatly as if the spread had been a net. Muttering threats the entire way, he dragged the struggling, yelping dog to the bathroom, pushed him in—comforter and all—and slammed the door.

Leaning against the door, he wiped a hand across his face—then his body sagged as he took in the carnage. Streaks of mud covered everything, from smudges on the rugs and floor to hair-encrusted splatters all over the walls and furniture. Slowly he walked into the living room. There were muddy paw prints everywhere.

"Well, I certainly hope you're satisfied."

He turned—and stopped cold. Amanda was covered with mud, and her hair was a snarled, mud-splattered mess. At the sight of the usually picture-perfect woman in such disarray, something quirked Mackenzie's mouth.

"*What* are you smiling about?" She stormed toward him, her arms flailing about. "Your house is destroyed—but it looks far better than you do!"

He glanced down. He was as wet and muddy as the dog. He shook his head slightly, struggling against the surprising urge to laugh himself silly.

"Mackenzie St. Clair, you wipe that absurd look from your face this minute!"

His head came up and his eyes narrowed. No one took that tone with him. Before he could respond, the doorbell rang.

"Saved by the bell." He crossed the room and opened the door.

Kylie's eyes went wide. She scanned the living room, and he followed her gaze to the cushions strewn about the room, the turned-over furniture, and, finally, Amanda's glowering visage.

"Oh, my goodness." Kylie's gaze came back to him. "Did I . . . interrupt something?"

Suddenly bloodcurdling screams split the air, and the two spun to see Amanda on the floor, the dog in her lap, paws on her shoulders, licking her face with gusto. She was swatting at him—with no effect—and screeching like a banshee.

"Oh!" Kylie put a warm hand on his arm. "You got a husky! How delightful!"

Mackenzie, who was trying to figure out how the beast had escaped the bathroom, turned to Kylie, his mouth falling open. An enraptured smile lit her face, and the woman glided across the room. She took hold of the dog's collar, gave a tug that drew him from Amanda, and led him away, talking to him in a low, sweet voice.

Amanda struggled to her feet, muttering some things Mac was glad he couldn't hear. Without a glance his way, she strode over to grab her coat from the rack. With one furious motion, she pulled it on, and attempted to smooth her hair—only succeeding in rearranging the mud—then headed for the door. With her hand on the knob, she turned to pin Mackenzie with her fury. "Thank you, my *dear* Mackenzie, for the most horrid experience I've had in my entire life!"

The door slammed behind her.

Mackenzie pursed his lips and blew out a long breath. *OK, Lindsay, so much for item number five.*

"Don't worry."

He turned to find Kylie sitting on the couch, the now-docile dog at her side. She gave the dog's ears a rub. "Your girlfriend will get used to him."

He moved toward them, took hold of the dog's collar, and tugged him off the couch. "This animal isn't staying long enough for *anyone* to get used to it."

She straightened. "Surely you wouldn't get rid of him before he's even had a chance to fit in? That wouldn't be fair at all."

"Wouldn't be—" He stopped himself before he said something else he'd regret. "It's not a case of fairness. This animal showed up on my doorstep a few hours ago. Someone tied him out there, though who or why, I haven't got a clue."

"Maybe someone thought you needed him."

"You make it sound like someone left a *gift* on my doorstep!"

She looked from the dog to him, as though something just occurred to her, and another smile crept across her features. "You can never tell."

"Oh, yes I can. This animal is not mine. Apparently he's not anyone's. I've already called Animal Control and as soon as they show up, he's gone."

Kylie looked at her watch. "You do realize it's ten o'clock?"

"So?"

"Well, Animal Control closes at nine. So I'd say this guy isn't going anywhere tonight."

Now *he* was getting a headache. "I don't suppose you could take him?"

"I'd love to—"

Thank heaven!

"—but I don't think I can."

He crossed his arms over his chest. "Don't think?"

She cupped the dog's fuzzy face, looked into those intent eyes, then gave a slow shake of her head. "Mac, I'm happy to help out—"

"Mackenzie."

She looked up at him, her brows creasing. "Excuse me?"

"Mackenzie, not Mac. I don't do nicknames."

She bit her lip, though he had a feeling it was more to keep from laughing than from any sense of propriety. "Ah. OK, *Mackenzie.* I'm happy to help you out with this fine boy, but I think taking him off your hands would be a mistake."

"A mistake?" Wasn't she a vet? Dedicated to caring for animals? "No. Leaving him with me, *that's* the mistake—"

She was already shaking her head.

"What am I supposed to do with a dog?"

She stood, handing him the clothesline, which she'd secured again to the dog's collar. "Tell you what. I'll help you clean up here, and I'll help you get the dog settled. I've got an extra crate that you can use, a collar, a leash, and bowls." She ticked the items off on her fingers. "All you'll need to do is buy him some food. And take him for a walk from time to time. Oh—" she plucked some mud from the dog's fur—"and give him a bath."

Now that was going too far. "I'm *not* a dog groomer."

"No"—she glanced around his house, then back to him—"but you like your place clean, yes?"

"Of course."

"Your best bet on that front is to get the dog clean."

His fingers fisted on the clothesline. "This is ridiculous. It's entirely too much work for some stray animal—"

A warm hand on his arm halted the words. "Mackenzie."

Something about the tone of her voice . . . and he stilled. Met those sincere eyes.

"I know this isn't how you'd planned to spend your evening—"

A master of understatement, this one.

"—but for whatever reason, God put this animal in your care."

"God? You think *God* tied this dog to my railing?"

"Of course not. But I do think this is a unique opportunity for you to help someone out."

He narrowed his eyes at that. "Help who out?"

"Don't know." She walked into his kitchen, and he followed, beast in tow, watching as she opened the pantry door, then closed it and scanned the room.

"What are you looking for?"

She glanced at him over her shoulder. "A broom and dustpan."

He fastened the clothesline to his belt—no way this dog was getting loose again—and went over to the hall closet. At least that's where he thought his housekeeper kept them. Yes. He held them out to her.

Tools in hand, she went back to the living room and started sweeping clumps of drying mud into the dustpan.

He stood watching her, then realized the dog was sitting right beside him, leaning against his leg. He lowered a hand to scratch the dog's soft ears. "Hey"—he glanced around—"where's your dog? I don't think I've ever seen you without it."

"Her."

He frowned. "Her?"

"Zsuzsi's a female. She's a her, not an it." She focused on her sweeping as she talked. "And she's at home. She had a long day and was ready for a snooze, so I dropped her off before I came over." She glanced at him and paused, taking in the way he and the dog stood there together. A small smile played at her lips. "Looks as though he's taken to you."

He angled a look at her. "Yuh-huh. So, again, who am I supposed to be helping here? And why?"

She carried the dustpan over to the trash can, then searched under the sink and came up with a couple of dish towels and spray cleaner. She held one of the towels and a spray bottle out to him. "You take the coffee table, I'll tackle the couch."

As he started in on the streaks with the glass cleaner, she wiped off the mud on the white leather couch. "As for who, well, the dog for one. And, if he has any, his owners."

Mackenzie spritzed the table again. How much mud could one dog transfer to furniture? "All strangers to me."

"Doesn't mean you shouldn't help them out, does it?"

She had him there.

She went on. "You're simply making sure this animal is cared for and safe. Tomorrow we can take him to my office, and I'll check to see if he's been chipped. If so, we can contact the owners and get him home."

Mackenzie admired the now clean coffee table, then turned to the dog still tied to his belt. "Stay off it, beast."

"Nice work."

He looked over and nodded at the couch, which was once again spotless. "You, too. Think you missed your calling."

She grinned. "I've had lots of practice cleaning up messes like this. I had Siberians for a lot of years."

She held her hand out for his dirty dish towel, and he gave it to her. Odd how it felt like the most natural thing in the world to be with her like this. Talking, working together—

"Time for a bath."

He blinked. "Excuse me?"

At the look on his face, her cheeks turned pink. "For the dog." She took hold of the clothesline and tugged it. He took a step closer to her.

Vanilla. She definitely smelled like vanilla.

Another tug. He peered down at her. "I don't think I can get much closer."

More pink in those cheeks. He liked that color on her.

"Untie him, you nitwit."

His lips twitched. He'd rather stay right there, but he did as commanded. "You want my help?"

"Better you vacuum while I've got him closed up in the bathroom. Just come on in after you're done so you can help dry him off."

He snapped a salute, and she swatted at him with one of the towels. He watched her walk down the hall, the husky trotting along beside her as though bewitched.

He knew exactly how the dog felt.

Kylie brushed her damp hair back and picked up the large, fluffy towel Mac had given her. No, not Mac. Mackenzie.

I don't do nicknames.

She shook her head. The man really needed to chill.

She eyed the dog now sitting in front of her. The bath had been, as they almost always were with huskies, a wrestling match. For the most part, Siberians hated water. Were afraid of getting wet. Some deep instinct warned them that letting that dense undercoat get soaked meant they'd freeze to death. In their natural environment, that was true. But for owners who didn't live in Alaska or Siberia, it made bath time a definite challenge.

Still, Kylie had had enough experience with her own huskies to win out, and the dog was well and duly clean. Now all she had to do was get him rubbed down.

Far easier said than done.

She'd been trying to corner him for the past five minutes, towel at the ready. The dog, of course, thought it was a grand game and did everything he could to dodge her in the confined space. She finally got him cornered—back in the now-empty bathtub. She opened the towel. All she had to do was envelop the husky and rub.

"Hey, comin' in."

Before Kylie could holler out a warning, Mac opened the bathroom door.

The dog leaped out of the tub and bolted toward the door, so Kylie had no choice. She threw herself at it.

And at Mac.

He yelped, caught her, towel and all, and slammed back into the door. Kylie sighed her relief when she heard the door click shut.

"That was close." The words were muffled against his chest.

"Everything OK?" He wasn't letting go.

She nodded, her nose brushing against his shirt. She should step away, she knew. But there was something about being held like this that was . . . well, so nice.

A doggie whine snapped her back to reality, and she pulled away so fast she almost stumbled. Strong hands gripped her arms, steadying her. She looked up, caught the glint of humor—and something else, something indefinable—in Mac's eyes.

Kylie knelt beside the dog and surrounded him with the towel. "So, everything cleaned up out there?"

"Until you let loose the hound." He knelt too and helped with the last of the drying.

Kylie gave the husky's fur one final rub, then looked around for the dog's collar. It suddenly dangled in front of her. She glanced at Mac again—it was as though he'd read her mind.

She took the collar, fastened it around the dog's neck, then attached a leash she'd fetched from her car. Far better than the clothesline. Leash in hand, she stood and glanced at Mac. "Well, you know what they say—"

He pulled the bathroom door open. "Once more unto the breach."

Kylie walked out of the room, not sure what surprised her more: the uncharacteristic grin on Mac's face—

Or the fact that he'd said exactly the words she had in mind.

Mac leaned back against the soft leather of the couch. Kylie sat at the opposite end, sipping fresh-brewed decaf—how did he know?—from a mug that seemed almost too big for her hands, watching the dog lying on the floor at Mac's feet, head on its paws, snoring softly.

He, on the other hand, watched Kylie.

"So"—she looked up at him—"have you considered my proposition?"

He cupped the coffee mug in his hands. "OK, you want to use the pictures you've taken of the dog with your cell phone to post about him online. And you'll pass on the info to other vets and Animal Control, so they can spread the word about him."

She gave a slow nod. "And you?"

"You want me to keep him until we hear from his owners."

Why, exactly, he would agree to such a thing was beyond him. He'd have to be nuts to even consider it.

Kylie rubbed the sleeping dog's back with her bare toe. "Three weeks. If the owners don't show up in three weeks, he's yours."

"No, thanks to both. Too long, and I am not looking for a dog." He noticed the slight crease in her forehead. "What?"

Her gaze met his, and the look in her eyes stirred him deep inside. "If Zsuzsi were lost, I'd pray that the people who found her would give me every opportunity to claim her."

"You're asking me to upend my life for three whole weeks, and for what? A dog? Why would I do that?" He kept his tone firm. So much so that he woke the dog. The beast stood, circled a few times, then plopped down—with his head resting on Mackenzie's foot. The dog breathed in, then uttered a low, long sigh.

Kylie directed twinkling eyes at Mackenzie. "He seems to have taken to you."

"No comment." Mackenzie rubbed the dog's ears. At least there was one creature that didn't consider him an unapproachable, heartless brute. The soft texture of the dog's fur was like velvet, and the way he tilted his square head and half closed his eyes made Mackenzie smile.

He looked at Kylie again. "You do realize I don't know anything about dogs."

"I'll help out."

"You already have. The crate and other supplies you brought over will be a great help, once you get them set up." At least he could keep the dog contained.

"I have an idea."

Mackenzie looked at her, waiting.

"Instead of asking me why you should consider this idea, why don't you ask God?"

She had the oddest notions.

"You really think the God of the universe cares about a stray dog and what I do with it?"

He'd expected some flippant answer, but she paused, considering the question. "Let me ask you this. If you had a child, would you care how he treated a stray dog?"

"I suppose so. I'd want him to treat it right, maybe learn something about treating other creatures with respect."

Kylie's face glowed. "Exactly. As a father, you care that your children live their lives in the best way possible, right?"

"Right . . ." Where was she going with this?

"Well, God is interested in everything we do, too. He's our Father, we're his children. He wants us to live our lives in the best way. Even in a situation like this."

"Seems to me the Almighty has better things to do with his time than worry about how I treat some stray dog." Mackenzie tried not to sound sarcastic, but he could tell he hadn't been very successful.

She studied him a moment. "'For I was hungry, and you fed me. I was thirsty, and you gave me a drink. I was a stranger, and you invited me into your home.'"

"Oh, come on now, he was talking about people—"

"'Then these righteous ones will reply, "Lord, when did we ever see you hungry and feed you? Or thirsty and give you something to drink? Or a stranger and show you hospitality?—"'"

He crossed his arms over his chest, but his obvious resistance didn't stop her recitation.

"'And the King will say, "I tell you the truth, when you did it"'"—she rested her hand on the dog's furry back—"'"to one of the least of these, you were doing it to me."'"

Mackenzie met her now laughing gaze. "You know you're taking that verse out of context."

She just smiled and leaned back against the couch arm.

Mackenzie looked from her to the dog. She was wrong. The almighty God of the universe wasn't involved in this fiasco.

And why not?

He pushed back against the voice in his head. *It's just a lost dog— Didn't he tell Peter, "Feed my lambs"? And didn't he say that he cares for the birds of the air? Isn't this animal as much God's creature as the birds and lambs?*

Mackenzie looked down at the sleeping dog. Maybe it was the late hour, or the events of the day, but he couldn't deny the strong sense that there was more going on here than just a stray dog landing on his doorstep. That there was some . . . purpose at work.

Do you want me to do this, Lord?

He hadn't intended to pray about it. The question just jumped free. No sooner had it slipped from his mind, flying toward heaven, than his furry invader stirred, yawned, and sat up. He leaned against Mackenzie's leg, and when Mackenzie looked down at him, the animal's two-colored gaze caught him for a moment. Then the dog put his paws on Mackenzie's thigh and reached up to deliver a quick lick to his face.

He stared at the animal. Was that supposed to be some kind of sign?

The dog licked him again.

Mackenzie closed his eyes, shaking his head. *I must be nuts. . . .*

"All right, I'll do it." He nailed Kylie with a stern look, daring her to gloat. "But just for three weeks."

As firm as he'd made his tone, now that the decision was made he had to admit that he kind of liked the idea. Somehow with Kylie's exclamation of delight floating around him and her warm, approving gaze resting on both him and dog, keeping it seemed the best decision he'd made in a very long time.

CHAPTER
Six

Kylie stepped back to study the room. One corner of Mackenzie's spacious living room was now a warm and welcome custom-designed doggie domicile.

She'd taken a run to the pet store for some supplies, then went home to retrieve one of Zsuzsi's older crates. The large container was constructed of heavy molded plastic, had side windows, a swinging gated door, and plenty of room for a dog of the husky's size to stand and turn around. A sleeping cushion and food dish completed the accommodations.

Kylie pulled the crate nearer the fireplace, reaching over to move the still-undecorated Christmas tree as she did so. She glanced over her shoulder at Mac—that really suited him so much better than his oh-so-formal full name. He was seated on his couch, watching her every move, a bemused look in his eyes.

She fingered the tree's needles. "You'd better get this beauty in a stand with some water or it will start to lose its needles. And there's nothing sadder than a dried out, undecorated Christmas tree."

"There's not?" His gaze drifted to the tree, then back to her.

She shook her head, leaning the tree against the wall. *See, Father? I told you he thinks I'm nuts.* She'd seen that slightly confused look on his face before—every time he saw her, to be exact. It was full of perplexity, as though she were an oddity that he couldn't quite analyze or categorize.

There was something sad—and strangely endearing—in that look. It reminded her of a little boy watching a parade from an enclosure, wanting desperately to join in the fun but not quite sure how to escape his confines. It made Kylie want to make her somber, dark-eyed neighbor smile or laugh.

Or put her arms around him and hug him close . . .

"Is something wrong?"

Oh, good grief. She was staring at the man. A man who was practically engaged, for heaven's sake! What was wrong with her?

"Oh . . . ah . . . no. Not at all." She turned back to the crate.

"You really think this dog will go in there without a fight?"

"Let's give it a try." She pulled a large dog biscuit from her pocket and held it out to the husky. When he trotted toward her, she gave the treat a toss into the crate. The dog hesitated just long enough to give the crate a sniff, then went inside and snapped up the biscuit. He circled once, twice, then settled down on the cushion, the biscuit between his paws.

Kylie turned to Mac. "I think he likes it."

Grudging respect shone in his eyes. "I admit, I'm surprised. I thought sure he'd fight you."

She moved back to sit on the couch again. "Dogs generally like crates. Remember, they're den animals, and crates are like a den to them. Just be sure you use a happy voice whenever you put him in there, so he doesn't connect the crate with being punished."

"A . . . happy voice?"

She met his dubious gaze. "I'm not saying you should sound like a Munchkin, Mac."

"Mackenzie."

"*Mackenzie.* Right. Just use the voice you'd use to praise him for doing something good."

He stifled a snort. "This dog? Do something good? You are such a dreamer."

She restrained a smile. In the time it took her to get the crate and other things from her house, Mac had lost three shoes, a towel, and a Mont Blanc pen to the husky's ever-busy jaws. Using a "happy voice" was likely the furthest thing from the man's mind.

She shook her head. "You'll need to close the dog in the crate when you're not at home."

"Oh? I can't just close him up in the garage?"

She did her best to hide her amusement. "Not unless you want a disaster. Huskies are notorious for being escape artists. Especially males. Add the fact that they're high in problem-solving abilities, and that makes for an incredibly destructive animal when they're bored or frustrated. And generally they're both when they're alone."

From his expression as he looked at the dog, it was clear Mac was wondering what he'd gotten himself into. "You're sure you can't take him?" The man was all but whining.

"I'm afraid so. He and Zsuzsi just aren't going to work." She moved to the table and started pulling items from a large bag.

"What did you do? Buy everything in the pet store?"

She grinned. "Hardly. That place is enormous. Next time you'll have to come along. We can even take your dog with us."

He snorted. "They let dogs in the sto—" He broke off and fixed her with a glare. "He's not my dog."

She didn't reply. He could argue all he wanted, she'd seen the way he looked at the husky when it leaned against him or rested its head on his leg. When she'd prayed for help with Mac, the last thing she'd had in mind was a dog. But there could be no denying that the man was smitten.

Of course, if she dared suggest such a thing, he'd get all huffy again. Much better to just hold her peace and give Mac time to listen to his heart.

No matter what anyone else said, she was sure he had one.

CHAPTER

Seven

Mackenzie watched with increasing discomfort as Kylie rummaged in a paper sack on the table.

"I know it's in here somewhere." Her long hair fell in a golden mass around her face, and Mackenzie felt an odd constriction in his throat. Watching her from out a window had been disturbing enough. Her eccentric actions had amused and confounded him, but he'd never felt any need to try and understand her.

Now, watching as she exclaimed with triumph and pulled a large plastic bone from the bag, he found himself struggling with the inexplicable desire to discover *why* she did the things she did.

Why, for example, she had stood in the middle of his living room a few moments ago staring at him, a strangely tender look on her face. It had taken every ounce of self-control not to jump off the couch and go to her and . . .

Forget it, St. Clair! She's not your type. Remember? Do yourself a favor and stick with a woman you can relate to.

Amanda. She was his type. Sleek. Sophisticated. A woman who thought the way he did, whose every action was logical and easily understood. You'd never find her standing there, tearing the packaging of a dog bone apart as though it were some wonderful treasure.

Kylie directed a smile his way. "It's a chew toy. Chicken flavored. Zsuzsi's favorite. I figured our friend here would like one too." She held it out to the dog.

"You got him a toy?"

"Of course."

"Let me get this straight. You spent good money on a *toy* for a *dog*?" Her expression told him she didn't see the problem. "I suppose your dog has a closet full of toys."

Her mouth curved. "Not exactly. She has a Nylabone that she likes to chew in her crate, a tennis ball she loves to chomp on while we're sitting on the couch watching TV—"

"You let that beast of yours up on your furniture?"

Kylie's bell-like laughter rang out. "Sure. A couch is just a couch. It doesn't bring me joy or comfort or laughter. Zsuzsi does all of those things and more." She shrugged. "Possessions are to be used, Mac. What does it matter if it's me using them or Zsuzsi?"

"Mackenzie."

She didn't seem to notice. She was too busy kneeling beside the crate, petting the dog. Well, this was one habit he intended to break before it got started. "It's Mackenzie, not 'Mac.'"

She stood to brush the fur from her jeans—the dog seemed to leave a cloud of it wherever he went!—and moved to lay out a small rug near the crate.

"I already told you, I don't do nicknames." The sternness he'd injected into the sentence seemed to have no effect. She filled one bowl with water and watched as the dog trotted over to circle the rug three times, then plop down with a contented sigh. Kylie turned and beamed that beautiful smile at him, but he refused to be moved.

"I don't believe in them." He was talking through gritted teeth now.

She blinked. "In what?"

"In nicknames—" He frowned. "Have you heard a word I've said?"

Her expression was one of utter innocence. "Oh dear, were you talking to me? I'm sorry! I thought you were scolding the dog again."

How did she do that? Melt away his determination to be firm and unmoved. Maybe it was her eyes. They were an extraordinary shade of green—

"Now, what were you saying?"

He'd never seen eyes quite that color before.

"Mac—I mean, Mackenzie?"

They were a deep, rich green in the center, circled by a ring of darker green. But what struck him even more than the startling color of her eyes was the artless serenity they held. It was . . . "Beautiful."

She started, her eyes widening a fraction. Then a slight grin quirked her mouth. She moved over to tap her knuckles against his forehead. "Hello? Anybody home?"

The warmth of her touch jarred him, and he stiffened.

She pursed her lips. "Are you OK?"

"Fine. Absolutely. No problem."

"OK, then what did you want to tell me?"

"About what?"

"About whatever you were saying to me."

"When?"

She laughed. "When I wasn't listening."

Oh yes. The nickname.

"Are you sure you're OK?"

"Yes, I'm fine." Though he felt far from it. Maybe he was coming down with a fever. "As for whatever I was saying before, well, never mind. It doesn't matter." If he and his peace of mind were lucky, she wouldn't be around often enough to call him much of anything.

Her shoulders lifted. "All righty then. So, what are you going to name him?"

"Name who?"

She looked at the dog, then back at him.

The dog? She wanted him to name the dog? "Why would I give it a name? I'm not going to keep it."

"You have to call *him* something."

He crossed his arms over his chest. *"Dog* should suffice."

"It most certainly will *not* suffice!"

Mackenzie fought a grin at her vehemence. But the grin won out when he took in the spark in her eyes, the mutinous tilt of her chin, her arms crossed over her chest.

"I don't know why not." That won him another glare.

"Well then, contrary to popular opinion—meaning your own—you obviously *don't* know everything, Mac*kenzie."* She whirled away from him and knelt beside the dog, burying her fingers in the animal's thick fur. "I know"—the look she cast him was pure mischief—"how about 'Bubba'?"

"Bubba?" She couldn't be serious.

"No? Well . . . there's always 'Buddy.' Or how about 'Spot' or 'Precious'?"

"I refuse to call that animal—or anything *else,* for that matter—'Precious'!"

"Fine." She stood with a flourish. "Then *you* come up with a name. Unless, of course, that's too much of a challenge for you. You know, too creative?"

He fixed her with a warning look, which only resulted in a burst of muffled laughter. He gave the dog a long look. So the beast needed a name, did he? "I've got it." He looked at her, but his voice caught in his throat when their gazes connected. She really did have the most amazing eyes—

"Yes?"

He started. Oh. Right. The dog's name. "Ivan."

She looked at the husky. "Ivan." She seemed to be testing it. The dog stretched, yawned, and tipped his head back to peer up at them. "Ivan." Her excitement was almost contagious. "It's perfect. I had a friend in college whose name was Ivan. If I remember correctly, it's the Russian form of John, which means 'gracious gift from God.' It fits."

He looked at the dog, then back at her. "Actually"—oh, she was going to hate him for this—"I was thinking more of Ivan the Terrible when I suggested the name, not Ivan the gift from God."

She planted her hands on her hips. "Mac!"

"Hey, he nearly destroyed my house."

She bit her lip.

"And my white towels—which, I might add, are *very* expensive—will never look the same."

She glanced at the dog and laughed. "Well, OK, so we know your meaning is appropriate. But I still think—" she waggled her eyebrows—"my meaning is better."

He laughed. "Never say die, eh?" He glanced down at the dog, who watched them with an adoring look in his mismatched eyes.

Kylie started for the door. "And isn't it nice that you have three weeks to discover whether or not I'm right?"

Before he could come up with an appropriate retort, she slipped out the door. But he could hear her chuckles all the way down the walkway.

Mackenzie stretched and yawned. It had been a long day—his gaze drifted to Ivan, who sat beside him on the floor, leaning against his leg. After Kylie left, he'd spent the rest of the evening cleaning up the dog hair.

The stuff seemed to materialize out of thin air!

As though sensing Mackenzie's attention, Ivan looked up at him, intent eyes wide.

Mackenzie frowned. "What is it, boy? What do you want?"

Ivan stared at him, then at the couch where Mackenzie was sitting.

"Forget it."

The dog kept staring.

"No way." Mackenzie crossed his arms. "You're not getting up here."

If anything, Ivan only looked more forlorn. "Manipulator. You're as bad as my sister." She knew exactly how to get around his most determined refusals. Well, he was not going to be cajoled by a four-footed fur ball.

Mackenzie leaned down to look Ivan in the eye. "Couches are for humans. Floors are for dogs."

Ivan licked Mackenzie's nose.

Mackenzie straightened, aware of an odd warmth somewhere in the region of his heart. He glanced at the couch cushion beside him. *I can't believe I'm even considering this. This couch cost me a bundle! No way am I going to let this fur machine up on it!*

At a gentle touch, Mackenzie glanced down to find the dog resting one paw on his knee. *"A couch is just a couch."* Kylie's voice echoed in his mind.

"Just a minute." He sighed, got up, and went to rummage in his cedar-lined linen closet. A few moments later he returned with a large beach towel in hand. He spread the towel over the cushion, then sat down—and patted the spot beside him.

Ivan jumped up, circled three times, then plopped down. By the time the movie Mackenzie had clicked on was rolling the credits, Ivan's head was in Mackenzie's lap. He stroked the soft ears, amazed at how calming the action was.

Shaking his head, he patted Ivan's side. "Up and at 'em, boy. Time for bed. Which means you go in your crate."

Ivan stretched and slid from the couch. He followed Mackenzie to the crate and went inside without argument.

"Good boy, Ivan. Now go to sleep."

He headed for his bedroom. Why on earth had he been worried? This dog thing was a breeze.

A horrific wailing sound split the night.

Mackenzie scrambled from bed, grabbed his robe, and raced for the living room. Ivan sat in his crate, staring at him, howling his heart out.

"That's enough!"

Ivan stilled, but his expression clearly told Mackenzie that his heart was breaking.

"Save it for the women, buster." Mackenzie turned and stalked back to bed.

No sooner had he slid beneath the covers than the howls began again. The mournful sounds bounced off the walls and reverberated all around Mackenzie. With a groan, he pulled his pillow over his head.

It didn't help.

He jumped up and went into the bathroom. He threw open the medicine cabinet, grabbed a handful of cotton balls, and stuffed them in his ears. All it did was waste the cotton.

Nothing blocked out the pitiful sound of Ivan's anguish. Finally, around 3 a.m., Mackenzie threw back the covers.

"All right. You win."

He opened the door of the crate. Ivan bounded out, jumping in ecstasy, dancing around Mackenzie like a Mexican Jumping Bean. "I should have named you Tigger." Ivan raced down the hallway, and Mackenzie followed, certain Ivan would be in the middle of the bed when he got there. But much to his surprise, the dog was sitting beside the bed, waiting for him. Too tired to question, Mackenzie slipped under the covers. Ivan stood up, turned three circles then lay down with a plop—*beside* the bed.

Mackenzie reached down and rested a hand on the dog's soft head. Just before he drifted off to sleep, Mackenzie felt a grateful lick on his hand.

CHAPTER
Eight

Ten days later, Mackenzie was just coming out of a deep sleep when something butted up against his backside. He cracked one eye open, then pushed against the lump.

"C'mon, you bed hog. Move over."

As though he'd been waiting for Mackenzie to wake up, Ivan jumped to his feet and spun in circles, stopping with a jolt. He stood there on the bed, head down on his front paws, backside up in the air, tail wagging, that husky grin on his face.

Mackenzie laughed. "So I take it you're ready for breakfast?"

Ivan rooed deep in his throat. Kylie called it yodeling, but the dog's "talk" sounded more to Mackenzie like a long, low "roo." In the week and a half the dog had been with him, the beast had grown more and more talkative.

Mackenzie loved it. But he'd seldom admit it, not even to himself.

He'd just set Ivan's dish down on the floor when the phone rang. "Eat up, boy." He scratched the dog's ears, then reached for the phone.

"Darling—" Amanda's voice, low and warm, came through the receiver. "Where have you been? It's been forever since I heard from you. And I'm so . . ."

Her voice drifted on as Mackenzie leaned against the kitchen counter, watching Ivan eat. Any dog he'd ever been around inhaled its food. Not so Sir Ivan. The Sibe would lie down with the dish between his two paws, then pluck one piece of the dry food from the dish. He'd chew, drop it, sniff at it, then pick it up and start all over. The mutt was nuts.

"Mackenzie?"

"Oh, sorry, Amanda. Yes, you were saying?"

"I *said,* I'm so sorry for our disagreement."

"So am I." He eased into a chair.

"That creature was terribly filthy—"

"He was, indeed."

"I've never been terribly good with animals, you know—"

"It's OK, Amanda. I wasn't either." Until now. He was actually getting pretty good with the dog.

Ivan rolled onto his back, stretching his legs straight, and yawned.

"Please, dear, do say you'll forgive me?"

"Hmmm?"

Ivan rose and came to sit beside him, leaning his body against Mackenzie's leg.

"I said—"

Mackenzie grinned. Apparently he needed a shower. Ivan was licking his hand from fingertips to wrist.

"—forgive me?"

He tuned back in to the phone call. "Of course I forgive you." Ivan chose that moment to climb into Mackenzie's lap and yodel into the receiver.

Mackenzie pulled the phone from his ear. "Hush, you!" He brought the phone back to his ear.

"Mackenzie! What was *that?*"

He chuckled. "Ivan. I think he's jealous."

"Ivan? Who in the world is Ivan?"

"The dog—"

"The *dog!* You still have that creature?"

He sighed, rubbing Ivan's ears. Apparently the dog could hear Amanda as well, and from the way he was hiding his face in Mackenzie's chest, Ivan considered her voice less than melodious.

"Just for a couple more weeks."

"*Weeks*? Mackenzie, really! Are you mad?"

"It's not that bad. My neighbor—"

"Oh, I'm certain your neighbor has made herself most indispensable—"

"Now, hold on, Amanda." He broke in on her frigid tirade. "Kylie has—"

"I *don't* want to hear about it! Any more than I want to hear about that . . . awful animal!"

A weariness settled over him. "What would you suggest I do?"

"Get *rid* of it."

He struggled to hold onto his patience. "I can't very well do that, now can I? He belongs to someone, and it doesn't seem right to ignore that fact. Besides, it's only for—"

"Yes, I heard you. 'A couple more weeks.' I refuse to step one foot into your house with that beast in residence!"

"He's not that bad."

"He's disgusting! And it sounds like you'd rather spend time with some mangy dog than with me."

"Amanda, don't be ridiculous—"

"If anyone is being ridiculous, it's you!"

"I'm doing what I have to, Amanda." His voice had hardened.

"As am I. Good-bye, Mackenzie."

"Amanda, wait." He really didn't want to end the call this way. "Look, why don't I take you out to dinner tonight?"

There was a pause. "Well . . ."

She was weakening. He lowered his voice. "Chateau Michel's shouldn't be too busy. We'll ask them for the corner table near the fireplace, away from everyone else. You can order veal, just the way you like it."

"Oh, honestly, Mackenzie. Very well. Pick me up at seven."

"I'll be there." He hung up the phone and took hold of Ivan's face, rubbing the sides of his muzzle. "I can work this out, boy."

The dog shook his head, then went to lie down, his back to Mackenzie. Clearly, he wasn't buying it.

Mackenzie could only hope Amanda would be at least as . . . well, unreceptive.

CHAPTER
Nine

Mackenzie finished making lunch—a perfectly created Western omelet—and took it to the kitchen table to eat. Ivan danced around him as he walked, pressing up against him as he cut off a bite of the still-hot omelet

Mackenzie tolerated the dog's interference for as long as he could, then barked, "Ivan! Lie down!"

The dog gave him one mournful look, then padded to his crate and laid himself down. Mackenzie stood there, mouth agape. The animal had actually obeyed him! And without much hesitation. So little, in fact, that it didn't really qualify as hesitation. It was more of an "Are you sure?" pause before doing as his master had ordered.

Mackenzie rose and went to stand in front of the dog, who now rested with his head on his paws. "Ivan, come."

Within seconds Ivan was sitting in front of him, gazing up at him.

"Ivan, lie down."

The husky did so.

"Good boy, Ivan." Mackenzie gave the dog a satisfied rub. He couldn't remember the last time he'd felt so pleased. He scratched Ivan's head. The husky panted happily and pressed his face into Mackenzie's hand.

Two realizations came to Mackenzie: He liked having Ivan around, and he was going to miss the dog when his real owners showed up.

Pushing that thought away, Mackenzie gave Ivan one final pat, then rose and went to dump his omelet down the garbage disposal. He wasn't hungry anymore. He grabbed his coat from the rack. Pulling a doggie treat from the tin, he tossed it into Ivan's crate. The dog entered the crate and polished off the tidbit before lying down.

When Mackenzie went outside, he stood on the porch. Where should he go? He stepped off the porch and started out, but his step slowed when he came to Kylie's gate. He paused, studying the tidy, white house. True, she had Christmas decorations up, but at least they didn't cover every inch of her house and lawn. The display was attractive, he had to admit.

Luminaries lined the walkway, though they weren't lit at the moment. An elegant wreath adorned the door holding a red banner sporting the simple message, "Immanuel: God With Us!" White lights were strung on the two trees in her front yard and along the eaves of the house. Inside he could see a crèche set up in front of the large plate-glass window. If he remembered correctly, it was lit in such a way that those passing by at night could see it.

"Oh, good! I need an extra hand."

He looked over to see Kylie standing in her doorway, smiling at him. Her golden hair flowed about her face, looking almost like a halo. He glanced around, surprised to discover that he'd come through the gate and was standing on her front porch. Heat washed his cheeks.

"I . . . I was just passing by."

She stepped forward and laid her hand on his sleeve. "You can't leave. Like I said, I need some help. Won't take but a minute . . ." and he let her lead him inside. He followed her into a bright kitchen decorated with sunflowers. It was the perfect setting for her, he decided, looking around.

"Here you go." She pulled his hands out and stuck hot-pad gloves on them.

He stared down at his hands. "What—?"

"Hold still. I have to get this tied on." She reached around him from behind.

He looked down to see she'd slipped an apron around his waist and was tying it in place.

She came around to cast a critical eye over him, then smiled. "Wonderful. You're all set."

"For what?"

An electronic beeping sounded, and she shooed him toward the oven. "For that! Pull the pan of cookies out and set them on the table. There's a flipper there to take the cookies off the pan and set them on the cooling racks."

Had he heard correctly? "Cookies? I don't—"

"You'll be fine. Here, hold the flipper like this. But you'd better hurry or they'll burn!"

There was something warm and enchanting in her eyes. He fumbled with the oven door. How was he supposed to do anything with these ridiculous mittens on his hands? He wrestled the door open, pulled the pan of golden-brown cookies from the oven, spun around—and bumped right into Kylie. The sifter of flour she'd been carrying went flying, dousing him with a cloud of white.

He coughed and sputtered, then froze when he heard her laugh. Blinking the flour out of his eyes, he stared at her, fully intending to tell her how little he appreciated being laughed at, but the words stopped in his throat.

She stood there, flour smeared on her cheek, dusting her hair, her eyes sparkling.

He'd never seen anyone more beautiful in his life.

She bit her lips to stop her laughter and grabbed a damp cloth from the sink. "Here, let me help."

A smile tugged at his lips. Lindsay was right. The woman was contagious.

She wiped his shirt front, rinsed out the cloth, then went on tiptoe to wipe his face. At her touch on his cheek, their eyes met—and all at once the very air around them seemed charged.

Kylie lowered her hand and stepped back. He watched her lick her lips and understood. His own throat and lips had gone bone dry.

"I . . ." She cleared her throat. "Maybe you should do this yourself."

She held out the cloth, and he took it from her, grateful for something to do. He moved to the sink and washed his face, pondering the uproar his emotions seemed to be in. If he were smart, he'd get out of there. Fast.

He turned to face her, and he realized he had absolutely no desire to do the smart thing. He shrugged. "Well, since I've been baptized by flour, I may as well help you finish this little venture."

The smile Kylie gave him confirmed his belief that being smart wasn't all it was cracked up to be.

CHAPTER
Ten

"Rudolph, the red-nosed reindeer, had a very shiny nooose. . . ."

Mackenzie belted out the song, letting the water from the shower fill his mouth and making the words sound gargled. He swallowed, laughing.

He felt good. No, great! He hadn't felt this way since . . . He frowned. Ever. He'd never felt this good. He and Kylie had spent the afternoon baking cookies. Then, when the treats were cooled and lined up on strips of wax paper, they'd decorated them. During it all, they'd talked and laughed and found they had more in common than he'd imagined. They shared interests in books, foods, walking, camping, horseback riding, even the kinds of movies they enjoyed.

And, of course, dogs.

He smiled again as he shut off the water and stepped from the shower. He'd have to let Lindsay know she was right for once. A quick glance at his watch reminded him he had just enough time to get dressed and head out to pick up Amanda. He pulled on his clothes in record time, calling for Ivan as he did so.

When the dog didn't come, Mackenzie went into the living room. "Ivan," he called again, looking around. No exuberant dog bounded toward him. A frown creased his forehead as he called again, fighting the sense of dread beginning to build inside. He went to the crate and pulled Ivan's favorite squeaky toy from inside. Feeling totally absurd, he squeaked it. Ivan was probably just snoozing soundly somewhere. He glanced around the room, and his gaze came to rest on the sliding doors. The air in his lungs came out in a rush.

The doors were open.

He rushed to look outside. "Ivan!" No response.

Huskies are famous for being escape artists. . . .

He groaned. "You dumb dog!" He went back inside. "Well, so be it. He's not my dog. If he wants to take off, I can't exactly stop him." But the words didn't ring true, even to his own ears. There was a decided ache in his chest, and he imagined the look in Kylie's eyes when he had to tell her Ivan was missing. He grabbed his coat. "Five minutes. I'll look for five minutes."

An hour later, Mackenzie came trudging back to his house. Ivan was gone. Mackenzie's throat was tight; his heart felt constricted. He'd done everything he could, looked everywhere he knew to look. He slid the key in the lock, then paused, resting his forehead against the door. There had to be something else he could do.

How about pray?

This time, he didn't argue. "God, I'm sure you have better things to do than find a lost dog, but I'd appreciate any help you could give me here."

He unlocked the front door and went inside—then paused. Someone was in the backyard. He hurried to the sliding doors and pushed them open. A group of neighborhood kids were there, gathered in a circle. Mackenzie walked over to find Kylie in the center kneeling beside a mud-encrusted, ecstatic Ivan.

"Oh, you're home!" Kylie brushed a hand across her forehead, leaving a streak of mud there. "Look who the gang found at the park."

He came to kneel beside her, stunned at the relief flowing through him. "Thank God."

Kylie's surprise brought a small smile to his lips.

"When I couldn't find him, I took your advice and prayed." He cupped Ivan's face in his hands and rested his forehead against the dog's furry muzzle. "I don't know how he did it, but he got the sliding doors open somehow."

Kylie's eyes told him she understood his feelings. "Huskies are notorious escape artists."

"Well, he's living up to his name, aren't you, Ivan the Terrible?"

Kylie pulled her knees to her chest and circled them with her arms. "I could swear someone around here told me he didn't believe in nicknames."

"I thought you weren't listening when I said that."

"Oh?"

He angled a look at her over the dog's head. "Seeing as you call me Mac all the time."

Her dimples peeked out. "Some things are better ignored."

A boy of about eight stepped forward. "Hey, mister, can we come play with your dog tomorrow?"

"He's not my—" Mackenzie's denial was cut off when the other children crowded closer in the excitement.

"Yeah! He was a lot of fun!"

"Your dog is vewy pwetty," a small girl said softly.

Mackenzie tried to stem the tide of exuberance. "He's not—"

"Is he your only dog?"

"HE'S NOT MY DOG!"

Five heads turned toward him and five pairs of wide eyes regarded him. He looked at Kylie, who was struggling with laughter.

"Did you steaw him?" the small girl finally asked in that sweet, angelic voice.

"Of course not!"

Kylie finally stepped in. "Ivan is a stray. Mr. St. Clair is taking care of him until we can find his owners."

"Wow," one of the other boys exclaimed. "God must like you a lot to bring you such a great dog, huh?"

Mackenzie directed his gaze at Ivan, who seemed pleased as punch at being the center of all this attention. For all that Mackenzie wanted to be angry, frustrated—*something*—he had to admit all he felt was relief. And happy.

He tousled the boy's hair. "Yes, I think God does."

CHAPTER
Eleven

It took some time, but the children finally went home.

"How about some coffee?"

Kylie leaned her elbows on the kitchen island. "I wouldn't refuse a cup of cocoa."

"You've got it." He opened the cupboard, then his eyes fell on his watch—and his hand froze mid-reach. Oh good grief.

Amanda.

He glanced at Kylie. "I'll fix it in a minute. Right after I make a phone call."

She must have seen something in his expression. "Everything OK?"

He forced a smile. "Sure. I just realized I forgot an appointment."

She nodded and went into the living room, Ivan padding along beside her. Drawing a deep breath, Mackenzie lifted the phone and dialed Amanda's cell.

She answered before the first ring was finished. "Mackenzie?"

Hoo boy. She was fuming. "Amanda, I can explain—"

"Do you realize I've been sitting here for two hours?"

He rubbed his eyes wearily. "Amanda, please, Ivan got away."

"Ivan? Who in the world is Ivan?"

"The dog—"

"The *dog?*"

Her screech pierced his eardrum, and with a grimace he held the phone away. Even with the receiver at arm's length, he had no trouble hearing her.

"Do you mean to tell me that you *stood me up for a dog*? How *dare* you treat me in such a cavalier manner! Well, I have had enough. *More* than enough. I do not, I repeat, *do not want* to hear from you again." A pause. "Until that . . . that *thing* is gone!"

The click of her phone rang in his ear like a receiver slammed down, and Mackenzie sat in silence for a moment. Then, very carefully, he hung up the phone.

Kylie glanced at the clock as she slipped into bed. One-thirty in the morning. She couldn't believe she'd stayed so long at Mac's.

They had talked into the wee hours, discussing everything from family to favorite foods.

"Hmm, peanut butter," she'd said. "Now God did himself proud when he moved somebody to invent peanut butter."

Mac almost choked on his cookie. "You really think God had anything to do with peanut butter?"

"I believe God cares about the things that move and delight us. Just as an earthly father cares about the things that delight his children." She crossed her arms, hugging herself. "I remember watching once when my older brother was sick. My dad sat beside him, washing his fevered face with a cool cloth, talking to him. And crying."

"Crying? Why?"

"Because his son was in pain, and he was helpless to stop it. But what my dad felt was only a small reflection of what God feels as he watches us. He's far more affected by our joys and our pains than any earthly father can be." She shrugged. "That's just the kind of God he is. When we hurt, he hurts. When we are in pain, he longs to help us and ease our suffering. Because he loves us."

"So why doesn't he stop the hurt?"

Mac sounded so . . . somber. She had the feeling the question went far deeper than the conversation they were having. She formed her response with care. "Sometimes he does. But God never said we wouldn't suffer. He just promised to be with us in the hurting. And he provides us with the help we need to get through it."

"Let me guess. You're talking about angels."

She smiled. "Sure, sometimes, or people." Her gaze drifted to Ivan, who was snuggled next to Mac. On the couch, no less. No one could tell her that dog wasn't getting to him. "Or others who bring us joy or comfort." A rebel yawn forced her to glance at her watch. When she groaned, Mac took her wrist in his hand and tilted her watch so he could see the time. He had looked at her then, and their eyes met and held.

She could still feel the way her heart had tripped and her breathing grew ragged at his nearness. Something flickered in his eyes. Kylie watched, unable to move, barely able to breathe, as he cradled her wrist in his large hand, then lifted it to his lips and pressed a gentle kiss there.

"Thanks for all your help." His low voice resonated through her, touching and warming her from the inside out. "If anyone's been an angel lately, it's you."

Kylie's cheeks felt warm now as she remembered wanting to lean forward and press her lips to his. Instead she'd managed to choke out, "Anytime," before she disengaged her hand from his and rose to leave.

She rolled over, punching her pillow into submission, then flopped down with a confused sigh. *What is it about this man, Lord? And why did he look at me that way tonight? He's nearly engaged to that socialite. Shouldn't he be saving his meaningful looks for her?* She punched the pillow again. *And while we're at it, why does one look from those blue eyes almost stop my heart?*

No answer came, but that didn't matter. She knew it already.

Mackenzie St. Clair had gotten to her. Big time. In just over a week they'd gone from virtual strangers to . . . what? Friends? No, it was more than that for her. She sat up and covered her face with her hands. She cared about the man. Cared for him. After just a few days together . . . How pathetic was *that?*

She hit her pillow again. This was all her mother's fault.

She'd been fine, content to focus on her career, until her mother had fallen in love. Again. Gotten married. Something about her mother's new life, about the love she saw between her mom and Jericho every time they looked at each other, had moved her. Deeply.

Suddenly Kylie's career wasn't enough. She wanted what they had. Longed for it. But when she'd prayed for God to bring the right man into her life, she'd never thought—

You've got to be kidding, Lord. Mackenzie St. Clair? She rolled onto her back and stared at the ceiling. Until the last week, she'd pegged her neighbor as distant and cold, a man far too focused on controlling his life and environment. Oh, Lindsay had told her time and again, there was more to Mac than that. But she hadn't believed the sister's perspective.

Until now. She'd seen another side of Mackenzie. A softer, tender side. She'd seen him smile and laugh and take a stray dog into his home. And into his heart. She pictured the way he'd rest one hand on Ivan's head as the dog slept beside Mac on the couch. This Mackenzie St. Clair was a man she liked, a man she enjoyed being around.

A man she could grow to love.

She threw her arm over her eyes. *Father, this is impossible. He's going to ask Amanda Carr to marry him, and that's all there is to it.* She pictured the woman in all her elegant perfection, and her heart sank. Why wouldn't Mac—strike that . . . *Mackenzie*—want to marry someone who looked like that? Amanda Carr matched him perfectly. Far better than Kylie ever could.

Wait...

The word whispered through her, stilling the morose thoughts rattling around in her head.

Wait on the Lord.

She wanted to. Really she did. But Amanda Carr's image wouldn't leave her alone. Perfect hair. Perfect teeth. Perfect clothes. *Perfect, perfect, perfect.*

Kylie hated that word.

With a final punch to her battered pillow, she reached a decision: Mackenzie St. Clair, with all of his charm and endearing boyishness, belonged to someone else. That made him off limits.

And her stubborn, disagreeing heart was just going to have to live with that.

CHAPTER

Twelve

It was no use.

He'd been trying to focus on work for the past several hours. Trying hard. But every time he'd start reading, his mind drifted off to other things. Well . . . one other thing.

OK, one other *person*.

Mackenzie leaned back in his chair. "This is ridiculous." A soft huff told him Ivan agreed. He lowered a hand to scratch the husky's ears. Amazing how second nature that action had become.

The doorbell sounded, and Mackenzie was up and out of his chair. He pulled the door open, anticipating the smile on Kylie's face. "I was just thinking about you—"

His sister's eyes widened. "You were? Really?"

A flash of disappointment hit him, but it was fleeting. He hadn't seen Lindsay since she stormed out that day almost four weeks ago. He'd tried to call her a couple of times, but he'd gotten only voicemail. He opened the door wider. "Come on in, Sis."

She did so. "I can't stay for more than a few minutes, but I wanted to stop by." Were those tears in her eyes? "I've missed you, Bear."

"Missed you, too, Changeling." He took hold of her and drew her into a hug. He knew she was surprised by the action—he'd never been big on hugging—but he didn't care. Seeing her face made his heart happy.

"Well"—she followed him into the living room—"I should stay away more often if I'm going to get a greeting like that."

"Tell you what. You forgive me for being a total goon, and I'll greet you that way every time you come around."

With a tip of her head, she studied him. "A total goon?"

He led her to the kitchen, lifting the coffee carafe and casting a questioning glance her way. She nodded, and he poured her a cup and handed it to her. "I've been thinking. A lot, actually. And well, Amanda and I . . . actually, I'm not convinced we're right together."

Lindsay whooped, jumped up from the stool where she'd lighted, and wrapped him in a crushing hug, raining kisses on his face. Ivan danced around them, yodeling like crazy.

When Lindsay finally calmed down and sank back onto the breakfast stool, Mackenzie patted the dog beside him. "Ivan, lie down."

The dog went to his crate in the living room, circled three times, and plopped down. Mackenzie reached down for one of Ivan's squeaky toys—once he discovered that Ivan would chew on them rather than shoes, he hadn't hesitated to buy a dozen of them—and tossed it to the husky.

When he looked up, Lindsay was staring at him, a strange expression in her eyes. "So, this is the stray that's turned your life upside down?"

"In the furry flesh."

She sipped her coffee. "I've got to say, I was amazed by the message about him you left on my machine. At first I thought it was a brotherly ploy to get me to come back so you could apologize."

He grinned. "Now there's an idea. I wish it had occurred to me."

Lindsay studied him for a moment.

"What?"

She met his curious gaze. "Are you sure you want to get rid of Ivan?"

The question took him aback. He'd forgotten about that. Ivan wasn't his. "I'm not getting rid of him. It's just . . . well, he doesn't belong to me."

"Suppose he doesn't belong to anyone else? I mean, what if no one claims him?"

The words had an odd effect on Mackenzie: hope seized his heart and emotion tightened his throat. He looked at Ivan, who stared at him, an adoring expression in his doggie eyes.

"You're sure not going to find anyone else in this world who looks at you like that!"

Mackenzie didn't respond. He couldn't get any words past that tight throat.

Lindsay came to wrap her arms around his neck. "That dog has been a gift to you, Bear. He's made you laugh again. If for no other reason than that, you should think about keeping him." She stepped back, then went to pull a small bundle from her purse. She set it on the coffee table.

"What's that?" he asked.

"A gift. From Kylie."

From Kylie? "Why didn't she bring it over herself?"

"I don't know, Bear. She just asked me to give it to you."

He leaned forward and picked it up, then looked up at his sister. "She's giving me a Bible?"

Lindsay nodded as she moved toward the door. "Kylie said she marked places that pertained to your discussion the other night." She angled a look over her shoulder. "Sounds as though you two are getting along pretty well."

He started to respond, but she halted as she noticed her tree.

At least it was in a stand now. Mackenzie bought one the day after Ivan showed up. And he'd been watering it faithfully, though he wasn't quite certain why. It was still as bare as the day Lindsay hauled it through the door.

"Bear—"

At the reproach in her voice, he held up a hand. "I've had a few things on my mind, Linds. And they were a bit more important than putting tinsel on a tree."

"Hmmm. You might be surprised how important that really is." She opened the door and cast a glance back at him. "Think hard about keeping Ivan, OK?"

"I will." He followed her and stood by the door. "When I have time." But he knew, as he watched her walk away, that he'd probably think of little else for the next several days.

Mackenzie couldn't believe he was doing this. If Kylie wanted to see him, she'd come over. What was he doing on her doorstep. He wasn't some love-struck teenager.

Still, since he was here . . .

He lifted his hand to knock on the door just as Kylie pulled it open. She stared at him, wide-eyed—and he felt his heart surge. He opened his mouth to speak and found his throat was dry as a desert. Clearing it, he tried again. "Hi."

She leaned against the door jamb. "Hi."

He frowned. Something was wrong. She seemed distant. He slid his hands into his jeans pockets, suddenly uneasy. "I wondered if you had a few minutes to talk."

Something flickered in her eyes—a gladness, a warm eagerness—and then it was gone, locked behind a remote veil that he'd never seen in her expression before.

"I don't know." She glanced around as though seeking some excuse.

"If it's a bad time—" He wasn't sure what confused him more—her behavior or the sharp hurt washing over him. He had the oddest feeling he was losing something precious, and he didn't even know what or why. His head spun, and his chest ached as though an anvil were sitting on it. *Get hold of yourself, St. Clair! So she doesn't want to see you. Big deal.*

Exactly, his heart echoed. *Very big deal.*

He had to get away from there. To think. "Well, never mind. I'm sorry to bother you." He spun and walked away with long, rapid strides.

"Mac—Mackenzie!"

She was too late. He was gone. And she couldn't blame him after the way she'd just acted. Kylie went back inside, more miserable than she'd felt in a very long time. Sinking into her rocking chair, she leaned her head back as tears began to slide down her cheeks.

Father, help me. I don't know what to do.

Fear not.

Kylie stilled. The words came again.

Fear not.

But . . . she wasn't afraid. She just wanted to do what was right. And poaching another woman's man definitely wasn't right. True? Besides, Mac had never said he was interested in her. She could just see baring her soul to the man only to have him give her a pitying look. After all, it wasn't like she belonged in Mac's world. The world of the wealthy. She wasn't Amanda Carr. She was just a vet, a woman who loved animals and kids and nature. She'd be out of place in Mac's world. In his life. And she'd probably embarrass him left and right—

Fear. Not.

Kylie closed her eyes. *I hear you, Lord. I do. But . . . I'm just not sure.*

With a sigh she pushed out of the chair and headed for her bedroom. What she needed was a good night's sleep. Things would make more sense in the morning. And if they didn't . . .

Well, she'd deal with that when she came to it.

CHAPTER
Thirteen

The jangling noise wouldn't stop. It kept nagging at her, poking her, pulling her from the warm cocoon of sleep.

The phone. It was ringing and ringing. Kylie forced her eyes open and tried to focus on the clock. The iridescent red numbers blinked at her.

3:30 a.m.

She grabbed for her phone, pulled the receiver from the cradle, and laid it next to her ear on the pillow. "Hullo?"

"I need you."

She blinked. "W . . . what?"

"I need you. Now!"

She frowned. It sounded like Mackenzie's voice, but it couldn't be. "Mac, is that you?"

"Stop asking ridiculous questions and get over here, now!"

"Mac, what in the world—?"

"He's sick."

Kylie sat up. Mackenzie wasn't angry, he was frightened. She could hear it in his voice. "Ivan?" Even as she asked, she knew it was the husky. "What's wrong with him?"

"I don't know." He sounded miserable. And desperate.

"Then how do you know he's sick?"

"Let's just say my two-thousand-dollar Persian rug will never be the same."

"Ah." She threw back the covers. "I'll be right there."

The sight of Ivan lying in the middle of the bathroom floor, panting rapidly, his tongue hanging out, sent a chill through Kylie. But that was nothing compared to what the sight of Mac's haggard face did to her.

Without thinking, she went to him and folded him in her arms. He stiffened, then sagged against her.

"Has Ivan eaten anything different?"

Mackenzie straightened and gave her a wry look, then pulled a large gold box from the trash container. "Not unless you count five pounds of the finest Belgian chocolates."

"Oh, wow."

At her low exclamation, Mackenzie turned to look at her, his stance and expression alert.

"What?"

She bit her lip. "Chocolate, well, it's toxic to dogs in large quantities."

His eyes narrowed. "How harmful?"

She didn't respond, and he took her hand, gripping it so hard it hurt. "Kylie."

Licking her lips, she met his gaze. "It could kill him." Mac's face paled, and she squeezed his hand. "Listen, we probably caught it in time. The best thing we can do now is take him to my clinic." She looked down at Ivan's limp form. "And pray."

Several hours later, Mackenzie and Ivan were back home. The husky was sick, very sick, but he would recover.

"Let's get Ivan set up in the bathroom, Mac."

He carried the dog in and laid him down on the cushion Kylie had brought in. He sat on the floor, next to Ivan, stroking the dog's ears.

"He's going to be OK, Mac."

Mac didn't look at Kylie. He just nodded, his gaze fixed on the dog. She straightened and started to leave the room. Mac reached out to capture her hand. "Kylie, I—"

He appreciated all she'd done more than he could say. But what meant the most to him was simply her presence. She'd been a source of comfort and calm.

Their eyes met, and she nodded. "I'll check on you tomorrow." She squeezed his hand, and then she was gone.

Mac listened to her footsteps, heard the door open and close, and leaned back against the wall. He looked down at Ivan's sleeping, exhausted form. "I didn't know . . ." The whisper came out raw, broken. "I didn't know chocolate was dangerous. Or that it would hurt so much to see you in pain and not be able to help you . . ." He turned his cheek against the cool wall. "I didn't know caring could hurt so much."

God is affected by our joys and pains. . . . When we hurt he hurts. . . . That's just the kind of God he is. . . .

When Kylie first said those things, Mackenzie hadn't understood. Now . . . "I don't know, Lord. I'm not sure it's worth it."

The feel of a wet tongue on his cheek startled Mackenzie, and he opened his eyes to find Ivan standing beside him, shaky but upright. The husky's mismatched eyes, filled with trust and devotion, were fixed on him. Mackenzie slid his arms around Ivan's neck, burying his hands in that deep fur. Ivan licked him again, then bent his head to tuck it beneath Mackenzie's chin.

"Good boy," Mackenzie murmured. "You're going to be OK." And in that moment, as he sat there, Ivan leaning against him, Mackenzie knew nothing was more worth the risk, and the pain, than loving.

CHAPTER
Fourteen

When the morning sun streamed in the windows, Mackenzie was already slipping into his coat and heading for the door. He needed to talk to Amanda. He reached for the door just as the bell rang. Surprised, he opened it and found Kylie standing there.

She met his gaze steadily. "We need to talk."

He nodded. No point in pretending he didn't understand. "Yes, we do." He held out his hand, and she placed hers in it. As his fingers closed around hers, he noticed how their hands seemed to fit together. Just like their hearts.

He led her into the kitchen. "Coffee, right?"

She nodded. He had it ready in minutes, then handed it to her. As she took the warm mug, he let his fingers do what they'd itched to do for days: caress her face. "I want you to wait here for me." He hadn't intended to make the request, but the second he saw her he knew he wanted her there when he got back.

"You're going somewhere?"

"I have to talk with Amanda." She stiffened slightly, and he cupped her face. "I need to tell her that things have changed." He brushed back a stray strand of hair. How he loved that wild hair of hers. "And I don't feel right about doing that over the phone."

She held his gaze, her eyes searching his face, and then she nodded. "I'll be here."

Relief swept him. "Good." He smiled, amazed at how light he felt. "I'll be back soon."

He grabbed his car keys and headed for the front door. Everything was going to work out. He was sure of it. Whatever this was between him and Kylie, it was right. For the first time in a long time, he felt as though his life was on the right track. And he could hardly wait to see where it would take him.

He pulled the door open—and ran right into a policeman who stood there, hand poised to ring the bell.

"Mr. St. Clair?"

Kylie came to stand beside Mackenzie as he nodded. The policeman inclined his head. "I'm afraid I have some bad news, sir."

Mackenzie froze.

"It's your sister. She's been in an automobile accident." His eyes gleamed with compassion. "I'm sorry, Mr. St. Clair, but it's serious."

Mackenzie tried to contact the aunts, but two days after the accident, he still hadn't been able to locate them. "I believe they intended to take a rather rambling tour of the countryside," a woman from the Paris conference informed him. He'd called the airlines and left messages. That was as much as he could do.

He sat in the ICU, holding Lindsay's hand, staring at her. He understood the doctors well enough: his sister had been thrown from her car when it was rear-ended by a truck. She suffered head trauma and was in a coma. The prognosis was not good.

What he couldn't understand, however, was why. Why Lindsay? Why now?

"Mackenzie?"

He stiffened at the cold tone and looked up. Amanda stood in the doorway, a nurse at her side. "Would you please tell this . . . woman that I'm part of the family?"

At Amanda's haughty tones, Mackenzie rose and went to take her arm, ushering her back to the waiting room. She gave him a disapproving look, but followed without comment. Until they reached the waiting room.

"You haven't called me."

At the cold accusation, Mackenzie stared at her. "I believe you told me not to."

She made a dismissive gesture. "Don't be ridiculous. I only meant while the dog was there."

"Well, he's still there, Amanda, and he's staying."

Her look told him she thought he'd lost his senses. "Staying? What do you mean 'staying'? I won't allow it, Mackenzie."

His head was starting to pound. "Listen, Amanda, I can't talk about this now—"

"Not with me, anyway. I understand you've been talking plenty with your little fuzzy-headed neighbor."

Anger swept him at the disdain in her tone. "Kylie has been an enormous help."

"Oh, I'm sure."

Mackenzie narrowed his eyes. Amanda's tone had turned downright nasty.

"Your sweet little veterinarian filled me in on quite a lot when I encountered her this morning as she was leaving your house." Her eyes were even more frigid than her tone. "She rambled on about all you've suffered, how her God saved your dog. She actually asked me to pray for you." She sniffed. "The way that woman talks about God is juvenile. But then, that doesn't seem to bother you. Not any—"

Her words halted, and stunned understanding filled her eyes.

"Amanda—"

"You're in *love* with her!"

"Look—"

"Don't waste your breath trying to deny it. You're in love with that absurd woman." She gave a harsh laugh and turned from him.

Mackenzie stood there, staring at the back of Amanda's well-tailored suit. "I don't intend to deny it."

She spun around, eyes narrowed. "I beg your pardon?"

Mackenzie had had enough. "And so you should." He took a step toward her. "You march in here, when my sister is lying in a hospital bed, when I don't know if she's going to die, and start telling me how I've treated you badly?"

Amanda held up an imperious hand, as though to halt his words. He ignored her.

"Let me tell you something, Amanda. Something I've only begun to realize. Neither you nor I have a clue about what it means to love someone. All we've been concerned about is whether or not we're a good match socially and financially. But that's not enough. Not for me. And it shouldn't be for you, either."

Her perfectly manicured hands balled into fists. "What exactly are you saying to me, Mackenzie?"

"Mac." The correction surprised him almost as much as it did her. "Call me Mac. I like it better."

Her mouth dropped open. "Since when?"

"Since now. As for what I'm saying to you, it's very simple. I thought you and I were a perfect match, but I was wrong. I'm not right for you—"

"You most certainly are not!"

"And you're not right for me. I need someone who is warm and loving, who knows how to laugh at herself and find joy in everyday life. I need someone who understands that at this moment, the only thing that matters to me is whether or not my sister lives. And, Amanda, you're not that someone."

She lifted her chin and glared at him down that elegant nose. "And all I can say to that is, thank God!"

Mac did something then he hadn't thought possible until that moment. He grinned. Which only offended Amanda more. As she spun on her heel and marched to the elevator, Mac leaned a shoulder against the wall. He knew he should feel some sense of loss that she was leaving, never to return. But all he felt was relief.

As the elevator doors opened, Amanda paused and turned to fix him with an icy glare. "You might want to ask your paragon of faith and virtue one thing, Ma*c*kenzie." Bitter sarcasm punctuated each word. "Where was her almighty God in *this?*" She swept her hand toward the ICU. "He cared enough to save your silly dog. Why didn't he save your sister?"

She stepped into the elevator and was gone.

Kylie set Ivan's bowl of food down, then stepped back.

"There you go, boy. Have at it."

Ivan just looked up at her, then laid his muzzle on his paws. She sighed and knelt beside the morose animal. "I know, pup. I miss him, too. But he'll be home soon." She sat back on her heels. "I just wish there was something I could do. . . ." Her gaze came to rest on the unadorned tree.

It was clear. She rose and went to work.

It was amazing how quiet the hospital hallways were around midnight. Mackenzie had grown somewhat used to the constant bustling of nurses, doctors, orderlies, and visitors during the daytime. Now, with the lights dimmed and the activity almost nonexistent, the hallway had a strange, melancholy emptiness to it.

Like a tomb.

The thought sent a chill up Mackenzie's spine, and he quickened his step back to Lindsay's room. He'd stepped out to get a drink of water. He knew he probably shouldn't stay night and day, but he didn't want to leave Lindsay. He needed to see her. To talk to her.

As he entered the ICU, the only sound was the ping of her cardiac monitor and the gentle *swooshing* sound of her respirator. Mackenzie sank into the chair he'd pulled next to the bed. "Hey, Changeling."

No, that rough, ragged voice wouldn't do. He cleared his throat—then shook his head. What did it matter if he sounded like he was about to cry? This was his *sister* lying here! Truth was, he wanted to put his head on her bed and bawl like a baby.

He stared at Lindsay's pale face. It didn't even look like her. All the animation, the luminous personality that drew people from the moment she entered a room, was gone. She lay there, passive, as though she were already gone.

"Don't." He drew in a ragged breath. "Don't let this happen." He felt the dampness on his face, grew aware that he was crying. He reached out to take Lindsay's limp hand and hold it between his own. Bowing his head, he placed a soft kiss on her fingers.

God, God . . . help us.

He started talking. Anything to break the stillness. "It's Christmas Eve, Linds. Bloomingdale's called me this morning all upset that you haven't been around."

He smiled. She would have appreciated the joke.

"Ah, Linds, you can't do this, hon. You can't leave me. How can I face Christmas without you? How can I face life without you? Don't you know you're the only spark I've got?"

He leaned his forehead on the white sheet. "You said my life was ho-hum, boring. Remember? You were right. But I don't know how to be different, Linds. I need you to show me . . ." Choking back a sob, he lifted his head and pressed her knuckles to his lips. Memories of their past life flitted through his mind, pictures of them as children, as teens, now as adults.

"Remember that first Christmas we stayed with the aunts?" He turned his head to gaze out the window. It was snowing again. "I was so steamed at Mom and Dad for dying. And at the aunts for being the ones who were alive. They understood, and they let me be mad. Until I yelled at you. Then they took me aside and told me to remember you were my little sister. That you needed me. I think they knew the truth, though. It was really I who needed you. I needed your laughter, your delight in every little thing. You missed Mom and Dad, but you loved being with the aunts. I thought they were kooks. You thought they were magic. Especially when we went after the tree."

He could see as though it were happening again, how they'd gone into the mountains, trudging through the deep snow, examining every tree in the forest—or so it had seemed to his teenage mind—until they found The Tree. That was how his aunt Ophelia had said it. *The Tree.* As though it were some precious treasure.

He had to admit it, though, once they brought it home and decorated it—an event that took an entire evening—even he had thought it was worthy of such respect. It had been magnificent.

"It was like spending Christmas with Beaver Cleaver and the gang," he muttered, looking at his sister's ashen face. "Christmas carols playing on the radio, the smell of fresh-baked cookies and pies in the air." He chuckled in spite of the pain in his heart. "I swear we watched every TV Christmas special ever produced!" His gaze rested on her face. "You made me watch the Grinch with you five times. Five times, Linds! I should have gotten a medal of some kind." He closed his eyes, savoring the memories of laughter, singing, praying together. . . . "It was pretty amazing, wasn't it? You said that year was full of Christmas magic. I pretended I didn't care, but I did. I still do."

Emotion choked him, stopping the flow of words. He stood and went to pour himself some water from the pitcher on her bedside table. He swallowed the tepid liquid, willing it to soothe the tightness in his throat, in his chest. "You hounded me into going caroling with you," he went on, staring out the window again. "Told me it would be my fault if you and your little friends got mugged. I groaned about it, complained every step of the way, but do you know, I can still remember the songs?" He smiled crookedly. "I can still hear you singing, your sweet voice floating on the air. . . ."

In a hushed voice, he started to sing.

Joy to the world, the Lord is come,
Let earth receive her king.
Let every heart prepare him room,
And heaven and nature sing. . . .

The last note came out ragged, and he turned and left the room with quick, almost desperate strides.

Kylie leaned over to pull a pan of cookies from the oven when she felt it . . . a strong sensation, an urging.

She needed to pray for Mac.

She set the cookies on the cooling rack and moved into the living room. Ivan padded beside her, watching her with that intent gaze. She sat down, and he situated himself beside her, leaning against her leg as though offering his support.

Laying her hand on the husky's velvety head, Kylie closed her eyes. . . .

CHAPTER
Fifteen

Let earth receive her king . . . Let every heart prepare him room . . .

The words echoed over and over in Mackenzie's mind, accompanied by a multitude of burning questions.

How do I do that, God, when I'm so full of anger, so full of fear? How do I receive you? How do I prepare my heart? What if I don't want to do either one?

The last question struck him hard, like a sledgehammer pounding the middle of his chest. He believed in God, didn't he?

"Yes," he whispered, knowing it was true.

He trusted God, didn't he?

He opened his mouth, but no response came. And as he considered the question, he saw a huge, gaping darkness within himself. Fear, sharp and piercing, sliced through him. *How can I trust you*—desperation flooded him—*if you take Lindsay away from me, how can I ever trust you?*

He waited, hoping, praying for a response. But there was only silence. And the fear grew.

The streets were dark and silent when he pulled up his driveway and into his garage. He stepped from his car feeling more weary, more bruised and abandoned than he'd ever felt in his life.

Are you there, God?

He moved inside, slipping out of his coat and letting it fall to the floor. He started down the hallway to his room . . . then stopped, startled by something drifting in the air. What? He turned toward the kitchen and saw a strange light in the living room, a glow of some kind. Moving as though in a dream, he forced himself forward, and what he saw took his breath away.

The tree, Lindsay's tree, stood there, resplendent in ornaments, tinsel, and delicate white lights. Gifts of all shapes and sizes were wrapped in colorful Christmas paper and piled beneath the full branches. The soft strains of Christmas carols floated around him as he moved toward the tree.

A cool nose nudged his hand, and he looked down. Ivan stood there beside him, as though he'd been waiting for Mackenzie to come home. The dog licked his hand, then fell into step beside Mackenzie as he walked to the tree. He fingered the needles, inhaled the scent of evergreen, drank in the delicate beauty of the ornaments.

It was real. He wasn't going crazy. Somehow, suddenly he was a teenager again, standing in his aunts' living room, surrounded by Lindsay's magical Christmas.

His knees went weak, and he went to sit on the couch. Ivan followed, settling at his feet. Mackenzie leaned back against the couch cushion, intensely aware of . . . something. A presence.

"Jesus . . . Jesus, please be here."

His gaze fell on the Bible Lindsay had placed on the coffee table. He reached out and lifted it, opening to one of the sections Kylie had marked. He reached up to turn on a lamp, then began to read.

I will strengthen you and help you. . . . My help comes from the Lord, the Maker of heaven and earth. He will not let your foot slip—he who watches over you. . . . the Lord will keep you from all harm—he will watch over your life; the Lord will watch over your coming and going both now and forever more. . . . God is our refuge and strength,

*an ever-present help in trouble. . . . If you make the Most High your
dwelling—even the Lord, who is my refuge—then no harm will befall
you, no disaster will come near your tent. For he will command his angels concerning you to guard you in all your ways; they will lift you up
in their hands, so that you will not strike your foot against a stone. . . .*

Understanding swept through Mackenzie, wonder washed
over his heart, filling him with the sense that he was not alone,
that God was, indeed, in that very room, touching him, loving him.

Let every heart prepare him room . . .

The carol rang through him again, and this time Mackenzie
understood.

God was present.

He always had been. Day in and day out, the Almighty was
there, watching over his children, involved in their lives. In *his*
life. Scenes from Mackenzie's life played over in his mind—his
aunts and their solid, everyday faith, Lindsay and her unflagging
determination to draw him back to real faith, Kylie and all she
had shared with him in the past weeks.

Even Ivan and the laughter he'd brought into Mackenzie's life.

It was all from God. For him. He just hadn't been willing
to see it.

Tears coursed down his cheeks as he faced the truth: After
his parents died, he convinced himself that it was better, safer, to
not care. To keep his heart shielded, protected. Against anything
that could hurt him.

And so he'd pulled away. Convinced himself that order and
control were his protection. But they hadn't protected him.

They'd become a prison.

They'd formed a wall between him and the people he cared
about. Lindsay. The aunts.

God.

It was so much easier to believe God was distant, unconcerned about the details of his life. But what was easy wasn't

what was true. He saw that now. These last weeks with Kylie and Ivan . . . seeing Lindsay in that hospital bed . . .

He couldn't lie to himself anymore. God did care, intimately, about the details of his life. About the big things and the small.

Mackenzie bowed his head. "I'm sorry. I couldn't see you, couldn't make room for you because I was so sure I was right. So sure I knew the truth. Forgive me. Father, please, forgive me."

Do not be dismayed, for I am your God.

The assurance resonated within him. Slow but certain, peace spread through him. He was not alone. Nor was Lindsay. They were both being held in loving, all-powerful hands.

He jumped up from the couch, startling Ivan who had been dozing beside him. He knelt and hugged the Siberian. "Did you know you're an angel sent to guide me?"

Ivan tilted his head as though considering the question, then delivered a lick to Mackenzie's face. He laughed, rubbing the dog's head. Ivan, Lindsay, even the old man whose words had so haunted him. All angels in God's hands. "And so was someone else. Someone I need to talk with."

A small knock sounded on the sliding doors, and Mackenzie turned to them. A quick glance at the clock on the mantel told him it was close to two in the morning. He moved to pull the blinds back—and his joy multiplied. He unlocked the doors, slid them open, and reached out a hand.

Kylie laid her hand in his and stepped inside. Her glorious hair was pulled back with a Christmas ribbon, her eyes were shining with tears. And love. He felt it almost like a physical blow. It washed over him, warming him inside and out, leaving his head spinning with the intensity of the experience.

"I'm sorry to come by so late. But I saw the light and wanted to see if there was any news on Lindsay."

"You did all this, didn't you?" He indicated the decorated room, and a slight flush filled her cheeks. She nodded.

His gaze held hers. "Why?"

"I wanted you to come home to Christmas."

He lifted a hand to touch her cheek. She placed her hand over his, her gaze never leaving his. For a moment he couldn't speak.

"You're in love with her!" The accusation rang in his head, and he said it again, this time as the truth. He was completely, totally, irrevocably in love with Kylie Hawk. With her glowing eyes, her laughter, her flowing hair, her sweet spirit . . . every crazy, illogical, absurd thing about her called to him.

All he had to do was answer.

"It worked." He cupped her face. "I came home. To Christmas, and to God."

Joy lit her face. "Oh, Mackenzie, I'm so glad!"

"Mac." His lips twitched at the surprise on her face. "I much prefer Mac. But now I need to know something. I need to know if I can come home . . . to you."

Her lips parted in a silent *O,* and it took all his will to not kiss her. But he needed to finish this. To tell her what was in his heart. "My life has been crazy over the past few weeks, but one thing remained constant. Seeing you, talking with you, spending time with you . . . that brought me joy."

He took in every detail of her face. "*You* brought me joy. And a sense of peace. Tonight, God brought my faith and my heart back to life. He showed me that my faith belongs to him. And my heart"—he placed his hand over her heart—"belongs to you. I love you, Kylie. I don't want another moment to pass by without you knowing how I feel."

He saw her answer in her eyes, read it in her face, but he still wanted to hear it. She didn't disappoint. "And I love you. When God put you in my heart, I thought it was *for you.* To help you see him. But now I know it was for both of us."

He nodded. "Immanuel."

She smiled, understanding. "God with us. Now and forever."

He drew her close, cradled her in his arms, and rested his chin on her head. "I don't know what will happen with Lindsay. But I do know God is here, with us. With me. And I'll be all right because I have him. And I have you." Glancing up, his eyes came to rest on a small sprig suspended from a string. He looked down at her with a grin. "I see you didn't forget the most important decoration of all."

She colored. "It isn't really Christmas without mistletoe."

He lowered his head until his lips met hers—and as her arms slid around his neck, he could almost swear he heard angels singing.

"*Glory to God in the highest, and on earth, peace, good will to men!*"

CHAPTER
Sixteen

"Well, boy, your idea worked."

Brendan Hawk leaned back in his chair. "Of course it did."

Gramps swatted at him. "Don't be so smug. Leaving that dog on Mac's doorstep could just as easily have backfired."

"With my sister's love of huskies? I don't think so, Gramps. And I only had to go to four shelters to find a Siberian."

Brendan moved over to throw another log on the fire pit. They were sitting in his grandparents' backyard, a roaring fire keeping them warm as they sipped hot chocolate. "Well, it worked out fine, for your sister and for the dog."

"And for Mac." Thank heaven. Brendan would never admit it to Gramps, but he'd been worried. When he tied the husky to the railing outside Mac's door, he'd figured the man would take the dog inside as soon as he saw it. That's what Brendan would have done.

Mac was another story. After the third time Mac opened the door and yelled at the husky, Brendan had pretty well decided it was time to give up and take the poor husky home himself. But just as he was about to do so, Mac finally gave in.

"Well, that wraps up this operation." Gramps tossed on another log, watching the sparks fly into the air.

"You trying to burn down the neighborhood?"

He grinned at Brendan. "Nope. Just like a good fire. Especially on a cold January night."

A small, burning twig had bounced out of the fire pit and landed at Brendan's feet. He put it out with the toe of his boot. "So I hear Mac's sister is doing better."

"That's what Kylie said. She and Mac have been spending a lot of time with his sister, helping her through her physical therapy. Girl's lucky to be alive."

Brendan cupped his hands around the warmth of his cocoa mug. "I'll have to meet her one of these days. Kylie says Lindsay is something special."

"So she tells me."

Brendan looked at his grandfather. Something about the tone of his voice . . . "Gramps, what are you up to?"

The man shrugged and poked a stick into the fire. "Not a thing, boy."

Brendan leaned forward. "My life is fine as is."

"Of course it is."

"I don't need you to find me a woman."

"Of course you don't."

"Gramps!"

The old man looked at Brendan, a broad grin on his face. "Don't worry, boy. I'm not planning anything for you."

Brendan searched his grandfather's face. Gramps was an old schemer, but this much was true: he didn't lie. So if he said he wasn't planning anything . . .

He settled back in his chair, watching the smoke rise into the night. His mom was settled, his sister was engaged. The two women he loved most in the world were happy. And he had Gramps's promise that the old man wasn't going to try and meddle in his life. All was right with the world.

He lifted his mug to his grandfather. "Mission accomplished, Gramps."

Gramps raised his mug as well. "Indeed it is."

Brendan hesitated. Gramps promised. So that smug smile on the old schemer's face had nothing to do with him.

He sighed and sipped his cocoa.

Time to stop worrying and relax.

Valentine Surprise

Slowly, steadily, surely, the time approaches when the vision will be fulfilled. If it seems slow, do not despair, for these things will surely come to pass. Just be patient! They will not be overdue a single day!

(Habakkuk 2:3, The Living Bible)

MISSION CONTROL A

"Kylie St. Clair, you promised not to meddle."

Kylie couldn't help it. She smiled. It still gave her shivers whenever she heard her new name. Especially when her new husband said it. She shook water from the head of lettuce she'd been rinsing in the sink, then carried it to the bowl waiting on the kitchen island. "I know. But this isn't really meddling."

Mac didn't respond. His raised brows did the talking for him as he took another tomato and placed it on the cutting board.

Kylie dried and then tore the lettuce leaves into the bowl. "I just think it's time Brendan and Lindsay met. After all, we've been married over a month now."

"Too bad Brendan had to leave the wedding right after the ceremony. That would have been the perfect time and place." Mac scooped the cubes of tomato, added them to the bowl, then set to work on a red onion.

"I know. But Brendan had that trip to a new gallery set up months before. And we did decide to get married kind of last-minute."

He came to stand behind her and wrapped those strong arms around her. "So I didn't want to wait. So sue me—hey! Knock it off, beast." He swatted a hand at the Siberian husky, who'd shoved his way between the two of them.

"Ivan just wants his share of the hug, that's all."

"Hmm." He planted a kiss on her neck and went back to chopping the onion. "He needs to take a lesson from Zsuzsi and not interfere when I hug my wife."

Kylie smiled at her dog, sprawled out in the middle of the living room floor. "Face it, hon. Komondors are just more laid back than Siberians. Now, back to my brother and your sister."

"Kylie—"

She lifted a hand to forestall further objections. "Remember, Brendan came to me. He asked my advice."

Mac cast his gaze upward. "Foolish, foolish man." He looked at Kylie. "And, I might add, he only asked after you inserted yourself into the situation."

Kylie tossed a piece of lettuce at him. "My brother needed me. And all I did was tell him what I thought he should try. Just a simple suggestion, that's all—"

"You sent the man to her door, Kylie."

"And if, in the process, they hit it off the way I think they will, well, all the better. I just want to provide them with the opportunity."

Mac picked up the tongs and tossed the salad, then added dressing. "Wouldn't it be easier just to invite them over for dinner?"

"That would never work. Lindsay would know we were setting her up. And you know she's sworn off dating."

He laughed. "And you don't think she'll know it anyway."

A slow grin spread across her lips. "Not if I don't tell Lindsay that Brendan is coming."

Mac's eyes narrowed. "Hold on. I thought you told your brother you'd call Lindsay and let her know to expect him."

She went to him, silencing his objection with a kiss.

"Well"—he managed when she finally pulled back a bit—"when you put it that way . . ."

It was her turn to laugh. She rested her cheek against that broad chest. "Your sister is in serious need of the element of surprise. If I warn her, she'll just think up reasons to send Brendan home as soon as he arrives. But this way . . ." She sighed. "I just want them to be as happy as we are."

"Hmm." His voice resonated against her ear. "I know. And I promise I won't interfere with your plan."

She hugged him. "It will work out, Mac. I just know it. This is going to be perfect."

MISSION CONTROL B

"So, sisters, are we all in agreement?" Cecelia Coulter added a splash of cream to her tea, then lifted the china cup to her lips.

Ophelia and Amelia looked first at each other, then back to her.

"Yes"—Amelia brushed a cookie crumb from her skirt—"I believe your plan is the most efficacious solution to the problem."

"Not," Ophelia was quick to add, "that we consider dear Lindsay a problem."

"Of course not." Cecelia sipped her tea. "But the fact that such a talented—"

"—beautiful—"

"and loving—"

"young woman," Cecelia went on, not even breaking stride at her sisters' insertions, "has yet to find a man who realizes what a gem she is . . . well, it's just not acceptable. And since time is marching on, I do believe it's wise for us to step in. Especially after speaking with Kylie's grandfather at the wedding."

Amelia sighed. "It was a lovely wedding, wasn't it?"

Though Cecelia didn't often share her youngest—by five minutes—triplet's bent for romanticism, she had to agree. "It was, indeed. Mackenzie and Kylie seemed very well suited."

"And so happy." Amelia sighed again.

Cecelia set her tea cup in the saucer. "I have to confess, it was inspirational hearing how Kylie's grandfather managed to bring just the right people into his daughter's and granddaughter's lives. And to see how content they both are now."

"Which is exactly what we want for Lindsay." Trust Ophelia to get them back on track. "So, Cecelia, you've vetted this young man, I assume?"

Cecelia pinned Ophelia with a look. The oldest of the three by ten minutes, Ophelia always felt the need to ensure her sisters had done proper due diligence. "Of course. I spoke to him myself, and his answers to my questions were more than satisfactory. He's intelligent, trustworthy, and kind."

"Good heavens, Celie, you make him sound like a German shepherd." Amelia's nose wrinkled. "Is he handsome?"

She nodded. "Yes, I believe so. But not so handsome that it's off-putting."

"Excellent." Ophelia took another cookie from the plate in front of her. "Now, how did Kylie's grandfather put it . . . ?" She frowned, then her face cleared and she smiled. "Ah yes, Operation Lindsay is hereby activated."

Amelia pressed her hands over her heart. "Oh, this is going to be perfect!"

Operation Lindsay

CHAPTER

One

Roses are red,
Violets are blue,
My gift is a date especially for you.
Dress casual, be ready by 10:32—
He'll be on your doorstep.
Love, Auntie Two

Lindsay St. Clair stared at the valentine in her hand.

Smiling cherubs and bright pink and red hearts shouted up at her. She couldn't believe Aunt Cecelia had bought anything so garish, even a greeting card. But it was the so-called poem written in her aunt's neat hand that held her attention.

"Cecelia"—she read it through again—"this had better be a joke."

She spun toward the phone. Aunt Celie was just going to have to call this thing off! No way was she—

Her thoughts were cut short when her foot encountered a solid object: Doofus, her snoozing basset hound, grunted and pushed himself up, which only made him a slightly taller obstacle for her scrambling feet. The dog accompanied her headlong tumble with a sonorous howl. Normally Lindsay found Doofie's bellows hilarious. Low and oddly melodious, they seldom failed to elicit a grin from her. This time, however, she added her own howl, filling her apartment with an impromptu duet.

"Aaarooooooo! Aaaroooo!" Doof sang out.

"Aaaaaaaahhhhhh!" she accompanied as she bounced off the back of the sofa and landed, face down, on the carpet.

She lay there, absorbing the shock of the fall, wondering if she'd broken anything. A cold nose pressed heavy snuffles against her ear. Lindsay couldn't help it . . . she grinned. Sometimes Doof sounded more like a walking sinus infection than a dog.

Groaning, she rolled onto her back. Doof responded to this sign of life with a glad wag of his thick tail—which set his entire hindquarters wagging—and lumbered forward to lay his heavy head on her chest. As one long ear fell over her face, Lindsay laughed and hugged the animal close.

"Fifty-five solid pounds of pure love, aren't ya, fella?"

Doofus wagged his hindquarters harder, ecstatic that she was not only alive but still able to serve her most important role in life: paying homage to him.

Lindsay patted the dog's broad head and scooted into a sitting position, leaning against the sofa. Doofus pressed against her leg, gazing up at her with those sweet, droopy brown eyes. His tail thumped the carpet.

She hugged him again. "Who could resist such devotion?" She laughed. "I'll tell you, Doof, men could take a lesson—"

Men. Oh, good heavens. Celie's ridiculous valentine.

Lindsay slid onto the couch and reached out to grab the phone. She dialed Celie's number. One ring, two, and then—

"Salutations!" Celie's refined voice greeted her, but before Lindsay could say anything the voice went on. "This is the Williams residence."

Ugh. Voicemail. Lindsay hated voicemail. She tapped her foot.

"We are unable to speak with you at present, but if you'd be so kind as to leave a message, we'll return your call in as expeditious a manner as possible."

"Cecelia Rose—" she began in frustration, but she was cut off again.

"And if this is Lindsay, you might as well hang up. I refuse to talk with you until tomorrow. And, no, I will not call it off. And don't try to appeal to Amelia or Ophelia for aid. We all think you need to do this. Besides, this man is quite perfect for you. So go get ready and, for heaven's sake, have *fun!*"

Lindsay barely heard the beep that followed this pronouncement. She just stared at the phone in her hand as though it had grown a head and a set of horns.

"Have fun?" she sputtered. "Have *fun?*" She slammed the phone back into the cradle, taking a perverse pleasure in the thought that the sound probably recorded and would make her aunt's ear ring.

So the aunts thought she needed to do this, did they? Well, who appointed them Grand Poobah Decision Makers in her life?

You know they only want you to be happy.

"I know." Lindsay sighed and settled back against the soft cushions. "And I want the same thing, Lord. You know I do." Her gaze wandered to the pictures on her fireplace mantel and came to rest on her aunts' pictures. Lindsay stood and went to study them.

The Three Aunties, with a soft "A," as Lindsay and her brother, Mac, called them (much to their chagrin), were triplets. Though fifteen years older than Lindsay, they'd been born when Lindsay's mother was ten, a surprise to all concerned. As was their prodigious intelligence. It hadn't taken long for Lindsay's grandparents to realize they had three brainiacs on their hands.

Perhaps that was part of the reason they seemed such worlds apart from Lindsay.

Ophelia, Cecelia, and Amelia all boasted a peaches-and-cream complexion and blue eyes. All tall and willowy, and possessed of long, flowing hair and angelic features, they were a sight to behold, together or apart. Celie was a physicist; Phelia, a law researcher; and Melia, a senior professor of mathematics and statistical methods at the university. All wonderful, well-paying, judicious professions. Not "jobs," mind you, but "professions."

Interestingly enough, all three held a particular dislike of anything domestic, be it cooking, cleaning, sewing—even decorating their homes was left to "someone with a flair for such things."

Namely, Lindsay.

She sighed. If she'd had a choice, she would have opted for being brilliant, like her aunts and her brother. Then, maybe, she wouldn't feel so . . . well, lonely all the time. It wasn't much fun to be the family oddity. And it wasn't just on the personality side that the three didn't mesh with her. Lindsay was different from them in almost every way.

Shorter than The Three Aunts, she was more athletic in build than willowy. And her hair shone a deep auburn, which made her stand out from her aunts like a sore thumb. Still, she thought her hair color went rather well with her forest-green eyes. As for her *profession*, well, it was something she absolutely loved, but it stymied The Three: Lindsay was a creative consultant. And though her aunts didn't understand what she did— or why—they all were proud of the fact that Lindsay's work was in high demand across the country.

If only they could be proud of her because she was doing what she loved, rather than because she was successful.

She longed to share her dreams with her aunts, to share her deepest feelings and hopes for the future. But she'd learned early on that The Three weren't particularly nurturing concerning that side of their niece. Oh, they were creative in their own ways. In very . . . *linear* ways. But when it came to Lindsay's everything's-possible, just-close-your-eyes-and-you're-there manner of thinking, their minds didn't work that way. She remembered once, when she was quite young, going to her aunts and asking, "What if we're really the reflections in the mirror, only *thinking* we're the real thing?" The Three gave her blank looks and shook their heads in that pitying, at-least-she's-a-pretty-child way. They loved her, she knew that. But they were more comfortable with each other.

That was probably why Lindsay had formed such a solid friendship with Kylie Hawk. No, she corrected herself with a smile, Kylie St. Clair. Her friend was now her sister. OK, sister-in-law. But Lindsay didn't bother much with technicalities.

Kylie was her sister, plain and simple.

She'd felt like her sister long before she and Mac got married. It was such a delight to Lindsay to find someone with as creative a bent as she had. Someone who understood the way Lindsay thought.

Unlike The Three Aunties. When it came down to it, about the only thing she shared with her aunts was their faith in God. Lindsay would always be grateful that her aunts had been devout in their faith, had insisted that she and Mac attend church. The aunts did all they could to help Lindsay and her brother develop a sincere relationship with God. And they'd succeeded. Lindsay always knew she could ask her aunts to pray for her or even with her. And, for that moment, they would be connected.

But it seldom happened other times.

Lindsay thus had focused her energies on finding outlets for her creativity. Painting, writing, photography, sculpture, origami—it all fascinated her. Many of her favorite creations were displayed in her spacious apartment, giving it a personality that was a delightful mix of gracious beauty and lighthearted whimsy.

In the past several years, cooking had become one of her favorite pastimes. And though The Three Aunts found Lindsay peculiar, they were delighted whenever she brought her culinary abilities to their kitchens.

In fact, when she went to cook dinner a few weeks ago for Ophelia, it was the first time her aunt had ever ventured into that particular room of her own house.

"Oh, my," Ophelia had remarked as she surveyed the kitchen. "It's yellow. How . . . cheerful."

Lindsay shook her head. Her aunts were, well, unique.

And ridiculously determined to see her settled. In other words, married.

Her gaze drifted to the collection of wedding photos on her fireplace mantel, traveling from one to the next . . . what was that old saying? "Always a bridesmaid, never a bride." Yes, that was it. And that was the story of her thirty-five years of life. She'd been in so many weddings of so many friends, she felt like a professional bridesmaid.

She rose and went to pick up one of the pictures, the one of Terri, a friend from high school. Terri's eyes positively shone with happiness as she gazed up into her groom's smiling face. As for the groom, he looked as though he'd won the lottery.

It was the same in all the photos. Her friends were blessed in love. Each had found the man of her dreams—the proverbial tall and handsome, as well as devoted to God and family, in that order. As for Lindsay . . . well, she had Doofus.

That counted for something, didn't it?

Lindsay glanced at the photo again. The Three Aunties had known Terri, too, and never failed to comment on the fact that Lindsay's high school friend and her husband only grew happier with each year. That they lived a lovely life in a lovely home, complete with their two lovely children.

It was enough to make a person sick.

Lindsay set the picture back in its place with a loud thump and turned to Doofus. "I love my aunts. You know I do," she told him.

Doofie gazed up at her. His tail gave one hesitant thump on the carpet—a sign he wasn't sure if she was upset or not.

Well, that was only fair. She wasn't sure, either.

"They just can't wait for me to be in a state of marital bliss." She paced back and forth in front of the fireplace.

Doofie's head swayed back and forth as he followed her movements.

"It's not like I haven't tried!" Lindsay heard the slightly hysterical tone in her voice, but she didn't care. "I mean"—she jerked to a halt and planted her hands firmly on her hips, staring at Doofus—"I was practically a candidate for the Queen of Dating, for Pete's sake! Well, wasn't I? Think about it. How many dates did I go on?"

"Rowf!"

"Exactly!" Lindsay's arms flailed around. "About a million! And how many of them were enjoyable?"

"Rowwruf!"

"That's right! Zero. Zilch. Nada. Zippo." The last word surprised her by coming out as a squeak because of her suddenly tight throat. She clenched her teeth. She was not going to cry. She moved to the sofa, dropped down on it, and pulled her knees up to her chin. Doof scooted toward her and laid his own chin on the couch beside her. Swallowing hard, she looked down at him.

"I tried, Doofer. I really did. I prayed about it and I trusted God to bring Mr. Right into my life. But all I ever met were Mr. Wrongs." She choked back a sob. "Or Mr. Not-on-Your-Lifes. There just wasn't anyone out there who . . . fit." She leaned her head back and blinked rapidly against the tears. "And I just got tired of it all, you know? Of meeting, and getting to know each other, and trying to sort the image from the reality. I got tired of the games . . . especially since I'm so rotten at them."

The tears won out. They ran down her face in hot streams. Good grief. Pathetic.

A small whimper drew her attention. Doof looked for all the world as though he was about to bawl right along with her. The incongruous thought made her smile despite the depression threatening to settle over her.

"Declaring a moratorium on dating was the smartest thing I ever did. I know The Three Aunts were horrified, but that last date was sooooo bad! Do you remember?" She leaned down close to Doofus's ear. "Remember . . . Gary?"

Doofus jerked back with a growl, and Lindsay laughed. It worked every time. Gary Brower—the last man with whom her well-intentioned aunts had set her up—was more than a disaster.

He'd been the nail in the coffin of her dating life.

"You're both creative types," Celie had said. "You have a great deal in common."

"Creative, eh? What does he do?" Lindsay had been skeptical. The Three Aunts' definition of *creative* and her own were worlds apart.

"He's an editor." Phelia spoke with such confidence.

"And a writer, I think," Melia added.

This caught Lindsay's interest, then—

"For a computer company." Celie's victorious smile flashed. "He works on books of some sort, to guide people as they work with their software or hardware."

Lindsay's heart sank. "He writes . . . computer manuals."

"Right." Celie beamed at her. "Sounds perfect, doesn't he?"

"And you barely even notice those thick glasses." Melia's wide, innocent eyes were so sincere.

Phelia frowned. "Though you'd think he could find frames in some color other than black. . . ."

Lindsay should have stopped it right there. She knew she should have. But she didn't have the heart to pop her aunts' hopeful bubble. Instead, she'd suffered through two dates with Mr. Creative. Not only had he bored her to tears with detailed descriptions of the importance in society of algorithms, but he'd taken one look at Doofus and started to sneeze.

"Allergic," he managed from behind a handful of Kleenex. "To dogs. Unsanitary beadsts. Can'd imagine why anyone would hab one id their hombe." He sneezed again, then fixed her with a look of pure censure. "Do you hab any idea the bacteria one finds id a dog's mouth?"

Doofus had felt the same dislike. All Lindsay had to do was mention Gary's name, and the usually easygoing basset growled. And snorted. And—she would swear to this in court—sneezed.

All three had been relieved when Lindsay told Gary she didn't think things were working out between them.

The Three Aunts, on the other hand, had been less than pleased. Especially when Lindsay informed them that she was finished. She wasn't playing the dating game any longer.

"Are you *insane*?" Celie had screeched the words—a surprisingly emotional display. "You'll never meet Mr. Right hiding in your apartment!"

"Cecelia, please." Ophelia had stepped between them. "I'm sure Lindsay isn't at all serious."

"Yes, I am."

Amelia planted those elegant hands on her tiny hips. "Do you truly believe this is what God wants for you?"

Cecelia brushed her youngest triplet aside. "Do you truly want to spend the rest of your life with no one to talk to but your *dog*?"

"He's a better conversationalist than Gary was!" Lindsay shot back. Seeing her aunt's crestfallen expression, she went to put her arm around her slim shoulders. "Hey, you guys, come on. I've given Mr. Right plenty of time to show. Apparently he's not interested. And neither am I. Not anymore. As for what God wants, well, I don't know. But I trust he'll let me know if I'm off base."

Celie had stared at her. "You're hopeless."

She'd met this with her usual equanimity—she'd stuck her tongue out at Celie, then kissed each of The Three and headed for home.

A year and a half had passed since then, and Lindsay was enjoying every minute of the emotional peace and quiet that came from not being caught up in the search for a soul mate.

As for those nights when she cried into her pillow, aching for someone to talk with, for someone who could share her heart and hopes, well, that was just the price one paid for giving up childish fantasies.

Lindsay glanced at the mantel clock. Almost nine-thirty. Her valentine date would be here in an hour.

"Ohhhhhhhh . . . rats!" It looked as though The Three were going to have the last laugh this time. They'd suckered some poor guy into playing valentine date, knowing full well their Lindsay would never just take off or not answer the door and leave the man standing there.

She sat for a few moments, thinking, then an idea began to dawn. No, she couldn't . . . could she?

The truth shall set you free.

Lindsay felt goose bumps as the oft-repeated words of Scripture floated through her mind. "Really, Lord? Can it really be that easy?"

As if in answer, verse after verse flooded her heart: *When the Spirit of truth comes, he will guide you into all truth. . . . Hold to the truth in love, becoming more and more in every way like Christ . . . under his direction the whole body is fitted together perfectly. . . . Give me an understanding heart. . . .*

She closed her eyes, letting the words wash over her. The answer was so simple. Why hadn't she seen it before? She jumped up from the couch, startling poor Doofus snoring away beside her.

"Sorry, Doof, old boy." She leaned down to plant a kiss on his sloping snout, then cupped his droopy face in her hands. "It just feels good to know what to do, you know?"

With a little jig, she turned and headed for her room to get ready and to make a few phone calls in preparation—giggling all the way down the hall.

CHAPTER
Two

He couldn't believe he'd agreed to this.

He should have known better. Arrangements like this never worked. Especially not with women. If Brendan had learned anything in life, it was that he should just stick to his art and his motorcycles. That's where he felt confident, in control.

With women . . . well, all he ever felt was used.

Too many times he'd gone out with a woman only to find that what she was looking for was someone to "take her away." But he had yet to find a woman who wanted to go where he did, do what he enjoyed, and just spend time getting to know each other.

He'd been foolish enough to believe he'd found her once. He felt his teeth clench as Gwen's image drifted into his mind. He pushed it—and the anger it always brought with it—away. He wouldn't be that foolish again.

Truth be told, he was tired. Here he was, nearly thirty years old, and still going out on dates. Kylie, his younger sister, kept reassuring him that an older man was a much-desired commodity on the dating scene. Somehow that did little to encourage him. If anything, it just made him more tired.

Be honest, a small inner voice chided him. *There is one woman you'd like to get to know.*

The image of her face drifted into his mind, and he pushed it away. Yes, he was interested. Was he going to do anything about it? Not likely. Better to just watch from afar and imagine her to be wonderful than to meet her and find out she was just one more disappointment.

That's what he told himself, anyway. Until last weekend, when Kylie had insisted on accompanying him to the park. She said it was to get some fresh air, but he knew better. She wanted to scope out the woman who'd caught her brother's attention.

He spent the walk to the park informing his sister he wasn't interested in meeting the woman. Just that he found her . . . kinda, well, intriguing. They sat on a bench—the same one he'd sat on numerous times in hopes of seeing the woman and her dog go by—and waited. Sure enough, she showed, basset hound in tow. Brendan pointed her out. His sister's eyes widened as she turned to look at him.

"You're kidding."

He'd figured that would be her response. "Afraid not."

She turned back to watch the woman, who'd stopped to let a group of children pet her dog. "Brendan, that's Lindsay. Mac's sister. You saw her at the wedding."

"Exactly."

His sister's mouth formed a little O. "Are you telling me that all it took was seeing her, and you were—"

"Like I said, intrigued. If you must know, captivated." He leaned back, resting his arms on the back of the park bench. "That's what I'm saying. Crazy, I know."

"Not so much."

He glanced at her, saw understanding in her eyes. "You and Mac?"

"Well, not quite that fast, but yes." She pursed her lips. "You know, she does attend the same church Mac and I go to. You'd have met her by now if you'd only come to church—"

"No, thanks." He didn't like cutting her off, but he wasn't willing to get into the usual debate. "I love God with my whole heart. It's his people I can't stand."

"Hmmm, well, she's one of them. So are you sure you want to meet her?"

"No."

"Brendan!"

"I told you I wasn't interested in—"

She'd just waved his words away. "Protest all you want, but I know you too well. Besides, you've done nothing but talk about this woman for the last month and a half. Now, all we need is a plan. . . ."

He hadn't heard anything more from Kylie for a week, so he figured that was it. Determined to get on with life, he immersed himself in his work, resigned to the idea of being a bachelor from now to eternity. Sure, God said it wasn't good for a man to be alone. But it wasn't good to be disappointed over and over either.

Then, a few days ago, Kylie came up with a wild scheme. And, for some crazy reason, he'd agreed.

"Crazy is the word, all right," he muttered to himself now as he stood with his sister in a flower shop, arms outstretched.

"It's not crazy at all." Kylie shoved the flowers he'd purchased into his arms. "It'll work, Brendan. Trust me."

"Yeah, right." He peered at her over the blossoms. "And why should I do that? Oh, wait. Let me guess. Because you're a woman?"

She gave him a truly saccharine smile. "And all our friends call you dense. Why, they don't know you at all, do they, brother dear?"

"Hmmm." He headed for the door. "I don't know about dense, but sucker certainly would seem appropriate."

"You *can* do this. You can *do* this. *You* can—"

Ding-Dong.

Lindsay's pep talk came to an abrupt end. She was standing in the living room, staring into her favorite antique mirror. She shot a quick glance at the mantel clock. No fair! It was only 10:10! He was twenty-two minutes early—

Ding-Dong.

Her eyes flew back to her reflection in the mirror, noting the sudden panic on her features. She knew she should answer the door, but she couldn't move. She closed her eyes. *Please, God, just have him go away. Please, please—*

Ding-Dong.

"Rowf! Arrrroooooooooo!"

Her eyes flew open. No! The sound of Doofus in full voice spurred her into action, and she raced for the front door. If the basset really got going, the din of his howling could shake the walls. Her neighbors would not be amused.

"Hush, Doofus!" She scooted him away from the door and pulled it open.

The dog wasn't listening; he was caught up in the heat of the hunt now. "Arrrrooorrooooooo!"

The pictures on the walls started to vibrate.

"Listen, Doofus! I said knock it *off*!"

Startled at her raised voice, Doofus sat down and gaped at her—and at the same moment, a deep voice commented, "Sorry. No one answered the first few rings so I thought I'd try one more time."

Lindsay felt her face flame as she turned to apologize, but the words died mid-utterance. There, in front of her, was the most beautifully huge bouquet of flowers she'd ever seen. The fragrance was heavenly.

"Wow." All she could think of.

A deep chuckle came from behind the blooms. "I take it that means you like them?"

"Oh!" Startled, she stepped forward and reached out. "Here, I'll take those."

"I—"

"I know. You want to get going." Obviously, considering how early he was. "But do me a favor and just hang on for a minute."

He hesitated, and she took the opportunity to pluck the gorgeous bouquet from his arms. "Let me get these in water. It won't take a minute." She carried them to the kitchen. "Just wait right there."

Carefully, she placed the flowers on the counter, then buried her face in the fragrant blooms. Inhaling deeply, she smiled.

Well, at least he knew how to start things off right.

"These are really beautiful," she called as she found a vase and filled it with water.

"I'm glad you like them."

His voice was nice. Deep, resonant, and kind of warm. Like he was smiling.

She arranged the flowers in the vase, then carried it to the dining room table. She grabbed her jacket and headed back to the doorway.

What?

Her valentine date was kneeling down, petting an ecstatic Doofus. The basset was leaning his heavy body against the man's leg, gazing up at him with an expression he usually reserved for her.

Lindsay didn't know whether to be pleased or jealous.

Her date glanced up as she approached, and her steps slowed. Very nice looking, striking in a rugged sort of way. Kneeling there in his black leather jacket, a motorcycle helmet on the floor beside him, he reminded her a bit of a dark-haired, dark-eyed version of Harrison Ford in his Indiana Jones incarnation. Especially when he smiled. He had a slow smile that was lopsided and utterly endearing—

Stop it. She occupied herself with putting on her denim jacket. *You don't even know the man's name, and he's endearing?* She tugged at the bottom of the jacket, squared her shoulders, and put her hand out.

"Lindsay St. Clair, but please, call me Lindsay. And the beast at your feet is Doofus."

There was that lopsided smile again. "Great dog." He gave Doof one last pat before he stood to take her hand. "It's nice to meet you."

"Thanks. It's nice to meet you, too."

His strong fingers all but engulfed hers. At the contact, an almost electrical jolt shot through her, and her eyes lifted to meet his, startled. Something flickered in those brown depths.

So he'd felt it, too.

She lowered her eyes and noted how Doof had managed to collapse across the man's feet. "Doof, go to your bed."

With a woebegone glance at her, the dog rolled away from his resting place and lumbered over to the dog bed near the fireplace.

A deep chuckle drew her attention back to her date. She really liked the way he laughed, and how his eyes crinkled, as though they performed that action on a regular basis.

She hadn't realized she was staring at him until he cleared his throat.

"I'm Brendan."

His expression was enigmatic, as though he wasn't sure about something. Her calm fled. Was she already falling short of his expectations?

Hold to the truth in love. . . .

Right. The truth.

She drew a steadying breath, and then plunged in. "OK, let's go." She moved past him and pulled the door shut behind them. She started down the hallway, then stopped when she realized he was still standing there, not moving, just watching her, a bemused smile on his face.

She marched back to him, leaned down to pick up the helmet, plunked it in his hands, and then took his arm, tugging until he fell in step with her.

"Are we leaving?" His question was filled with barely re-strained laughter.

She glanced at him. Planting her hands on her hips, she faced him, lifting her chin. "I'm sorry, Brendan. I'm sure this seems a bit odd—"

"Just a bit."

She raised an imperious brow. This was *not* a laughing matter. "It's really very simple. I don't know what you had in mind for today, but we're going to do this my way, or not at all."

His only response was a slight lifting of his brows. Good. A man who knew the value of silence.

"So here's the plan. We spend one day together. Just one. We don't waste our time or your money with a series of dates trying to figure out if we have anything in common. The only investment we make is one day, morning 'til evening, doing things together and being who we really are. No games, no pretense, no putting on a show to catch each other's interest."

She met his eyes, hoping he saw she was sincere, not crazy. "Come on, Brendan, admit it. Aren't you sick and tired of all the games we're expected to play when it comes to dating?"

A response flickered in his eyes, and he tilted his head. "As a matter of fact, I am."

"Well, then. What have you got to lose? I don't know if you're familiar with Bible verses—"

"As a matter of fact, I am."

That was good news. "Well, remember the verse about the truth setting you free? When's the last time you remember being truthful on a date? I mean, really truthful? Right from the start."

"I'm not sure I—"

"—have ever been that way. I know." She was interrupting, but she wanted to get this out. Clear from the get-go. "Dating is custom-designed for pretense. You try to make yourself who you think your date wants you to be. You're careful what you do and don't say, you reveal only as much of yourself as you think is safe. As a result, it takes forever to really know a person. And by that time, you've invested so much time and energy you feel like you've *got* to make it work. Even when you shouldn't. But it doesn't have to be that way. We can relax, feel free to be honest about how we feel or think, and by the end of the day it should be crystal clear to us if this is something we want to pursue."

He studied her for one beat, then two, and she felt her face grow warm. Did he think she was a total kook? She swallowed. Oh, good grief, why had she said anything at all? In fact, why had she even answered the door? She should have known he wouldn't understand.

Lord, this was a mistake! Why did you let me—?

"Makes sense."

She gawked at him. "It—it does?" The words came out in a surprised squeak, and he grinned.

"Yes, it does. So how do we decide what we do for the day?"

"Oh, I've got some things in mind." She wasn't sure if he looked pleased—or apprehensive. Either way, she had things planned. Things that would make their suitability—or lack thereof—clear very early on.

He leaned against the wall, shaking his head. "Now, that doesn't exactly seem fair, does it?"

She bit her lip. He was right. "No. I suppose not."

He pushed away from the wall and took her arm, walking down the hall toward the outside door. "Of course it doesn't." He held the door open for her and she stepped out into the brisk air.

She loved February in Seattle. Cold enough to let you know it was winter, but every once in a while a day like today, when the sun shone and the cold fled. She drew a deep, appreciative breath.

"So," Brendan went on, "how about you pick out the first activity, then I pick one? And we can go on like that for as long as we have time."

She paused, pondering for a moment. "OK, that sounds fair." She offered a hesitant smile. "So, are we set?"

"Absolutely."

She felt his warm smile all the way down to her toes.

CHAPTER
Three

"Do you think they're having fun?"

Ophelia gave Amelia a stern look and reached for the teapot. The three of them were gathered in Ophelia's kitchen. That was the safest place to hide from Lindsay. She'd never think to look for them there.

Admittedly, if their niece had intended to hunt them down for what they'd done, she'd have turned up by now. The odds, therefore, were very good that she'd decided to give in and go on the date Cecelia had devised for her. It would all work out, Ophelia was certain.

But if Amelia didn't stop worrying, Ophelia was going to scream. "Of course they're having fun. Cecelia chose the man, so you can be sure he's neither an idiot nor a dud. Please give him a bit of credit."

"Really, we've done all we can to make this a success," Cecelia added. "We just have to leave the details to him. And to Lindsay, of course."

Amelia's alarm was immediate. "That's an awful thing to say! Lindsay is an utter *disaster* at dating."

Well, there was no arguing with that. Ophelia lifted the tea bag from her cup. "Undeniably so. But she's still our niece and, as such, possessed of a high degree of intellect. She can handle this, I'm sure. Besides, she's a delightful person, fun to be around, interesting—"

"For heaven's sake, Ophelia, you sound as though you're giving a eulogy."

"She probably is," Amelia lamented, "for this date."

Ophelia clattered her cup down on its saucer, startling her sisters. "All right now, that's quite enough!" As the eldest, even if only by a few minutes, it had always been her duty to comfort and guide her sisters, but—as Lindsay would put it—she'd had it!

She stood and paced back and forth in front of the . . . what was that called? Oh, yes, oven. "We all agreed this was a worthwhile undertaking, didn't we?"

"Yes, Ophelia," the other two answered in chorus.

"And we felt this young man was, really, when it came down to it, a rather good match for Lindsay, didn't we?"

"Yes, Ophelia."

Cecelia remained silent. Ophelia fixed her with a stern look. "Well? Didn't we?"

She sighed heavily. "Oh, I suppose so. At least as good a match as we could find amongst our acquaintances."

"All right, then. It seems to me we simply need to relax and let things run their natural course."

"I suppose you're right." Amelia seemed mollified.

Ophelia inclined her head. Of course she was right. That was not open to debate. With a sigh, she sipped her tea, only to choke a moment later when Amelia added, "Even if Lindsay's most natural course with men is one that leads to disaster."

Wow.

It was the only word that came to Brendan's mind. He could scarcely take it all in. Nothing had happened the way he'd expected. It was better. Far better. So much so that he was nearly positive he was dreaming.

No . . . not even his dreams were this good.

Lindsay was seated behind him on the bike, her arms draped loosely around his middle as they made their way into traffic. He could feel her resting the front of her helmet against his back as they accelerated, and his breath caught in his throat.

Wow.

There it was again. That word. Well, it was about as appropriate as it got when you were faced with God working a miracle.

As the motorcycle's speed increased, Lindsay couldn't keep the grin from her lips. With each burst of speed, she'd had to hold onto Brendan a bit tighter. Just for safety's sake, of course.

What a shame there were speed limits.

She tightened her grip even more as the bike made a sudden move to the left.

"Sorry!" Brendan called back. "Debris in the road."

"No problem." And it wasn't. Not in the least.

If only The Three Aunts could see her now.

Soon—too soon, in fact—the ride was over. Lindsay slid from the back of the cycle and pulled off her helmet. Tucking it under her arm, she turned to survey the building in front of them.

"Ready?"

His smile was cocky. "Always."

She knew her responding grin was decidedly fiendish, but she couldn't help herself. "We'll see."

She led the way through the glass doors of the library, then down the stairs to the children's section. Gaily colored decorations greeted them as they entered the room.

"Lindsay, over here!"

She turned to see her friend Amy, the children's librarian, waving her and Brendan over. Amy was one of the calls she'd made that morning. She'd been delighted to take part in Lindsay's plans. "Just leave your helmets on the desk there and come join us."

In a circle at Amy's feet sat about thirty children of various ages, all watching, eyes wide, smiles eager.

Lindsay didn't dare look at Brendan. She was too close to losing it.

"Let me guess, story time, right?" His voice was low and right next to her ear.

She nodded.

"And I don't suppose there's any chance you're the reader?"

She shook her head. "Nope. No chance at all." She glanced up at him. "Amy was thrilled that a man was willing to read to the kids. Unless, of course, you'd rather not. Remember, no pretense."

He studied her for a moment. "Do I get to pick out the book?"

"I suppose so."

With that he turned and disappeared between the shelves. *What is he up to?* She went to join Amy and the children.

"You're right on time." Amy patted Lindsay's arm. "That's great. The children are all ready, aren't you, gang?"

"Yeaaaaaahhh!" they chorused.

Amy glanced behind Lindsay. "Where did your friend go?"

"To—" she started to explain, but suddenly Brendan was right there, his hand on her shoulder, finishing for her.

"—pick out a book. Can't do story time without the best materials." With a quick squeeze to Lindsay's shoulder, he stepped past her and went to sit in the storyteller's chair. Kind of a small one, but he fit himself into it, book at the ready.

"OK, who's ready for a story?"

The children cheered as he began. At the first few words, Lindsay's eyes widened. He'd chosen one of her favorite books, *I Love You, Stinky Face.* It was a fun story of a little child at bedtime asking his mother if she would love him, even if he were all kinds of terrible things. Lindsay adored the mother's responses. She always said she'd love him, no matter what, even if he smelled so terrible that his nickname was Stinky Face.

Amy and Lindsay stood watching as Brendan read, changing his voice to match each new terrible creation, gesturing wildly when the creature was a slimy, swamp-dwelling monster or a space alien. . . .

The children were mesmerized.

So was Lindsay.

Amy leaned against her. "Where did you *find* this guy? Are there any more of him around?"

Lindsay chuckled. "I didn't find him. The Three Aunts did."

Amy's jaw dropped. "The *Three* found him?" She shook her head. "I don't believe it." Her eyes narrowed as she studied Brendan. "Maybe he's some kind of robot they made—"

"Amy!" She choked back a laugh, unwilling to admit she'd entertained similar thoughts.

"Or a cyborg. Or a clone. That's it. I'll bet he's some kind of mutated clone your mad scientist aunt created." She gave a dramatic sigh. "I knew he was too good to be true."

Lindsay's chuckle was interrupted by Brendan's triumphant "The End!" followed by the children's jubilant applause.

The sweet-faced little girl sitting beside Brendan fixed wide, imploring eyes on him. "Read us another one! Please?"

Brendan reached out to tug her pigtail. "I will another day, I promise."

Amy looked as though she was about to swoon. "Oh, *honey*, if you don't keep him, *I* will."

"What if he decides not to keep me?"

Amy's smile was wicked. "Even better. Just let me know in any case." And with that she turned back to the children. "Well, wasn't that fun? Let's thank Mr. . . . ?" She looked at Brendan.

Before he could answer, the children surged forward, surrounding him, asking questions, all chattering at once. It took a few minutes for him to extricate himself, but soon he came to stand beside Lindsay.

"So, did I pass the test?"

She looked up at him. "Test? What test?"

"Ah, ah, ah. No pretense, remember? You wanted to know if I liked children, right? And if they liked me?"

She opened her mouth to deny it, then stopped. He was right. She'd convinced herself she was just having fun, but the truth was this *had* been a test. "Yes, I guess that's what I was doing."

"So, did I pass?"

"With flying colors."

He nodded, clearly pleased, then took her arm and turned toward the door.

"'Bye, you two." Amy waved at them. "And Lindsay, don't forget to let me know if that item becomes available, you hear?"

Heat filled her face. Brendan's curious look didn't help. "Item?"

She shot Amy a glare, then grabbed her helmet and headed out the door. "So where did you learn to get along with children so well?" Sidetracking was one of her best skills.

Usually.

Brendan stopped at the bottom of the stairs and leaned against the wall, a stance Lindsay was beginning to recognize. "The truth will set you free. No games, remember?"

With a sigh she sat down on the top step. "You. The item is you. Amy thinks you're wonderful, and she's offered to take you if things don't work out for us."

"Ah." He pushed away from the wall. "See there? Now don't you feel better?"

She watched him, bemused, as he came to the top stair and held a hand out for her. She took his hand and let him pull her to her feet. "That's it?"

He gave a nod. "Yup. Since I'm not available at the moment"— he paused and looked at her—"am I?"

"Definitely not."

A twinkle lit his eyes at her firm response, and he reached out to take her helmet from her and gently slide it over her head. "Well, then"—he fastened her chin strap—"it's not something we need to think about." He cupped her face briefly, his fingers warm against her skin. "Is it?"

It took a moment for her to find her voice. "No, it certainly isn't."

He pulled his helmet on and got on the bike, starting it up. She slid into place behind him, and he looked at her over his shoulder.

"Now"—there was no missing devilish gleam in his eyes—"my turn."

CHAPTER

Four

Brendan watched Lindsay as she slid from the motorcycle, took off her helmet, and saw where they were.

He restrained a smile as surprise touch her features. "The zoo?"

"Yup. The zoo."

He turned so she wouldn't see his amusement at her confusion, and led the way to the ticket booth. He'd be willing to take bets on what she was thinking. He'd heard it often enough from women, his sister among them, *"Men HATE going to the zoo."*

From what he'd seen so far of Lindsay's bent for honesty, he figured she was probably struggling, wondering if he'd come here because he thought it would please her rather than because he wanted to do it himself.

He glanced at her. Sure enough, disappointment painted her features. *Well, it never hurts to have your stereotypes shaken from time to time, does it, God?*

Clothe yourself with tenderhearted mercy and kindness. . . .

He looked away. There wouldn't be a need for kindness if she wasn't so quick to assume the worst.

Be considerate of the doubts and fears of others . . . do what helps them.

Why on earth had he thought it was a good idea to memorize Scripture? It always came back at the most inconvenient times.

The most important piece of clothing you must wear is love.

Fine. But he wasn't ready to give in. Not yet. She got to test him. Well, he had his own tests. Like whether or not she'd be willing to see him for who he really was, not for whom she assumed him to be. And if she could admit she was wrong.

Kindness makes a man attractive.

"Knock it off!" he muttered, then cast a quick look at Lindsay. She was staring at the zoo, immersed in thought. . . .

The words were out before he could stop them. "You'd better be careful."

"About what?"

"Getting too much exercise without stretching out first."

She frowned. "Exercise?"

He shrugged and took her arm, turning them toward the entrance. "You know, jumping to conclusions, leaps of logic, that kind of thing."

Pink tinged her cheeks.

Bingo. He waited for a sense of gratification, but all he felt was mean-spirited. Probably because that's what he was at the moment. Time to man up. He turned to tell her the truth when a voice called out, "Hey, Brendan! Long time no see, eh?"

Lindsay started, and Brendan turned to the ticket attendant, pulling out his wallet. "Hi, Chad."

"Hey, I've seen your pass a million times, bud. I don't need to see it again. But as for this lovely lady, here"—he focused appreciative eyes on Lindsay—"I'm afraid I'll have to ask for hers."

Lindsay bit her lip and looked away.

Well, he'd accomplished his goal. He'd taught her not to make assumptions. Pity it only made him feel rotten. "I'm covering her, Chad." He pulled money from his wallet.

"You got it, Bro."

Lindsay took the ticket from Brendan in silence and followed him through the turnstile. They found the lockers and secured their helmets.

Could he possibly feel any worse? Time to fess up. "Lindsay, I'm sorry."

She shook her head. "No, Brendan, I am. You were right, I assumed you picked the zoo because you thought *I'd* want to come here." She looked down at her hands. "That wasn't very fair of me."

So. The answer was yes. It *was* possible to feel worse. He took her hand. "Lindsay, I wasn't very fair, either. I could have told you right up front that I come here all the time. I wanted to teach you a lesson—"

She looked at him keenly. "You did."

He shook his head. "No, I didn't. At least, not the one I intended. I wanted you to give me a chance, to see me for who I am and not who you think men are in general. Instead, I just confirmed your stereotype."

A slight frown creased her brow. "How did you do that?"

"By being the typical insensitive, arrogant male. I treated you poorly, Lindsay, and I'm sorry." He looked away. "God told me this was a rotten idea, and I ignored him."

She surprised him by grinning. "That's never a good idea. I know from personal experience. Ignoring God only makes you sorry. And usually makes you look stupid."

"Guilty as charged. But I'm not near as stupid as I was five minutes ago." He met her gaze. "Forgive me?"

Her smile was a thing of beauty. It lit her face and sparkled in her eyes.

"Yes, on both counts." She looked around, then back at him, and her expression reminded him of a little girl on Christmas morning. "I really love zoos."

He took her hand. "So do I. It's a good thing my work brings me here so much."

She fell into step beside him. "Your work? What do you do?"

"I'm an artist. A painter, mostly, though I've worked in other mediums. But painting is my true passion. My primary subjects are animals. Or children. So I spend a lot of time in parks, too. Sketching."

She'd stopped cold. "An artist? You're an artist?"

"I take it that's good?"

"That's more than good. That's wonderful." Eyes sparkling, she told him about her work. He listened, watching the way her emotions played over her features. Excitement as she talked about her workshops. Joy as she shared her passion of helping others bring their creativity to life. Then a sudden sadness as she described her aunts. "They think I'm a bit odd." The slight shrug of her shoulders spoke volumes.

A powerful urge swept him as he looked at her. An urge to take her in his arms and draw her close. He wanted to protect her, to bring her smile back . . . to let her know she wasn't alone at all.

He was there.

Whoa, buddy. Slow down! Just because her family doesn't understand her is no reason to fall apart and pledge a lifetime of devotion to the woman.

No, it wasn't. Which only made it that much more astounding that that was exactly what he wanted to do. He was not a man easily swayed by emotion. Oh, he was as drawn to women as the next man—Gwen had more than proven that. But she'd also taught him to keep his emotions under tight rein, which he'd never had trouble doing.

Until now.

"Oh!" Lindsay's excited exclamation pulled him out of his thoughts. She was pointing to a crowd. "They must be getting ready to do something there."

"They are. I saw a sign that said they have a special Valentine's Day tour that would begin at the Tiger exhibit. We're just in time."

"Great! Let's see if there's any room in front so we can see everything." She tugged him along as she hurried toward the group.

They found a spot up front just as the zoo employee started talking. "Hello, and welcome to our Valentine's Day tour! We've put together a special program for you, to give you an insider's look at romance in the animal world."

Brendan couldn't help being a bit proud of himself. He leaned his head down to whisper to Lindsay. "I told you I knew the perfect place to start—"

"Or, in more accurate terms, the mating rituals and habits of the big cats."

Whoa! Brendan looked at the zoo employee. *The what?* A quick glance at Lindsay's suddenly pink cheeks told him he'd heard right. He took hold of her arm.

"I think we can do better than this on our own."

She followed him without question.

His prediction turned out to be accurate. They had a wonderful time. Of course, it helped that the animals—from the big cats to the monkeys to the polar bears—were unusually active and entertaining.

Then came lunch. Brendan couldn't believe it when Lindsay informed him she wanted hot dogs, cotton candy, jumbo-sized drinks, and doubled-dipped ice cream cones. "No pretense." She'd been positively gleeful as she licked dribbling ice cream from her fingers.

Their conversation had ranged from teasing and humorous to quiet and serious. They'd talked about their families, their hobbies—many of which they shared—and their faith, what they believed and how they'd gotten there. He'd been surprised to find himself believing her as she told him how much she wanted to reflect Christ in her actions and words. From what he'd seen, she was sincere. Not that she was a saint, but she wasn't just mouthing a bunch of convenient platitudes. She truly tried to live out what she believed.

Quite a conclusion on merely one day's acquaintance, isn't it?

The mocking question didn't surprise him. But his response did. *Yes, I've seen more of this woman's heart in this day than I've seen of anyone else's in months of being together. I trust her.*

So if you trust her so much, why haven't you told her about Gwen?

No answer for that, save one: he wasn't ready.

The high point came when they ran into a friend of his who was the manager of the big cat exhibit. He took them to the nursery, where they found three young tiger cubs. Brendan wasn't sure who'd had more fun holding and playing with the little beasts, Lindsay or him.

It was late afternoon by the time they left the zoo grounds and walked to his motorcycle.

"That"—Lindsay linked her arm in his—"was wonderful."

"The best."

"I hope not, seeing as it's my turn now."

He helped her onto the motorcycle. "OK, it was the best so far. How's that?"

"Much better." She dimpled.

"Though how you're going to top it is beyond me." He slid onto the bike in front of her.

She put her arms around his waist. "That's simple. I'm going to make you the best dinner you've ever had."

CHAPTER
Five

The idea to cook dinner at her place had been a spur of the moment thing, but Lindsay was glad she'd offered it.

She and Brendan went to Trader Joe's together, and shopping for groceries had never been so much fun. In fact, nothing had ever been as much fun as it seemed to be with Brendan. The most mundane activities turned hilarious; the briefest conversations held insight and discovery.

As they drove to her house, he pointed to a tall building on the way. "That's where I live." She'd looked at him in happy surprise. It wasn't more than a half a mile from her own.

He'd grinned. "I know, convenient, eh? I thought so, too. You'll have to come see my place soon. Apartment 1101. End of the hall. I think you'll like it."

"I'm sure I will." Why wouldn't she? She liked everything about the man so far. She had to keep reminding herself she'd known him less than a day. It felt as though he'd been in her life for as long as she could remember. And she found herself, as she unlocked her apartment door, hoping he'd stay in her life for a long time.

Maybe forever.

He's the one, isn't he, Lord? She was almost afraid to give voice to what she was feeling. *He's the one I've been waiting for.*

"Aaroooo! Aarrrooooo!" Doofus greeted her with his usual vocal exuberance. It never mattered how long or brief her absence, he always acted, upon her return, as though he'd been afraid he'd never see her again. His low-slung, solid body would wag itself from one end to the other, and his ear-splitting "roo" would bounce off the walls.

Brendan followed her inside, watching as she did her best to quiet the wriggling basset. "Now that's what I call a heartfelt welcome home."

"Oh, it's that all right." She hugged Doofus and clamped her hand over his muzzle in the same motion. "I just wish there was a volume control."

"Why don't you let me try to calm him down while you get started on dinner?"

"Hungry, are we?"

"Count on it!" He scooped the dog up as though he were a poodle rather than fifty-five very solid pounds.

With a shrug, she hefted the bags of groceries and went to the kitchen. Some fifteen minutes later she laid shish kebobs on the grill on her balcony.

"Hey, would you like something to drink?" she asked, coming into the living room.

The scene that met her stopped her in her tracks. Brendan was sitting on the couch, leaning back, completely at ease. On the cushion beside him was an equally relaxed Doofus. The basset hound was in his favorite position: stretched out on his back, his legs dangling in the air, paws relaxed and drooped. His massive head was all but draped across Brendan's jean-clad lap. Contented snores rumbled from Doofie's snout as Brendan's lean fingers scratched the dog's long ears.

Brendan looked up at her. There was the lopsided smile again. She liked it more each time she saw it—and she liked the way it did something to her, making her heart dance and ache all at the same time.

Brendan held his hands out. "He does seem rather . . . content, don't you think?"

"Ecstatic is more like it." She moved toward the love seat opposite him. Obviously Brendan had passed the Doofie test. The basset was smitten.

"He's a good dog."

Brendan had the nicest dark brown eyes, and she really liked the way they were smiling at her. And the way they could grow serious and attentive when they discussed something serious. If the eyes were a window to the soul, then Brendan's soul had to be in a class all its own—a very appealing class.

Maybe The Three Aunties were right about him . . . maybe he was perfect for her. Since this whole day was about being honest, she didn't even try to deny the fact that she truly hoped so.

"You look like you've got something on your mind."

His words snapped her back to the present. "The truth?"

Was she really going to say what she thought?

Don't do it! It's too risky! Her breath caught a moment. But she didn't care. She'd been asking Brendan for honesty all day long. She wasn't going to start dodging the truth now.

He captured and held her gaze. "Yes."

"I was thinking about us, about today. About the way I'm feeling and how it should scare me silly. But it doesn't."

He remained silent, but for some reason that encouraged rather than threatened her. It gave her the chance to sort through her thoughts and express them. "Brendan, when we started out today I hoped we'd at least have a nice time. If we were lucky, we'd get to know each other a bit better than usual in a dating situation. But what's happened is . . ." She searched for the right word.

"Extraordinary," he supplied.

"Remarkable," she agreed. "And rare. I mean, I've certainly never had anything like this happen before, have you?"

"Only in my dreams."

In any other situation, that would have sounded trite. But she knew what he meant. It was true. She'd dreamed of meeting someone—her soul mate—like this. But she never believed it would happen.

Forgive me, Lord. You promised me wonderful things, and I didn't let myself believe you. And now . . .

Tears sprang to her eyes, and for once she didn't try to stop them.

Brendan eased Doofus aside and came to sit with her on the love seat. He took her hand, his grip firm, secure. He lifted his free hand and touched a gentle finger to her cheek, capturing a tear.

"'You have collected all my tears in your bottle. You have recorded each one in your book.'" He looked down at her hand, as though studying it carefully. After a few moments, he looked up at her again. "Lindsay, I don't know where we're going. I don't know what God intends for us together. All I know is that he's done something today, something inside both of us. We agreed no games, no pretense, so I want to you to know this: you're not alone in what you're feeling. You move me like I've never been moved before. I want to care for you, to protect you, to be with you. And if I feel that way after one day, I can't even begin to conceive how it's going to be after a week, or a month."

She sniffed. It was as though he was expressing her heart, too. "I feel the same way. And I don't know whether to be thrilled or terrified."

"How about if we're just patient?" His smile was kind, tender. "Let's take this slow, and build on the base God has given us today. I know it feels as though we've known each other a long time, but the truth is we haven't. We have a lot to learn about each other. And I, for one, plan to enjoy that process."

She lifted their joined hands to her cheek and closed her eyes. "Where did you come from?"

"From the same place you did." His voice was choked with emotion, and he cupped her face with his hand. "From the heart of the Father."

"Wurf!" Doofus barked.

Lindsay barely heard him, so focused was she on Brendan and the feel of his hands against her skin. She could hardly breathe. "Brendan, I—"

"Rowrf! Aroooo!" Doofus insisted.

"I—"

"Aaarrrrroooooooooo!"

"What??" Lindsay spun to scold the dog for interrupting such a sweet moment. But the words died on her lips, and she jumped up from the love seat with a yelp.

"My shish kebobs!" She raced for the balcony, which was cloaked in a cloud of gray smoke.

"Oooooohhh." The blackened spears looked like columns of pure charcoal. "They're ruined." She looked at Brendan, who stood leaning against the sliding door, a bemused smile on his face.

"What?" She shook her head at him.

His slow smile was rueful. "I just think God has an interesting way of letting certain things burn out of control to keep other things from doing the same thing."

She turned to survey the remains of their dinner, then chuckled. "So much for the best dinner you've ever had."

"No sweat. Give me five minutes and everything will be fine."

She looked at him. "Five minutes?" He couldn't salvage those poor shish kebobs with five hours!

"Yup. That's how long it will take me to find the number for pizza delivery. You can't burn a salad, can you?"

She punched him on the arm, and Doofus took up another wail.

It was after ten when Brendan left. They'd agreed it was too soon to share a kiss. "Not until we're more sure about this."

She'd agreed with him, caught between disappointment and gratitude for his wisdom.

She'd followed him to the door, and he'd held her hands, then lifted one to place a soft kiss at the wrist, where her pulse beat. She'd read in novels about women nearly swooning when a man kissed her, but she'd always dismissed it as fiction.

Now she knew.

She grabbed at the doorway, dazed. When had she stopped breathing? And could someone please tell her how to start again? From Brendan's dazed look, he wasn't faring much better.

"Wow," he muttered, and she agreed. Wholeheartedly.

She closed the door behind him, then leaned against it wondering how something so small as a kiss to the wrist could have such an enormous impact.

"Wow," she mumbled, echoing Brendan's reaction. "Wait'll I tell The Three Aunts. . . ."

Better yet, why wait? It wasn't too late to call. She jumped on the phone with glee and punched in the numbers. She would owe them for the rest of her life for this.

Big time.

"Hello?"

"Celie! You're wonderful! And so are Phelia and Melia. You're all wonderful! I mean it."

Stunned silence met her enthusiasm. Then, "I take it the date went well?"

"'Well'?" Lindsay laughed. "'Well'? Oh, Celie, it was the most amazing day of my life!" She went on to recount the events of the day in detail, barely giving Celie a chance to comment.

"I mean it, Celie. I'll never be able to thank you three for introducing me to Brendan. He's the most perfect man—"

"Who?"

"Brendan. He's funny, and so sincere in his faith. I mean, I can tell he's got some issues—"

"Lindsay . . ."

"—but who doesn't?"

"Lindsay . . ."

"What really matters is that we—"

"Lindsay Renae!"

Lindsay stopped in mid-rave at the alarm in her aunt's voice. "What? What's wrong?"

"Who is Brendan?"

"What?"

"You said 'Brendan.' Who on earth is Brendan?"

A small alarm sounded somewhere in Lindsay's mind. "My date. The man you sent to take me out today."

"Lindsay—" her aunt spoke in slow tones, as though speaking to a dense child. "The man I sent was Alex. Alex Winters. From church."

The alarm was now a full-blown siren, blasting so loudly that she could scarcely think straight.

Cecelia went on. "This Brendan person may have been your date, but I didn't send him. Lindsay, I have no idea who that man is."

CHAPTER

Six

Despite a virtually sleepless night, Lindsay was surprised to find her anger had abated a little by the time she rolled out of bed the next morning.

There had to be an explanation. Brendan wouldn't lie to her. She was sure of it. She'd racked her brain all night, going over and over the things they'd said. One thing did stand out: the fact that she'd never gotten his last name. That alone made her feel like an absolute idiot. She was sure he'd given it at the library. At least, she thought he had. But it all was so clouded with emotion, she couldn't keep it straight.

Had he said he knew her aunts? That he'd been sent as her valentine date? She couldn't remember.

All she knew was that she had to find out, from Brendan himself, what was going on.

You can't go talk to him, the inner voice cautioned. *Not alone. Call one of your aunts—better yet, call all three!—and ask them to go with you.*

No. She'd gotten into this on her own, she'd get out of it the same way. Besides, she wasn't afraid of Brendan.

Aren't you?

Despair flooded her. No, she wasn't afraid of Brendan. How could she be?

She was in love with him.

Lindsay watched the numbers on the panel as the elevator rose. Eight, nine, ten . . .

Don't do this! You don't know what you'll find if you do.

She couldn't argue the point. *No, but I do know what I'll lose if I don't.*

Do you? Or was it all just make-believe? A remarkably well-acted fantasy that you were all too ready to buy into?

Thankfully, the doors opened, stopping the inner debate. She stepped from the elevator and glanced around. Brendan had said his apartment was at the end. . . .

He'd better be there. With answers. Her jaw tightened. *And they'd better be good.*

She made her way down the hall. 1110. 1108. 1106 . . . Ah, there. At the end of the hallway, just as he'd said. Apartment 1101.

She raised her hand to knock, then paused. The door was already open. Just a crack, but open nonetheless. Had he somehow known she was coming? No, that wasn't possible. . . .

She reached out a finger to push at the door. It opened wider. She pressed her face to the crack and whispered, "Brendan?"

No answer.

He could hardly have heard you, now could he? Her conscience scolded her.

It was easier to ignore that little bit of truth than address it. She stepped back and looked up and down the hall. No sign of Brendan. She leaned forward to peek through the crack in the door, and her eyes widened.

Pushing the door open the rest of the way, she went inside, then halted. It was beautiful!

A large, open room greeted her. The sun poured in through tall windows and skylights, making the room feel light and airy. The furnishings were simple, but not spartan. Elegant, colorful prints and an assortment of sculptures and art items were displayed with artistic abandon. The chairs were low and overstuffed; the tables, thick and wooden. Overall, the tone of the room was warm and inviting.

But what caught her attention and drew her like a magnet was the easel and paintings at the far end of the room.

Joy filled her heart. He's told her the truth. He really was a painter. Or, at least he had all the accoutrements. Lindsay went to one of the canvases sitting on the floor, leaned up against a chair leg. Kneeling, she studied it . . . and again her heart sang.

It was beautiful. She carefully tipped the painting forward to see it better. A child's face smiled up at her, so realistic in its depiction that she almost expected the little one to speak. The strokes were strong and sure, the detail intricate but not overdone. Soft angel hair framed a face that was the epitome of innocence and wonder. The round cheeks were flushed with excitement, the blue eyes sparkled with laughter. One small hand reached out toward her, as though wanting to make sure she was real. Floating in the air, all around the child, were dandelion fluffs.

It was a magical, captivating portrayal of delight, of childish discovery.

Brendan had, indeed, told her the truth. He was an artist. And a gifted one.

She looked at the lower right-hand corner of the painting. The signature was equally beautiful, rendered in a distinctive script: "HawkEye."

She frowned. HawkEye? Probably his last name. She never did get it from him. But then, she'd never asked.

And there, just below the name, was a Scripture reference: James 1:17–18. She would have to look that up when she got home.

She leaned the painting back in place, then stood, eager to see more. She went to the painting on the easel—and smiled anew. It was exquisite. A sleeping tiger cub lay curled contentedly in the curve of its mother's enormous paws. The blend of helplessness and power held at bay was surprisingly moving. Lindsay had a sudden image of God holding her in just such a way . . . surely, protectively, unconcerned for what might come against her, confident that the battle was already won.

Lindsay explored further, finding one treasure after another. Finally, she came to several canvases leaned against a wall, covered by a tarp. She pulled the covering back, and knelt with an exclamation of delight.

A basset hound looked out at her, his soulful eyes filled with adoration. "Doofus," she whispered. Indeed, if she hadn't known better, she would have sworn it was her dog. The coloring, the build, the expression all were vintage Doof.

She pulled the painting forward and looked at the canvas behind it—

Shock jolted through her.

It was like looking in a mirror. Her own laughing face looked out from the panel before her. Here, as with the other paintings, the detail was exquisite. So much so that she had the oddest sensation of having been thrown outside of herself, an out-of-body observer. Her hair was windblown, and she was framed by trees in the background, resplendent in their autumn foliage. Leaves of rich, muted colors rained down about her, and she had wrapped her arms about herself in an unconscious gesture of savoring the wonder of the moment. Her likeness looked out of the painting, laughing, her eyes filled with warmth, as though she were looking at someone she knew.

No . . . at someone she loved.

She pushed the painting away and jumped to her feet, her heart racing. She was no painter, but she knew something this detailed, this intricate, this . . . *intimate* took time. More time than she'd known Brendan.

A lot more time.

Then she remembered. One day last month she'd gone to the city park for a walk. It had been a perfect day, and she'd had a wonderful time drinking in the beauty all around her. One tree in particular drew her. It still had leaves. Then, in one magical moment, a gust of wind kicked up, shaking the limbs of the trees all around her, creating a shower of leaves. It was an experience that had stayed imprinted on her memory.

And, apparently, in Brendan's.

She frowned. But that was a month ago. A chill washed over her. How long had he been watching her?

She stepped back, and her foot slipped on something. Looking down she saw a manila folder. It must have been set against the painting of the basset, and she'd knocked it over—

The basset hound. Her eyes went back to the painting that had brought her such delight a few minutes ago. It didn't just look like Doofus. It *was* him.

She reached down to the folder, but she picked it up too quickly. Papers fell out and littered the floor around her. Muttering an exclamation, she bent to retrieve them—and froze again. They were sketches—some in pencil, some in charcoal—of her and Doofus. Some were of them together, others of them individually, others showed them with the children who always gathered so eagerly around Doofus when she walked him.

God . . . It was all her terrified mind could manage. *God, help.*

With quick, frightened movements she put the sketches back in the folder, set it against the painting of Doofus, and pulled the tarp back in place. Her heart racing, she ran to the door, careful to pull it nearly shut on her way out, then she hurried toward the elevator.

She held her breath, waiting anxiously for the doors to open. "Come on, come on," she muttered, heaving a relieved sigh when they finally slid to admit her. Inside, she reached out a shaking hand to punch the button for the lobby.

The real shaking didn't start until she was in her car, the door securely locked. *Lord, what are you doing?* She tried to steady her fingers enough to put the key in the ignition.

Trust in the Lord with all your heart.

Swift anger filled her. *I did* trust *you, and look where it got me. I spent the day with a crazy man!*

Do not depend on your own understanding.

She pulled into traffic with an angry jerk of the steering wheel. *I'll tell you what I understand. The best thing I can do about Brendan HawkEye—or whatever his last name is—is to stay as far away from him as possible.*

CHAPTER

Seven

"You what?"

Lindsay faced her aunts resolutely. "I went to Brendan's apartment. I wanted to get some answers."

"And did you?" Ophelia's disapproval rang in her tone.

"Yes." More than she'd wanted.

Amelia put her arm around Lindsay's shoulders. "Well, what did the scoundrel have to say for himself?"

"Not much, Melia." She'd be darned if she was going to tell them she went into the apartment without him there. Why give them yet another opportunity to tell her how crazy she was?

"Was this—this *imposter* telling the truth about anything?"

"Actually, Phelia, yes. He really is an artist. A painter."

"Hmpfh!" Cecelia snorted, a most uncharacteristic sound for her. "I'll bet."

"No, really." For some reason, she didn't want the aunts to think Brendan had lied on every count. "What I saw was exceptional." She smiled—amazing she could do so about anything that had to do with Brendan. "Even his signature on the paintings was beautiful."

"I assume it was his name?"

"I think so, though it's his last name. HawkEye, with the *e* capitalized."

"What did you say?"

Why was Amelia looking at her like that? "I said he signs his paintings HawkEye, with the *e*—"

"For heaven's sake, Amelia, what possible diff—" Ophelia began, but her triplet cut her off.

"Good heavens, Lindsay. You don't mean he's HawkEye? Not *the* HawkEye??"

Lindsay hesitated, blinking. There was a "*the* HawkEye"?

"Are you telling me you've never heard of HawkEye?" Amelia looked like she'd swallowed a toad. "You're the art-aware one in the family, for heaven's sake!"

"Amelia, would you be so kind as to dispense with the histrionics and explain yourself?" Ophelia was a bit fed up.

Amelia waved her hands at them. "Do you recall when I invited you all to the fund raiser for the children's hospital? The one cosponsored by the university a few months ago?"

"Who could forget? The food was substandard, at best."

Amelia shot Cecelia a quelling look and went on. "Lindsay, you couldn't come because you were out of town. But you two were there." She pointed to her sisters. "Don't you remember the art exhibit? They were featuring the work of a much-acclaimed artist who lives in the area."

Cecelia nodded. "Oh, yes. Those! They were wonderful! All depictions of children at play, and they were simply stunning. I could have sworn the figures were going to step right off the canvas."

"Yes, I recall it now—" Ophelia's eyes widened. "The artist was this HawkEye?"

Amelia clapped her hands. "Yes! I remember because he had a Scripture reference beneath his name, and one of the philosophy professors made an inane remark about faith in God being passé." She grimaced. "I wanted to upend my tea on his head."

"The verse"—Lindsay took her aunt's hand—"was it from James?"

"Yes. Chapter one, verses seventeen and eighteen, I believe. I looked it up when I got home that night. It was the section about every good thing coming from God, and that we are his children and his choice possessions." She smiled. "Rather appropriate, I thought."

"Lindsay, what were the subjects of your friend's paintings?"

Lindsay stared at Cecelia. Her *friend*? What happened to "the *scoundrel*"? "Children. And animals."

Amelia clapped her hands. "He *has* to be the same artist, don't you think? There can't be two with the same name in the Seattle area."

"I would think that highly unlikely," Ophelia said. "Do you two remember the prices on those paintings?"

"Quite clearly," Cecelia said. "I wanted one so badly I could almost taste it, but Roger would have shot me if I'd paid seven thousand dollars on a painting."

Lindsay felt her mouth drop open. "How much?"

"Oh, that was one of the bargains. There were a couple of large paintings of children playing in a field of flowers that went for three times that."

Ophelia stirred her tea. "Am I remembering correctly that the entire proceeds from the sale of his works were going to the children's hospital?"

Amelia nodded. "Yes, he didn't want any money at all. It was really quite remarkable."

The Three Aunts turned to scrutinize Lindsay in silence.

She crossed her arms over her chest. "What?"

"Well, my dear, it's quite improbable—"

"To say the least—"

"That an artist of such skill—"

"—and craftsmanship—"

"—and what would seem to be devotion to God—"

"Well," Phelia finished for The Three, "don't you see? It's just not likely such a man would be a common masher."

Lindsay lifted her chin. "Then perhaps he's an uncommon one."

"There's no need to be defensive." Ophelia's tone was the same as it had been when Lindsay was a child and said something unkind. "All we're saying is that the man must have a reason for what he did. And you really should give him the opportunity to explain himself."

"I tried that."

"Well, then, what did he say?"

Oops. Caught. "Ummmm, he wasn't home. But I saw something . . ." She looked away. "Something that convinced me I shouldn't see him again."

The Three waited, expectant.

"There was a painting."

Cecelia lifted her face to the ceiling. "Oh. Well. *That* explains it."

Lindsay pulled a face at her. "It was of me. And there was one of Doofus, too."

A mix of confusion and concern swiftly replaced the disdain on her aunts' faces.

"I confess, that does seem odd," Phelia said.

"It *felt* odd. And . . . invasive, somehow. And it means he's been watching me. For a long time."

"But Lindsay, it just doesn't make sense." Amelia's logic was hard at work. "He's well known and respected in the art world. And his philanthropy is well documented."

Ophelia nodded. "I'm afraid she's right, my dear. Perhaps we should go with you to talk to him."

"No!" Lindsay took a breath, trying to soften her horrified response. "Really. I'll think over what you've said. And I'll pray about it. I promise. If it seems right, I'll talk with him."

Thankfully, this seemed to satisfy them and they let the issue drop. She knew once they let it go, they most likely wouldn't give it another moment's thought.

If only she could do the same.

CHAPTER
Eight

Brendan stared at Lindsay's apartment building, torn between anger and feeling a total fool.

"What am I doing here, God?"

He was across the street, sitting on a bus stop bench. When he decided to go for a walk, he'd had no intention of ending up here. All he'd known was he had to get out.

Actually, he'd considered showing up on her doorstep several times over the last three weeks, but every time he headed for the door, he'd stopped. He couldn't explain it, but he'd had the distinct feeling that he needed to wait.

Tonight, though, he'd reached the limits of his patience. He'd tried calling Lindsay one more time, and again there had been no answer. He'd left messages on her voicemail, for all the good that had done him.

Now, after three weeks of silence, he was starting to wonder if Lindsay wasn't just another Gwen. Lots of talk about faith and honesty, but when it came down to it, that's all it was. Talk.

Judge not.

"Give me a break. If anyone has a right to judge here, *I* do. You know, Lord, seems to me you keep letting me care for people who don't deserve it."

He stood and paced. "Is this how it works, Lord? *Pow!* and it's over. No good-bye. No explanation. No nothing. What am I supposed to learn from this?"

I am the Alpha and Omega, the beginning and the end.

The words rang in his mind as clearly as if someone had leaned over and whispered them in his ear. His reaction was swift. "Then you should have seen this coming! You should have kept me from caring so much!"

Who is this that questions my wisdom? Where were you when I laid the foundations of the earth? . . . Who defined the boundaries of the sea? . . . Have you ever commanded the morning to appear and caused the dawn to rise in the east? . . . You are God's critic, but do you have the answers?

All the anger-driven energy drained out of him. He plopped back down on the bench. No. He didn't have the answers. Not for anything. He shoved his hands into his pockets, leaning back against the back of the bench. He couldn't deny it. God's words were as true for him as they'd been for Job. But he couldn't deny his anger, either.

What do I do, God? I want to yell, at you, at myself. I want to say I'll never trust a woman again. But I know that's not the answer, any more than blaming you is the answer. I just wish someone would tell me what to do.

He shook his head and glanced at Lindsay's building again. And then he stiffened, disbelief rippling along his spine.

Lindsay was leaving her building, laughing and smiling and talking.

With a man.

Brendan rose and stepped off the curb, fully intending to march across the street and confront her, when a horn blared loudly. He jumped back just in time to avoid being turned into a grease spot on the street by the six o'clock bus.

He sat back down on the bench with a thud, clenching his teeth so hard his jaw ached.

OK, God, he thought grudgingly. *You win. I'll wait. For a few hours more. But that's it.* He settled back against the bench. *Then I'm going to get some answers.*

God, if you don't get me out of this in the next ten seconds, I'm going to scream.

"Did you say something, my dear?"

Call me that one more time, and I'm going to let you have it between the eyes. She met her date's curious gaze. "Not a thing, Alex." She spoke as sweetly as possible when the words were forced through clamped teeth. Why, oh, *why* did she ever let The Three Aunties talk her into this?

"It's been three weeks, Lindsay," Phelia had said a few days ago.

"Thanks for the reminder." Lindsay had nearly snapped her response. As though she needed a reminder. She knew how many weeks . . . days . . . minutes . . . interminable *seconds* it had been since she walked away from Brendan.

Fortunately, Phelia didn't address her rancorous tone. "If you're not going to contact Brendan and resolve things, then it's time you got on with your life."

"And we have exactly what the doctor ordered." This from Amelia, who was doing her level best to look enthusiastic. "Alex Winters, your valentine date. He's willing to forgive you for going off with a total stranger and leaving him to stand in your hallway like a ninny."

"Oh, goody."

"Lindsay, please." Phelia cast a scolding look her way. "Alex is a fine man. Besides, he's perfect for you. Just what the doctor ordered."

Lindsay didn't trust her aunt's bland expression. "Oh?"

"Absolutely. He's a psychologist."

"Definitely what you need." Celie batted her eyes.

"Besides, you owe the man a date." From Melia.

She'd resisted, but they'd worn her down. And now here she was, in a nice restaurant, staring at Alex Winters, listening as he expounded on the fact that people brought their trials on themselves, how much better off they would be if they would only get over themselves and show even the smallest kernel of intelligence. Of course, one sign of this intelligence would be for them to buy his book, *Living Life the Way You Should.*

If he was what the doctor ordered, she'd rather be terminal. At least there'd be an end to the torture.

Quick shame over the unkind direction of her thoughts swept her. *Sorry, Lord. It's not Alex's fault I find him pompous and irritating.* She grimaced. Oops. She'd done it again. She never should have left her apartment.

With as much sincerity as possible, Lindsay feigned a huge yawn. "Oh, gosh, sorry about that, but it's getting to be past my bedtime."

Alex glanced at his watch and frowned. "You go to bed by eight-thirty?"

She nodded. "Oh, yes. Always have. I find it, uh, conducive to creativity."

He wasn't buying it.

This is a punishment, isn't it, Lord? For ignoring you when you've urged me to call Brendan. Well, I'm not calling. OK? I'm just not going to.

"Uh, besides," she pushed on, "I need to check on Doofus. He . . . hasn't had his dinner. And, you know, there's just nothing worse than a hungry basset hound."

"Indeed?"

"Oh, definitely. He'll start howling and crying. My neighbors wouldn't like it at all. In fact, they'd probably demand I get rid of him." She managed a trembling lower lip at the thought. "And I just couldn't bear that." She gave him her best imitation of Doofus's woebegone look.

Hey, it always worked on her.

And, wonder of wonders, it worked on Alex, too.

"Well, by all means then"—the pitying smile on his face set her teeth on edge yet again—"let's get you home to feed the little fellow." Alex signaled for the bill.

Ha! See there? I can handle things myself—

"And while he's enjoying his canine repast, we can treat ourselves to a spot of coffee and a nice little chat, eh? About this rather odd fixation you have on your dog? How does that sound, my dear?"

Only like her worst nightmare.

OK, Lord, I give. Uncle. You win. I'll call Brendan. I promise. Just, please, can you get rid of Mr. I-Can-Fix-You-if-You'll-Just-Do-Everything-I-Say before he gets past my apartment door?

Lindsay was nearly desperate.

She'd been hoping for a traffic accident, or a hold-up, an alien abduction . . . *anything* to distract Alex and convince him to go home. But her prayed-for reprieve hadn't materialized, and they were headed down the hallway to her apartment.

God? This is a test, right? You're not really going to make me go through this—

She stopped, frozen in her tracks.

There, leaning against the wall beside her apartment door, stood Brendan. He looked as wonderful as she remembered—except for something around his eyes that looked stiff and hard.

That was new.

He looked at her for a moment, then over at Alex. His lips thinned. Apparently Brendan wasn't any more pleased to have Alex walking behind her than she was.

"Hello, Lindsay." The greeting sounded pleasant enough, even if there was a definite edge to the words. "I hope I'm not late."

She blinked. "Late?"

Alex stiffened. Good grief, was he going to try to defend her from Brendan? She turned toward him, but she needn't have worried.

He was looking at her, not Brendan. And his expression was one of complete outrage. "Really, Lindsay, all you had to do was tell me you had another engagement and I would have dropped you at the door."

"I—"

"May I just say how thoroughly unsatisfactory this entire evening has been?" The man sounded like a petulant teenager. "I had hoped your unbelievable affront to me on Valentine's Day was an exception, but I can see you are that careless sort of woman who believes she can use men as she wills. Well, my dear, you shall not use me a moment longer."

The man spun on his heel and strode down the hallway and out the door.

Lindsay stood there, mouth agape.

"Nice guy. Astute. I like him."

Brendan's sardonic tone was the last straw. She whirled around to face him. "What are you doing here?"

His brows arched. "Fine, thanks. And how are you?"

She didn't answer. She brushed past him to shove her key in the door. Her annoyance only increased when she saw her hands were shaking. Before she could turn the key, his hand settled over hers.

"Lindsay."

She stilled, overwhelmed by the sudden wave of emotion. It took all her willpower not to bury her face against him and weep.

"We need to talk. That's all I want. To talk."

She rested her forehead against the door. *God, I know I promised. But I'm not ready. I can't do this. I can't.*

I am the Lord, the God of all the peoples of the world. Is anything too hard for me?

No. No, it wasn't.

She straightened and looked at Brendan. "Come on in. I'll make us some coffee."

I'm frightened, Father.

Lindsay stood in the kitchen, gripping the countertop as though it were a life preserver. The coffee had been ready for five minutes, but she couldn't force herself to go into the living room.

She knew she wasn't afraid of Brendan. When she'd seen him, she'd known he was safe. And sane. She couldn't explain it, but one look at him and she'd been filled with the certainty that he was everything he'd said he was.

No, what held her frozen in place, caught between hope and terror, was another realization that she couldn't escape, no matter how desperately she wanted to.

I love him.

The fact kept ringing in her mind until she thought she'd go crazy with it. On impulse, she reached for the phone and quickly dialed Ophelia's number.

Be home. Please be—

"Hello?"

She cupped her hand around the receiver and lowered her tone to a whisper. "Phelia, it's Lindsay."

"Lindsay? Do you have a cold? I can scarcely hear you."

"Phelia, listen, I haven't got much time. I . . . would you pray for me?"

Her aunt's response was immediate. "You know I will. What's happening?"

"Brendan is here—"

"Oh, my! Should I call the police?"

"No!" The word came out half laughing, half frantic. "No, Phelia, just listen. It's good that he's here. We need to talk. I—I care about him. A great deal. And I want to work things out."

"I see. So I take it he's Prince Charming again." There was a smile in the question.

A sweet warmth filled Lindsay. "Yes, yes, I think he is."

"All right then, dear. I'll pray for you. And I'll ask God to show you if this is the man to whom you can give your heart."

"Thanks. And Phelia . . ."

"Yes?"

"I love you."

There was a surprised pause, and then, "I love you, too, Lindsay."

Feeling more at peace, she hung up the phone and reached down to pick up the two mugs. *OK, Lord, here we go.* They would talk, bring everything out in the open. Maybe that way she could put this whole episode to rest.

Maybe that way her heart could stop aching.

She entered the room and experienced a sense of déjà vu. Brendan sat on the couch, Doofus snoozing beside him. She set one of the coffee mugs on the low table in front of Brendan, then settled on the love seat. She cradled her mug between her hands, staring at the steam drifting up. Where on earth should she begin?

Hold to the truth. . . .

The truth. What was the truth? That she was desperately unhappy? That she was sorry for her lack of trust, but unable to overcome it? That she was terrified?

Yes. All of the above.

"Brendan—"

"Look, Lindsay—"

They both broke off, and Lindsay felt a hysterical giggle in her throat. Leave it to them to start speaking at the same time.

With a tip of his head, Brendan indicated she should continue. "Please. Ladies first."

She grimaced. "I don't feel like much of a lady. More of an idiot." OK, so it was honest, but what a beginning.

He blinked. "Excuse me?"

Well, it *was* the truth. "I'm an idiot. I've been going crazy—"

"I haven't exactly been having a wonderful time—"

At his growled rejoinder, regret filled her. "I know. But . . . well . . . Brendan, I went to your apartment." Seeing his confused reaction, she rushed on. "The door was open, but you weren't there. I . . . I wanted some answers. I mean, you weren't the date The Three Aunts sent, so even though I was sure I could trust you, I didn't think I could. After all, you were an imposter. But I was almost sure you didn't *know* you were. I mean, you never said The Three sent you—"

"The *what?*—"

"—at least, I don't think you did. So I had to find out. Because I really cared—"

"Lindsay . . ."

"—and I was looking around, and saw your paintings, and it was so exciting because they're wonderful. You really are gifted, you know? And I was so thrilled that you'd told the truth about being an artist—"

"Lindsay . . ."

"—that I was ready to forgive you most anything, and I was sure God had brought us together, and then I found the paintings."

Stillness settled over him, as though he were alarmed.

"The paintings?"

She nodded. "The ones of Doofus. And of—of me."

He eased back against the couch cushion.

Say something, Brendan. Give me an explanation. One that will make the fear go away.

So, she found the paintings. Well, that at least explained a few things. It didn't excuse her behavior, but it did explain it.

He knew the constructive thing would be to explain, to tell her the truth about that day in the park and about all that had resulted from it. To tell her about Kylie's plan and how he'd agreed to do something he never would have done normally because he'd been captivated since he saw her at his sister's wedding—to her brother, just to complicate things further.

But he couldn't make the words come.

All he wanted to do was yell at her.

"*You left me hanging for three weeks because you saw a stupid painting? Did it ever occur to you to just ask me about it? What happened to being honest, Lindsay? Doesn't count when it seems scary? Is that it?"*

He clenched his jaws shut, holding the tirade back. Barely.

I want to blast her, God. I want to let her have it. . . .

He didn't, though. Because one thought kept running through his mind, over and over. It was the thought that had hit him square between the eyes when he'd seen her walking down the hallway. It was the thought that had coursed through him like fire as he fought against the urge to grab the man with her and turn him into silly putty . . .

I love her. God help me, I love her.

But he'd be darned if he'd tell *her* that.

The silence grew between them until Lindsay wanted to jump up and shake him. Just as she was about to give in to that urge, he sighed.

"Who are The Three?"

She started. "What?"

"The Three. You said you thought they'd sent me . . . ?"

Understanding dawned. "They're my aunts. I told you about them."

"The brainy triplets."

She nodded. "They sent me an . . . unusual valentine gift this year. A date. With a man."

"I didn't think it was with a kumquat."

A smile found its way through her uncertainty. "Anyway, he was supposed to show up valentine morning, at precisely 10:32."

Brendan's brows arched. "About the time I came with the flowers. You thought I was your aunts' gift."

She nodded. "Right."

"Well, that explains it then."

She shook her head, "No, that doesn't explain it. Not your part, anyway. Brendan, you were just there to deliver the flowers, weren't you?"

He paused. "Yes . . . and no."

"I don't understand. Why did you agree to spend the day with me? And what's the deal with those paintings?"

There was no humor in his face now. "I suppose you think I'm some kind of nut case."

"No, oddly enough, I don't. Not anymore."

"But you did. When you saw the paintings."

She nodded.

"I see. So that's why you pulled your little disappearing act? You saw the paintings, decided I was a stalker, and ran."

"You're angry."

He stared at her. She couldn't blame him. She'd just stated the patently obvious. "Well, it's not like it was that unreasonable an assumption—"

"Not if you didn't know me at all."

At the taut words, she looked away. Score one for Brendan. "I'm sorry. I was frightened." She squared her shoulders and met his gaze. "Brendan, I know now that I should have just come to you, asked you to tell me about the paintings. Well, I can only hope it's not too late to do so. Please tell me about the paintings."

Please. Please tell me something that makes sense of this love I have for you!

Brendan was torn.

He wanted to explain to Lindsay, wanted her to understand. But the anger was still there. She should have trusted him. *OK, so they'd only known each other for a day. But it had been a day like no other.*

It's not fair, God. I've trusted her, taken her at her word. Why couldn't she do the same for me?

Be considerate of the doubts and fears of others . . . do what helps them.

The words were as clear as a neon sign. He let out an exasperated breath. *You don't ever get tired of saying the same things over and over?* He already knew the answer to that. *I know, I know, you wouldn't have to if I would just get it, right? Right.*

He pulled his drifting thoughts together and studied Lindsay. She sat so silent, staring at her hands, waiting. "I told you before that I mostly paint children and animals."

She jumped at the sound of his voice. Apparently she hadn't expected him to answer her. The relief he saw in her eyes pierced him.

"Y-yes, you told me that."

"Because of that, I spend a lot of time at the zoo and in parks. It's a good thing I like them so much." He managed a brief smile, and an answering smile touched her lips.

"That's probably why your paintings are so emotive," she said. "I can see why you've enjoyed the success you have."

The success he had? She knew about his success?

"My aunts recognized your signature, HawkEye. They told me about you." Her tone softened. "Amelia works at the university, where they had a showing of your work a few months ago."

Interesting. She knew about his work and she'd still avoided him. So he didn't have to worry about her falling for him just because he had money.

No, you just have to wonder if she loves you, period.

He started again. "Anyway, I go to the park just down the block several times a week. You can imagine my surprise when I saw you there."

Her brow crinkled. Something wasn't making sense to her.

"I just didn't know you lived in this area," he tried to explain. "But about a month ago, I was at the park, sketching the kids at the playground. And I heard . . ." The memory of that sound caught him again.

Lindsay leaned forward. "You heard?"

He nodded. "Laughter. It was almost musical it was so light and uninhibited. I figured the child who belonged to that laughter would be a great subject, but when I turned, it wasn't a child at all." He met her eyes. "It was you. You were sitting on the ground, your dog jumping on you, children all around you laughing."

Even he could hear the sudden ragged quality to his voice. Clear evidence that the memory still got to him. "I don't know what it was about you. But from the first time I saw you, something inside of me clicked. It was as though someone whispered into my heart, 'That's her. That's the one.' For a moment . . . just for a moment, I believed it. I almost got up and came over to you right then and there."

Her eyes shimmered, and he realized it was tears. A powerful need to be near her, to comfort her swept over him. He nearly stood and moved to sit beside her. He wanted to be closer, to touch her hand, to find some way to help her understand what their day together had meant to him.

But it wasn't time for that. Might never be. So instead he stood and started pacing behind the sofa.

"I told myself I'd had too much pizza and anchovies the night before." Stupid thing to say, but he needed to lighten things up a bit—though whether for her sake or his, he wasn't sure. "But I couldn't forget you." He gave a short laugh. "I didn't have the chance. You seemed to be there almost as often as I was, walking Doofus, stopping to let the children adore him. And then, a few weeks ago, I was sitting there just enjoying the day, and I saw you make a beeline for what looked like the only tree that had leaves left on it. And then, this waterfall of color suddenly surrounded you, and you looked so . . . enchanted. And enchanting."

Just like she did at this very moment. The way she watched him, the way she sat, even the way she held her hands folded tight together . . . everything about her seemed filled with an air of anticipation.

"I almost came up to you then, but I couldn't. I was too afraid you'd be like—" No. Now wasn't the time to talk about Gwen. "Like too many others. Beautiful on the outside, but hollow where it matters the most. I couldn't let myself believe you could possibly be someone I could trust."

And she isn't, is she? How can you trust someone who so clearly doesn't trust you?

The thought jolted him into silence. For a moment he couldn't breathe. What was he doing? Pouring out his thoughts, his feelings? Hadn't Gwen taught him anything?

But . . . Lindsay wasn't Gwen.

How can you be sure she's any different?

How, indeed? He wanted to say, "By her actions." But they hadn't exactly been what he'd hoped. In fact . . .

He turned to face her. "Why didn't you call me?" The abrupt question came out harsher than he'd intended. So much so that it startled Lindsay. She stiffened.

"Call you?"

He had to know. "When you found out I wasn't the man your aunts sent, why didn't you just call me? Ask me what was going on?"

Pink blossomed in her cheeks. "I-I don't know. I was stunned. Unnerved."

"But after the day we'd just spent together . . ." He felt his gaze and tone harden. "Did you really think I was the kind of man who would lie to you? Take advantage of you?"

Silence followed his reproach. She lowered her head, stared at her hands. What she didn't do was answer him.

Disappointment became a bitter taste in his mouth. Turned his heart—and words—sour. "I was wrong."

She lifted her eyes to his face. "Wrong?"

Stop. Talk to her. Work this through. Don't make the same mistake she did.

He shook his head, his throat tight against the emotions pushing at him. "I'm sorry." He turned, walked to the door of her apartment, put his hand on the knob.

He couldn't risk this again. The pain. The loss. Better to stay alone than lose more of himself than he could afford.

He didn't turn to look at her. "I never should have come here." Not today. Not ever.

He heard Lindsay stand, move toward him. He glanced over his shoulder, and one hand was reaching toward him. "Brendan, please. Wait."

"For what? If you can't trust me, then what do we have, Lindsay?"

"I'm sorry. I should have called you. I should—"

He held his hand palm up, stopping the flow of words. She was so close to him. All he had to do was reach out, just a few inches, and he could take her hand. Pull her into his arms.

His hand fell to his side, and he turned from her, back to the door.

"If you leave now, don't—don't bother coming back."

He didn't turn. He didn't need to. He could tell she didn't mean it. Heard the regret, the pain, in her voice. The plea for him to stop.

He shook his head again. This was for the best. "I won't bother you again."

He turned the knob and walked into the hallway. When he closed the door, the decisive *click* echoed around him—a death knell on his hopes.

Tears ran down her face. Fell onto her hands, clutched in her lap. She was afraid to move. Afraid her heart would shatter into a million pieces.

He'd looked at her with such disappointment. No, it went deeper than that.

Grief.

That's what was in his eyes. A sorrow she didn't understand. Especially when she caught a flash of desperation in his eyes just before he turned away. It told Lindsay he didn't want this any more than she did. He didn't want it to end like this. To finish even before it started.

What a fool she'd been. No, she hadn't known him long, but she should have trusted what she did know of him. She could so easily have called him, asked him to meet with her and talk it all over. But she'd been afraid.

Apparently with good reason. First obstacle he hits and he walks out? What kind of relationship could you have with a man like that? Good riddance.

She wanted to argue. To fight through the defeat that threatened to swallow her. But what good would it do? Brendan had made his decision. She wasn't worth fighting for.

So be it.

He was gone, and there was nothing she could do about it. Even if he had taken her heart with him when he walked out the door.

Brendan stood on the sidewalk outside Lindsay's apartment building.

He rubbed aching eyes, then turned to study the brick building for a few seconds. He strode forward, stood next to the wall— and thumped his head against it.

"Idiot! Idiot! Idiot!"

After the fourth smack, he saw stars and staggered back. He rubbed the spot where a small lump already was forming. *So this is love, eh, God? One minute I'm looking at her, loving her, wanting to be near her, the next I'm running for the hills. No offense, but I'm not so sure I care for love if . . .*

He shrugged, turned, and started the walk back to his own apartment.

It was going to take some time to work through things. To figure out exactly what had happened tonight. What he'd reacted to.

Why he'd walked away from the one woman he wanted in his life.

It wasn't over. No matter what he'd said, what she'd said, it wasn't over. But before he tried again, before he faced Lindsay, he had to understand.

Had to find a way to let God free him of the sorrow and bitterness over Gwen.

Then, no matter how hard it was, he would find a way to convince Lindsay she should speak to him again.

Or at least listen.

CHAPTER
Nine

"You what?"

Lindsay faced her aunts. She would not cave. After all, she'd played this scene once before, so she could do it again. She would not let them make her feel foolish. *I made the right decision. Right, Lord?* Silence was her only answer, so she rushed on. *Of course I did.* And no one was going to tell her differently.

Fools think they need no advice, but the wise listen to others.

Nuh-uh. No way. She'd listened to others too many times. And look where it got her. Disappointed. Hurt.

Alone.

Tears stung at her eyes and she blinked them back.

She was not going to shed one more precious drop over Brendan HawkEye.

"I told Brendan I didn't want to see him again." There. Surely the aunts couldn't argue with something spoken in such a calm, reasonable tone.

"Why on earth would you do that?" There was no censure in Ophelia's tone, only total and complete confusion.

"I thought he was your Prince Charming." Amelia, too, looked utterly baffled.

"He turned out to be more of a toad." The words slipped out before Lindsay could stop herself. She felt the quick heat in her cheeks as The Three fixed her with chiding looks.

Per usual, Ophelia was the first to speak her mind. "Lindsay, I'm sure there is no need to be unkind."

A retort flew to her lips, and she clamped them shut. Phelia was right. Berating Brendan wasn't going to help anything. Besides, her heart wasn't in it. She didn't really think he was a toad.

And even if he was, her treacherous heart would probably find a way to like toads. A lot.

Help me out here, will you, Lord? How do I explain this to them so they'll understand and let it go?

An old adage flitted through her mind: "Better to keep silent and be thought a fool than to open your mouth and remove all doubt."

Well! What did *that* have to do with anything?

"Let's just say he wasn't what I thought he was."

Cecelia cocked her head. "Oh. He wasn't HawkEye?"

"No, he's HawkEye . . . uh, Brendan. Whatever. He's the artist." The image of his painting of her came to mind. She could still see the exquisite detail, the way he'd seemed to capture her personality—even her soul—on the canvas. Oh, yes, he was an artist.

"Did he explain the painting?"

She sighed. "Yes." Wait, did he? No, the conversation turned before he did so. "I mean, no. But that really doesn't matter."

"Oh?" Ophelia had the same expression she wore when she was trying to puzzle out a particularly stubborn theory.

This was not going well. "Yes, but there were things about him that I didn't know—"

"Don't tell me he's married!"

"No!" Her response was almost as aghast as Amelia's exclamation. "Of course not. It's not that at all. He's single, like he said he was—"

"Well, dear, which is it?" Ophelia sat ramrod straight on the couch. "Was he or wasn't he what he said?"

"Yes, he was what he said, but he wasn't what I thought."
Oh, good heavens. Even she could see the absurdity of this. Not
surprisingly, The Three pounced.

"For *mercy's* sake, Lindsay, make some sense!"

"What *are* you talking about?"

"That is the most illogical thing I've heard in *years.*"

The triplicate chorus rang in her ears, and her reply jumped
out, hot and angry. "*So what?* So what if it isn't logical? *I'm* not
logical. I never *have* been. And what's more, I have no desire to be!
Not if it means I have to ignore my feelings and intuition! When
will you people *get* that?"

Stop! Stop this now! But she wasn't listening. She was on a roll.

"I don't think the way you do. You three and Mac, you all
think the same. A equals B equals C. But I don't think like that. I
don't *feel* the way you do. I'm not you! OK? Considering how off
the charts you three are in IQ, I fail to understand why that's so
hard for you to grasp. But you have to let me be who I am"—she
couldn't keep the bitterness out of her voice—"no matter how
inferior you all think that is—"

She broke off, not so much because she was finished, but because her throat was too choked with tears to continue.

The silence in the room was deafening.

A sob caught in Lindsay's throat, and she shook her head.
How could she have said such hateful things? She couldn't bear
to even look at her aunts for fear of the anger she'd see on their
faces. Or, worse, the hurt.

She turned to leave, and suddenly they were there, beside her,
their arms encircling her, their faces pressed against hers.

"No, oh, Lindsay, no. Don't leave. Please. Not now."

The plea was filled with grief, and she looked into Ophelia's
face, stunned to find tears coursing down her aunt's cheeks.

"We can't let you go. Not believing such things."

"I—" The tightness in her throat cut off the words she so wanted to say. *I'm sorry. I didn't mean it. I'm an idiot! Forgive me. . . .*

She squeezed her eyes shut, but it did no good. The tears spilled out anyway. *God, God, forgive me. . . .*

"Oh, sweet Lindsay, don't cry." Amelia took hold of her hand and led her to the sofa.

Lindsay sat beside her aunt, leaning into the protective arm Amelia had around her shoulders. "I'm sorry," Lindsay finally managed to sob out.

"No, my dear." Cecelia knelt in front of her, patting her knee. "We're sorry. So dreadfully sorry that you thought we . . . that we made you feel . . . oh, bother! Ophelia, where's your blasted Kleenex?"

Soon all four of them were doing their best to mop up the tears. Ophelia blew her nose with enormous gusto.

They all froze, looked at each other, then dissolved into hysterical laughter, collapsing against each other on the large, overstuffed sofa.

Amelia was the first to regain her composure. She touched Lindsay's arm. "We love you, Lindsay. *I* love you."

Lindsay blinked back tears again. "I know, Melia. I never doubted that."

"But you doubt we *like* you." Ophelia's quiet words hit the nail square on the head.

Lindsay fell silent, not sure what to say. Finally, she nodded.

"Oh, my dear, we not only like you, we respect you."

Lindsay looked at Cecelia. "You . . . respect me?"

"A great deal." Ophelia sat down beside her. "Lindsay, you have so many wonderful qualities, so many gifts that God has given you. All three of us have watched you, the way you are with people, the ability you have to draw others out and bring them joy—"

"And we've envied that in you."

Amelia's comment was too much. Lindsay's mouth dropped open.

"It's true, Lindsay." There was no doubting Amelia's sincerity. "We've often wished we could reach people the way you do. Make them feel comfortable, rather than intimidated. But since it's just not in our makeup—"

"*Definitely* not in our makeup," Celie echoed, grinning.

"—we've been thankful to have you."

"You're our bridge, Lindsay." Ophelia took her hand. "The one who connects us with others, and even with ourselves at times."

Tenderness filled Amelia's gaze. "You're our heart."

"The wind beneath our wings," Celie chimed in, then sat back, clearly chagrined when her sisters glowered at her.

"What we're saying," Ophelia turned back to Lindsay, "is that we've always considered you a gift. Yes, Mackenzie is more like us. And we love him deeply, as well. But you. Well, God has used you to help us feel and to be honest about those feelings."

Lindsay tried to sort through what she was hearing. "I . . . I had no idea."

Ophelia pursed her lips. "I don't suppose you could have, since we've never said any of this before. I'm afraid we don't do particularly well expressing our feelings."

Amelia smoothed back Lindsay's hair. "But I promise you, if we had known you were feeling as you were—"

"Left out—"

"Lacking—"

Lindsay swallowed with difficulty. "Lonely."

Celie took her hand. "Oh, my dear, we would have done whatever it took to let you know how we felt."

"And that you are, most certainly, not alone." Ophelia gave a definite nod.

"Though, heaven knows, there have been times when you quite likely wished you were."

Lindsay shook her head. "No, I didn't want to be without you." At their knowing looks, she grinned. "OK, once in a while, maybe. But not often. I just wanted to feel as though I belonged. That I wasn't just . . . an oddity that you and Mac endured as best you could."

Ophelia lifted her chin. "If anyone in this family is an oddity, it's me. Actually, all three of us."

"After all, my dear"—Amelia's eyes reflected the awe in her words—"*you* can cook."

"And clean house." Phelia shuddered.

"And do all those puzzling acts of domesticity that most women learn at their mother's knee," Celie finished.

Amelia frowned. "Good heavens." She looked at Ophelia and Cecelia. "Do you realize, if you really contemplate the facts, Lindsay is the most *normal* of the four of us?"

"Now, *that's* the kind of logic I could learn to love!" Lindsay laughed, and her aunts joined in. This was what she'd longed for, prayed for so many years—this sense of belonging. If only she'd realized it was there all the time. If only she'd said something sooner.

The truth shall set you free. . . .

Oh, yes. Thank you, Father.

"Well, I for one will need some help recovering from that realization." Ophelia rose.

"Absolutely." Amelia's tone was filled with mirth. "In fact, I think it will take nothing less than something terribly gooey and replete with chocolate to get us through our trauma."

"Oh," sighed Celie, "if only some gracious, gifted, creative person would take pity on us—"

"—and bake a pan of double-chocolate—"

"—fudge-frosted—"

"—nut-filled brownies."

Lindsay's lifted her hands, signaling surrender. "All right, all right. I'll take pity on you." She looked at Ophelia. "I assume you have the necessary ingredients for brownies."

Ophelia's expression was blank.

"Margarine, flour, sugar, eggs," Lindsay listed hopefully.

"And I would find these items . . . where?" Ophelia glanced around.

"In the pantry!" Amelia supplied, tone triumphant.

"No, in the kitchen, in that cold thing," Celie countered. "What is it? Ah, yes, the refrigerator."

"Never mind!" Lindsay gasped out. "I'll go to the store. You three are hopeless."

"Indubitably," Ophelia said.

"Undeniably," Melia offered.

"Most assuredly," Celie finished.

And not one of them had the grace to look even a little bit repentant.

CHAPTER
Ten

Kylie and Mac had just settled down on the couch to read when the doorbell sounded. Amid the dogs' responding barks, Mac rose and went to open the door.

Brendan stood there, looking as miserable as Mac had ever seen him. Mac recognized that look all too well.

He'd seen it on his own features not three months ago, when he and Kylie were trying to figure out if they were in love or not.

Mac stepped aside. "Come on in, Brother."

Brendan did so. He petted the dogs, who greeted him with wagging tails and happy yips, then sank into an overstuffed chair.

Mac sat beside Kylie again, slipping his arm around his wife's shoulders.

Brendan got right to the point.

"OK, you two. You're the ones who got me into this."

Mac's mouth dropped open. "Me? I didn't have anything to do with it."

"Lindsay is your sister, isn't she?"

"Well, sure, but—"

"And you're the one who's been telling me how wonderful married life is?"

"Sure, but—"

Kylie laid a hand on Mac's arm, and he fell silent. She turned to her brother. "OK, brother mine. Spill."

He did so. Told them all that had happened since he showed up on Lindsay's doorstep. A couple of times Mac had to remind himself not to get defensive on Lindsay's account. Apparently his wife could feel him tense at those times, and she stroked his arm, probably to calm him.

As Brendan finished his tale of woe, Mac leaned back against the couch cushions. "Well, sounds like you're in a mess."

Kylie punched his arm.

"What? Doesn't it sound like that to you?"

She grimaced. "Of course, but that's not the point. Brendan knows he's in a mess—"

"Hellooo. Still sitting here." Brendan waved at them, but they both ignored him.

"—but it's our job to listen and encourage him—"

"And who is encouraging my sister in all this? Sounds like he's broken her heart."

Brendan waved his hand closer. "Yello! Haven't gone any-where. Can hear every word."

"We can call Lindsay after we've talked with—"

"Enough!"

Mac and Kylie jumped, then turned to look at Brendan, now standing. He glared at them. "I know I've made a mess of this. I didn't come here for you guys to tell me I did everything right. I know I didn't." He sank back down again.

Mac drew a deep breath. "So why did you come, Brendan?"

He leaned forward. "Because I need your help."

"To figure out Lindsay?"

Brendan met Mac's gaze head-on. "No. To understand myself."

"I think he's ready."

Mac looked at Kylie over the top of the newspaper he was reading. "Are you meddling again?"

"Of course not." She looked down at the dogs. The floor. The table. Anything to avoid her husband's probing eyes. "But it's been three weeks."

Mac didn't comment.

Kylie used the toe of her shoe to rub Ivan's back. "Don't you think Brendan's gotten past the Gwen issues?"

The newspaper rattled.

"You know he misses your sister so much it's eating him up."

Mac turned a page.

Kylie stood and reached over the table to snatch the paper from her husband's hands. "Mackenzie St. Clair!"

He crossed his arms and rested his elbows on the table. "Love of my life, your brother is an adult. He'll know when he's ready to see Lindsay."

"You're kidding me, right?" Kylie plopped back in her chair. "He's avoiding the issue."

"Then maybe he's not ready."

"Of course he is. He's just . . . stuck. I think he's worried she'll shut him down before he gets a chance to help her understand."

"So what, exactly, do you want me to do?"

Ah, surrender at last. "You? Nothing. But your aunts? I want to enlist them."

Mac rested his chin in a hand. "Enlist them?"

"For a mission."

"Lindsay needs our help."

At her oldest sister's comment, Amelia glanced at her. The three of them stood crowded in the doorway of Amelia's home, waving good-bye to Lindsay as she walked to her car.

Cecelia lowered her hand. "I believe you're right, Ophelia."

"Maybe it's just as well that she's given up on Brendan Hawk-Eye." But the words rang false in Amelia's own ears. "No, you're right. We can't leave things as they are."

"Absolutely not," Ophelia said as Amelia led the way to the living room. "Lindsay has finally found a man she cares about. We cannot let emotions muck up such a splendid match."

Cecelia settled on the couch. "Do you think he would let us have a discount on his paintings once he's part of the family?"

"Cecelia!" Amelia and Ophelia admonished in chorus.

She looked appropriately chastised. "Never mind, then. Now, how do we go about this?"

"I think"—Ophelia looked from Amelia to Cecelia—"we should deal with it the way Lindsay would."

Amelia stared at her eldest triplet. "You want us to . . . think like Lindsay?"

"Is that even possible?" Cecelia sounded as uncertain as Amelia felt.

"We've always said we can do anything if we put our minds to it." Ah, Ophelia, ever the confident one. "Now, if you were Lindsay, how would you get two people together."

"I'd cook a meal."

Ophelia pinned Cecelia with a bland look. "Don't be absurd."

Amelia leaned forward. Maybe Celie was onto something. "Ophelia, we have PhDs. I daresay we can put together one meal."

After a moment, the eldest nodded. "All right. We'll do it."

"I just have one question." Amelia bit her lip and peered over her shoulder toward the kitchen. "Who's going to tell us which of those contraptions we're supposed to use?"

CHAPTER
Eleven

The next day, Amelia paused on her way out the door of her home. Drat! The phone was ringing.

She should just let voicemail pick up, but what if it was one of the sisters asking her to pick up something else from the store? With a sigh, she hustled to grab the phone out of its cradle.

"Yes? Hello?"

"Aunt A?"

The deep voice brought a broad smile. "Mackenzie! How wonderful to hear from you. Oh, but I really haven't much time to chat, dear. I'm on a mission."

He chuckled. "Funny you should say that."

"Oh? Why is that?"

"Auntie A, I have a proposition for you."

Well, this sounded intriguing. If only she had the time for it. "Really, dear, that sounds lovely. But I have to meet the sisters."

"Perfect. When and where?"

She hesitated. "Mackenzie, exactly what is going on?"

"Love, dear auntie. Love is going on."

Well, she couldn't argue with that!

Kylie looked up as the bell on the flower shop door jingled. Three attractive, elegant women came in.

The Three had arrived.

"Greetings, ladies." Mac moved from Kylie's side to greet the women, and they showered him with praise and kisses.

"Oh, you look so happy, dear!" Amelia crooned. She turned her direction Kylie's way, and held out a hand. "And so do you, Kylie."

Kylie took Amelia's hand and hugged her. "I'm awfully glad you all agreed to meet."

"Well, we were coming here anyway in preparation of our own plan." Ophelia came to hug her. "So it only made sense."

Cecelia joined the circle. "Now, you two, tell us what this is about."

As Kylie explained, she watched the aunts for any sign of resistance. There was none. In fact, all three seemed delighted at her idea.

"It's quite perfect. It dovetails beautifully with what we had in mind." Amelia's eyes shone.

"Well, then," Ophelia glanced around them, "I think we should get started."

Kylie loved these women. "OK, we order the flowers—"

"I think we should order them to arrive while the meal is going on."

Ophelia pondered this, then tilted her head in a nod. "You're right, Amelia."

"And they should be from Brendan!"

"Cecelia, you're a genius," Amelia patted her sister on the arm.

Cecelia smiled. "Well, of course."

Kylie restrained a grin and followed the aunts to the counter. Mac kept his distance. Clearly he was preparing a case for plausible deniability.

"That one." Ophelia pointed to a large, beautiful arrangement. "That will do nicely."

The woman at the counter wrote the information on the order form. "And how do you want the card to read?"

Cecelia leaned forward. "'To Lindsay. With all my love, Brendan.'"

Within moments, the order was completed, and they filed out of the store. Kylie looked at the aunts. "Everyone know their assignments?"

"Absolutely." Ophelia's smile took in her sisters and Kylie. "We'll see you in two nights. At my place. And everything will be ready."

CHAPTER
Twelve

Lindsay hung the phone up. It had finally happened. She'd become part of a *Twilight Zone* episode.

Her aunts had just invited her to Ophelia's house for dinner tomorrow night. And they were cooking.

I wonder, is it 911 for the fire department?

"Where exactly are we going again?" Brendan eyed his sister as he drove down the road.

"I told you, to a dinner with some potential clients. They may want me to do the flowers for an upcoming wedding."

"And I'm going . . . why?"

Kylie tossed him a scolding look. "Because Mac couldn't make it, and I need you to be charming. And because when they found out you're a famous artist, they just had to meet you."

"Ah, of course."

"There it is . . . 422 Standish Drive." Kylie directed him to the house.

"Wow." Brendan pulled the car into the circular driveway and peered at the marble columns framing the front double-doors. "This could be quite a wedding. I might even want to come."

Kylie coughed, as though she'd choked on something.

"You OK?"

She nodded, motioning him out of the car and toward the door.

They walked up the wide stone stairs and rang the bell. No answer. They rang the bell again.

"Are you sure they're home—?" Brendan's question was interrupted by the door flying open, and he turned to face what looked like a tall, slim ghost.

"Well, don't just stand there," the apparition snapped. "Come in."

Brendan saw it was a woman, covered in a layer of some kind of white, powdery substance.

"Amelia?" Kylie sounded decidedly startled. "Is that you?"

"Don't be smug," Flour Woman snapped. "We've encountered a bit of an obstacle, but I believe we have it under control now. At least . . . I hope so."

At that moment, the sound of clanging and clunking came from the direction of what Brendan assumed was the kitchen, at the far end of the dining room.

"Pay no attention to the man behind the curtain," Amelia muttered. "This way, please." She brushed at her soiled apron as she led the way to a large, elegant dining room.

Well, the servants are a mess, but the home is strictly House Beautiful. He looked around, his artist's eye finding plenty to attract and please it.

"Have a seat." Amelia motioned them to the chairs. "We should be ready to start soon." Brendan took in the table. Two places were set, complete with fine china, sparkling crystal, and tapestry napkins. A large crystal vase filled with beautiful flowers was on the table to the side of the place settings. Out of the way, but near enough to add beauty and fragrance.

A frustrated howl came from behind the closed kitchen door, followed by the door flying open.

A woman stood there, gesturing like a crazed person. Smudges of flour and something dark ran across her face, and her hair stuck out in all directions, as though she'd been caught in a wind tunnel. "Amelia! Quickly! Ophelia's stuck in the—the icebox or whatever it is!"

And then she was gone again, back into what Brendan was beginning to think of as the black hole.

Amelia's smile was pained. "You'll excuse me. I believe I'm being paged."

They watched her trudge to the door and shove it open. Brendan bit his lips to keep from bursting out in laughter. Casting a cautious glance at his sister, he saw she was doing the same. She reached out for a glass of water and began sipping.

"I sure hope being a maid isn't their day job."

Kylie choked, sputtering and spewing water everywhere. Brendan went to pound her on the back.

"Sorry," she wheezed when she could speak again. "I had trouble swallowing."

"Well, at least we get to enjoy beautiful surroundings." He pulled the chair out for his sister.

She hesitated. "Um, I think I'll go see if I can help them in the kitchen."

"Are you sure it's safe in there?"

Just then the tones of a melodic door chime filled the air. Brendan glanced at the doorway, then back to his sister. "Were you expecting someone else?"

Kylie's eyes went wide. "Who? Me?" She stepped back, inching toward the kitchen door. "Not my house. Not my place to expect anything."

The door chime sounded again.

Brendan looked toward the front door. "Well, somebody's here."

Kylie took another step backward. "You're absolutely right. Tell you what, why don't you answer the door, and I'll just go see what's holding dinner up."

With that she pushed the kitchen door open and slipped through.

Brendan went to open the door.

"What's with the locked door—?"

Lindsay's question hung, unfinished. Brendan drank in the sight of her. She stood there, hair windblown, eyes wide, a half smile frozen on her face—and he thought his heart would burst with the feelings she stirred in him.

"I—" She tried again. "You . . . what are you doing here?"

"I believe I was invited. And you?"

She came inside, her expression wary. "The same. But I'm getting the distinct feeling it was for something far different than dinner." She looked around. They stood there until the silence between them grew unbearable.

"I'm going to find out what's going on," Lindsay said, turning to march away.

Brendan's hand shot out. He caught her arm and held on, halting her. "Wait. Please."

She stood frozen, her back to him.

"Did I ever tell you I was engaged once?" He knew he hadn't, but he didn't know how else to begin.

Apparently it was a good start. She turned to look at him.

"About five years ago. Her name was Gwen. We met at church, and it seemed so clear to me that God had brought us together."

Despite her still-closed expression, he sensed her vulnerability. "So you can imagine my surprise when Gwen called me about a week before the wedding to say God had told her he knew she wouldn't be happy married to a penniless artist and that she should marry Dewie Dortman."

Her lips twitched. "Dewie . . . ?"

He nodded. "Dortman. One of the more affluent members of the church. Gwen wished me all God's blessings, told me she'd be praying for me, and hung up."

Compassion was clear in her expression, and she placed her hand over his, where he still held her arm. "I'm so sorry she hurt you that way. She was wrong, Brendan."

The simple words hit him like a line drive. He stood there, his eyes fixed on her face, wanting nothing more than to have her in his arms. "Yes, she was, but I was wrong, too. With you. I was bitter because of Gwen. It didn't matter that you weren't her, I just gave in to the anger I had never surrendered. I couldn't see anything but deceit in every woman I dated. Then, when my work was suddenly in such demand, all I encountered were women who liked the idea of being with a well-known artist. So long as that meant parties and rubbing elbows with famous people. And money. But the places I wanted to go were to the beach, to the park—"

"To the zoo."

"That day at your apartment," Brendan said, "you asked me if I was tired of playing games. I told you I was, but I didn't tell you why. Nor did I tell you the reason I was so quick to believe you were just playing a role."

"Gwen."

He nodded. She fell silent for a moment, and he watched the emotions play across her expressive face. Compassion, frustration, regret . . . and then sadness.

Icy fear stabbed through him. "Lindsay—"

She shook her head. "I understand, Brendan. I do, but I don't know that it changes anything. You didn't trust me—"

"Any more than you trusted me." He regretted the words immediately.

"That's true"—her stricken eyes met his—"and that's what worries me. What if I can't be what you want me to be? What if I do something else, make another mistake—?" She broke off, and he saw tears in her eyes. "I want to be with a man I can depend on, someone willing to depend on me." Her lips trembled as she spoke. "What if we can't get past ourselves to find each other?"

*God, God, help us! I don't know what to say or do . . . and I'm
losing her.*

A screech from the kitchen jarred them both.

"Call 911! Somebody, call 911!!"

Lindsay and Brendan froze for a second, then raced together
toward the kitchen.

Lindsay stood in her aunt's kitchen, too stupefied to do more
than gawk.

The Three Aunts were a disaster. Their faces and arms were
covered in flour and who knew what else. Their usually immacu-
late hair was poking out in all directions, and their aprons sported
what looked like some kind of primordial goo.

But they were clean compared to the kitchen. The floors,
walls, and cabinets held a layer of grime that Lindsay was almost
sure must have come from a science lab somewhere. Bits of food
were splattered here and there, and dirty pots and pans and utensils lay littered all about.

It looked like an earthquake had hit.

Or maybe a bomb.

A near hysterical giggle bubbled inside Lindsay as she surveyed the wreckage. All humor fled, though, when she spotted
The Three dancing about the stove, flapping their hands at a pan
bellowing black smoke.

"Whoa!" Apparently Brendan had just spotted the problem
as well. "Kylie, there's a phone! Call 911."

Kylie? Lindsay turned and saw her new sister-in-law. What
on earth was Kylie doing there? And how did Brendan know her?

Before she could ask, Brendan rushed to grasp Ophelia's arm.
She spun to stare at him, and Lindsay saw that her aunt's flour-
dusted face had streaks all through it from her frantic tears.

"Where's your fire extinguisher?"

Lindsay knew the question was wasted on her aunt. She snatched a towel from the butcher block, then scooped up the pan lid and slammed it into place.

"Good job, sweetheart!" Brendan was suddenly right beside her, a towel in his hand as well. "Let me in there for a minute—"

Using the towel as insulation, he lifted the pan, holding the lid in place. As though this was a drill they'd practiced, Lindsay moved to the cupboard, grabbing the box of baking soda, then met him at the sink. He lowered the pan into the sink, lifted the lid. She dumped the baking soda on top of the still-burning grease, effectively snuffing out the fire.

Their eyes met, and they smiled. "Thanks, pardner."

Lindsay nodded, her throat too tight for words.

Brendan looked toward the ceiling at the thick cloud of smoke, then at the windows.

"Got 'em." Within seconds, Lindsay had thrown the windows open as he turned on the stove vent.

"All I wanted to do was make potatoes," Ophelia wailed.

"Water would have been helpful!" Amelia snapped.

Ophelia turned on her sister, and Lindsay rushed to get between them—only to find Brendan had beat her to it.

"Why don't we go outside." He spoke in low, soothing tones. Lindsay watched as he led a suddenly compliant Ophelia toward the door.

Lindsay slid her arms around Melia and Celie's trembling shoulders, then looked over her shoulder at Kylie. "Come on, everyone. I think we can all use some air."

Brendan stood watching in a bit of a daze as the firemen went in and out of Ophelia's house, busy making sure all was safe and secure in the battered kitchen.

He would never, as long as he lived, forget the sight of that kitchen and those three women. But what struck him the most wasn't the disarray, it was the love he saw between Lindsay and her aunts.

He wanted to know what it would be like to love Lindsay that deeply. Every day. For the rest of his life.

"I beg your pardon, but must you wear boots in my home?"

His lips twitched. Apparently Ophelia was recovering a bit from the trauma of trying to cook a meal.

"What are you standing here for?" a voice inquired, and he turned to smile at Kylie.

"Am I in the way?"

She shook her head. "No, but I think you'd probably be more comfortable"—she motioned with her head—"over there."

He followed the direction of her gaze, then turned back to her with a grateful smile. "Did you know I love you?"

"Of course."

He even forgave her for being smug.

Lindsay sat on the curb, staring at her shoes. No doubt about it. She was in the *Twilight Zone*.

"May I join you?"

She hesitated, then inclined her head.

He lowered himself beside her, not touching her, but filling her senses all the same.

"We made quite a team in there."

Tears choked her throat, stopping any words she wanted to say. She nodded.

"Not bad for only knowing one another for a day, don't you think?"

The tears streaked down her cheeks now. "Yes," she managed hoarsely. "It was."

"Lindsay. Look at me."

She closed her eyes, suddenly afraid.

"Please."

Slowly, carefully, she opened her eyes and turned to him. It was all there, in his face . . . the promise, the regret, the determination to hold onto what they'd found.

He opened his arms and she moved almost without conscious thought. No hesitation, no debate. She was coming home.

"I'm sorry," she whispered. "I should have trusted you, what I knew of you and your character."

"And I should have realized that a single day, no matter how wonderful, isn't enough for either of us to build trust." His arms tightened. "I was an idiot." He murmured the words against her hair.

"It's only fair. I was one first."

"Let's face it. You're both idiots."

Kylie stood behind them. Lindsay looked from her to Brendan. "How do you two know each other?"

Kylie's surprise was reflected in Brendan's features as well. "Linds, this is my brother, Brendan."

"Your . . ." It was too much to take in. She met Brendan's confused gaze. "So your last name is . . ."

"Hawk."

Lindsay nodded. "Not HawkEye."

Brendan took her hand. "That's my signature for my paintings. My company is Hawk's Eye Fine Art. Hence—"

"HawkEye." It was starting to come together.

Brendan narrowed his gaze and turned to Kylie. His sister. "You didn't call her, did you?"

Lindsay tipped her head. "Call me?"

"My sister was supposed to call you on Valentine's Day, to tell you I was coming by."

Kylie's face turned pink. "I . . . no, I didn't call. I didn't want Lindsay to decide she wasn't interested even before you showed up."

"Hang on." Lindsay held up her eyes. "You"—she looked at Kylie—"knew your brother was coming to see me?"

"He's been mooning over you since he saw you at Mac's and my wedding."

"I do not moon—"

Lindsay cut off Brendan's objection. "You saw me at the wedding? But I thought the first time you saw me was at the park?"

Brendan and Kylie looked at each other, then back at Lindsay. With a slow shake of his head, Brendan stepped toward Lindsay and held out his hand. "Hi. I'm Brendan Hawk. Professional artist and occasional idiot."

Lindsay hesitated only a moment. Then she made up her mind. She let him engulf her hand in his. "Lindsay St. Clair." She lifted her eyes to his. "I'm happy to meet you, Brendan. Your sister is a good friend of mine." She angled a look at Kylie. "Not always the smartest friend, but a good one."

His lips twitched. "Well, she never has been the bright one in the family—"

"OK, OK." Kylie's hands lifted. "If I had a white flag I'd be waving it. No more meddling. I promise."

Brendan eyed his sister. "Starting now?"

She looked from him to Lindsay, then started backing away. "'Nuff said. Think I'll go check on the aunts."

When she was out of earshot, Brendan turned back to Lindsay. "I have the weirdest family."

Lindsay laughed. "Oh no. I think mine's got that description tied up."

He arched a brow. "Have you met my sister? And then there's my matchmaking grandfather—"

"I'll meet your sister and grandfather, and raise you three brainiac aunts and a people-hating brother. Well"—she shrugged—"he was, until your sister got hold of him."

"Ha! So my sister is weird enough that she changed your brother. True?"

"OK." She couldn't help it. She was half laughing, half crying. "You win."

He reached out, lifting her chin until their eyes locked. "Do I, Lindsay? Do I really?"

She didn't have to ask what he meant. "I love you." The words seemed to free her heart.

Emotion flickered in his dark eyes, and she felt wrapped in an invisible warmth. "And I love you. Now. Always."

He lowered his head to kiss first her nose, then her eyes, and finally, her mouth.

When he lifted his head, she reached up to trace his face with tender fingers. "I take it we're serious about this, then."

The smile she'd come to love so well tipped his mouth. "Oh, absolutely." And he claimed her lips again.

Kylie nudged Ophelia, then motioned toward Lindsay and Brendan. "Well, this wasn't exactly the plan you told me about, but apparently it worked."

Ophelia and her sisters looked to where Brendan and Lindsay were engrossed in each other, then turned back to Kylie.

"Well!" Cecelia exclaimed. "It was all worth it then."

Ophelia shot her a dark look.

"Well done, Aunts. You went way beyond anything I would have done—"

Amelia gaped at Kylie. "You can't possibly believe we did this on purpose!"

She met their gazes blankly. "You're kidding, right?"

They didn't smile. Not even a little.

"But . . . you've all got PhDs."

"Exactly," Ophelia gave a firm nod. "We have far more important things to do than cook." But her trembling lips made this confident assertion less than believable.

Kylie slipped her arm around Ophelia. "Now, now, don't you worry. I come from a long line of culinary masters." She cast another glance at Brendan and Lindsay. "Since odds are good we're going to be family—again—what say I teach you a few things about that mean old kitchen?"

"I'm never darkening the doorway of that horrid place again!" Ophelia sniffed.

"None of us are!" Amelia wiped at her smudged face with an even more smudged hand.

"I am." At Cecelia's assertion, her two sisters turned to look at her. "Well, I am! I'm not going to let that beastly place beat me!"

"Well"—Ophelia pondered that—"I suppose you're right."

Amelia took hold of Kylie's sleeve. "You'll go with us? Protect us?"

"I promise." They hooked arms and started toward the house. "We'll start with something easy." She looked at them carefully, taking in the smoke smudges and bits of flour still clinging to their skin and clothes.

"So, how do you three feel about toast?"

ABOUT THE AUTHOR

KAREN BALL has been blessed to use her love of story during nearly thirty years in publishing. Currently the owner/operator of Karen Ball Publishing Services, LLC, and a literary agent with the Steve Laube agency, Karen built and led fiction lines for Tyndale, Multnomah, Zondervan, and B&H Publishing Group. She's acquired and worked with some of the top novelists in publishing, including Francine Rivers, Karen Kingsbury, Brandilyn Collins, Angela Hunt, Ginny Yttrup, and Robin Jones Gunn. In addition, Karen is a best-selling, award-winning novelist and a popular speaker. She lives in Oregon with her husband, her father, and three four-legged, furry "kids."

12. 25